BEST
CANADIAN
STORIES

2019

EDITED BY

CAROLINE ADDERSON

BIBLIOASIS

WINDSOR, ONTARIO

First Edition
ISBN 978-1-77196-327-5 (Trade Paper)
ISBN 978-1-77196-328-2 (eBook)

Edited by Caroline Adderson
Cover and text designed by Gordon Robertson

Published with the generous assistance of the Canada Council for the Arts,
which last year invested $153 million to bring the arts to Canadians throughout
the country, and the financial support of the Government of Canada. Biblioasis
also acknowledges the support of the Ontario Arts Council (OAC), an agency
of the Government of Ontario, which last year funded 1,709 individual artists
and 1,078 organizations in 204 com- munities across Ontario, for a total of
$52.1 million, and the contribution of the Government of Ontario through
the Ontario Book Publishing Tax Credit and Ontario Creates.

PRINTED AND BOUND IN CANADA

CONTENTS

INTRODUCTION

Caroline Adderson

Welcome to *Best Canadian Stories 2019*, an anthology of the stories published in Canada by Canadians in 2018 that most delighted me. An extraordinary variety of writing awaits you in these pages: long and short; traditionally realistic and fantastical; elegiac and comical; stories written in first, second and third points of view. There's even a story narrated in first person plural—by plants! So diverse are these works in tone, style and subject that, as you read, you may begin to wonder what arbitrary mind assembled this literary smorgasbord. Who put the pickled herring next to the pavlova? Is there even a cook back there? Is she drunk?

No, no, no. I had a strict criterion, as stated above: delight.

First, a bit about how I made my selections for the book. These stories thudded onto my doorstep in two large boxes in the early months of 2019. Boxes filled with magazines. I read every work of short fiction in them—that is, every story published in print form in a Canadian periodical. I also considered at least a score of stories published online. Added to these were a number of Advanced Reading Copies of story collections. As long as a story hadn't been previously published before 2018, it qualified.

Now back to delight.

I realize that delight is out of fashion these days. I'm writing this during what is starting to feel like the End Times, the summer of 2019, with wild fires raging for yet another year in British Columbia where I live, record heat in Europe (again), and still precious little meaningful political action on our climate crisis. Refugees are still streaming out of their hells. The issues that triggered #Metoo haven't gone away. Trump has not been impeached. The future sometimes looks hopeless and so does our past as we in Canada reckon with a dark history finally brought to light by the Truth and Reconciliation Commission. In times like these it's normal and right for artists to try to make sense of the world through art. Indeed, many of the stories I read reflected the despair of our times and moved this sometime activist and daily petition signer deeply. But they were not selected for this anthology if they didn't also offer delight.

John Gardner writes in *The Art of Fiction*, "At all levels, not just in high schools . . . novels, short stories and poems have for years been taught not as experiences that can delight and enliven the soul but as things that are good for us, like vitamin C." Though I'm not sure I believe in the soul, I agree with the point I think he's making; something shrivels in fiction when it's read, or written, for a moral or instructive purpose. When I want a moral or instructive experience I read non-fiction. (Actually, I listen to a non-fiction audiobook while taking a vigorous angry walk.) Issues can certainly be explored in fiction, but that shouldn't be its ultimate purpose. After all, any artless textbook can teach me something, but only fiction offers the astonishing opportunity to enter deeply, through the medium of language, into the consciousness of another being. There is, in fact, no other way to achieve this empathetic merging of consciousnesses. Ironically, when this merging of reader and character is achieved, fiction can have a similar effect as non-fiction; the reader can learn and even be roused to action, but these are, in my opinion, side effects.

I do want to emphasize that delight is not escape. It is not even necessarily pleasurable. (Consider the highly discomfiting "Alice and Charles" included here.) Delight is not a respite from our troubled world but a direct and more mysterious engagement with it. Through the vehicle of fiction I can understand what it means to be you, whoever you are: animal, vegetable, or mineral. It may sound idealistic and grandiose, but I believe that more empathetic understanding is actually what we need to save this world.

So what delights await you in this anthology? The audacity of the idea (Zsuzsi Gartner's "The Second Coming of the Plants"), a twist in the narrative (Kai Conradi's "Every True Artist"; Shashi Bhat's "The Most Precious Substance on Earth"), a telling detail that cries out "This is so true!" (that game called Red Ass in Zalika Reid-Benta's "Pig Head"), or a general strangeness that makes you feel completely outside your normal experience (Frankie Barnet's "Again, The Sad Woman's Soliloquy"; Camilla Grudova's "Alice and Charles"; Conradi again). But usually the delight is in the telling, the *way* the story is written, either its energy and exuberance (Richard Van Camp's "Young Warriors in Love") or its seductive melancholia (Christy Ann Conlin's "Late and Soon"; Cathy Stonehouse's "A Room at the Marlborough"; Barnet again) or its subversive humour (Troy Sebastian's "nupqu ʔak·ɬam̓/ A Long Time Ago"). This language is not necessarily fancy. Pared down rhythmical language is wonderfully effective. The telling should match the teller, after all. Sequins glitter on these pages, but not too many to be distracting, nothing Las Vegasy. Cree and Ktunaxa are sprinkled in; how thrilling to have these languages appear in our literature. If you're a writer, you may even feel a little jealous reading some of these stories, as I did. You may find yourself tingling simultaneously with recognition and surprise.

Pinned to the bulletin board above my desk is one of my favourite descriptions of fictional language at its best. It comes from *Startle and Illuminate: Carol Shields on Writing*. "I look first to language that possesses an accuracy that cannot really exist without leaving its trace of deliberation. I want, too, the risky articulation of what I recognize but haven't yet articulated myself. And finally, I hope for some fresh news from another country that satisfies, by its modesty, a microscopic enlargement of my vision of the world. I wouldn't dream of asking for more."

This is such a complex description, one wide open, like fiction itself, to interpretation. I thought it might be useful to break it down into parts and see how it applies to some of the stories I've selected for this book.

> *[A]n accuracy that cannot really exist without leaving its trace of deliberation.*

Shields is speaking here about prose that is so precise that if we stop to notice it, beads of sweat will appear on the page, the sweat of the writer deliberating over every word. But mostly we don't notice, because we're swept along by the narrative. In Adam Dickinson's "Commensalism" we do actually notice, for the story is so packed with arresting imagery it's practically a prose poem. The narrator's dog, for example, is "crossed with a switchblade"; the animals she kills and delivers are "wilted envelopes"; she wanders as "fluently as children". And that's just the first paragraph.

All Lisa Moore's work is built of layered images and sensations. Note the precision of description in "The Curse":

> *I saw her remove the top of the lipstick, and place it on the concrete windowsill of the store. The sill was slanted. The woman put down the little plastic top and her fingers—a giant ring of rhinestones or glass on each finger and even one thumb, it was a mystery how she got them over her arthritic knuckles—hovered, waiting to be sure*

> *the top of the lipstick wouldn't roll away and fall onto*
> *the sidewalk.*

It took me five times as long to type out those three sentences than the actual moment it describes. You can be sure Moore's labour was a hundredfold. In fact the entire story takes place as the narrator walks along a street in Saint John's, Newfoundland, with three young children, yet the virtuoso Moore expands and contracts time to give us crucial moments in three of those characters' lives while still lasering down, via her deliberate language, on the present moment.

> *[T]he risky articulation of what I recognize but haven't*
> *yet articulated myself.*

Frankie Barnet in "Again, The Sad Woman's Soliloquy," presents an awkward young woman having an affair with her creative writing professor. (Shocking! "'You can't write about me,' he had said. 'You know that, right?' Other than that we did everything.") She goes to a party with him, takes a drug called "youth" and ends up on the couch with the titular sad woman. "'My sadness,' recited the sad woman as if it were a poem,' is a dark, velvety distress . . .'" I read this whimsical, yet biting, story several times before I think I understood what Barnet was articulating about happiness, sadness, and being young. Ultimately, though, I stopped caring what exactly the story meant and was simply gloriously subsumed in a velvety sadness myself.

I'm still mulling over the creepiness of "Alice and Charles." Camilla Grudova has set her story in what seems to be the future, one where every unmarried woman is assigned a dog for her protection. Dog shit is everywhere. The sexes are strictly separated and—surprise, surprise—women's living conditions are like your worst university flop times ten. Sanitary protection appears to be non-existent. "I noticed that all the stains on her clothes and our furniture were now familiar, and there weren't any new ones, no fresh drips of blood on the toilet seat and floors." "Alice and Charles" is as funny as it is horrible. The narrator and her dog Alice begin a relationship with . . . a clown! It goes very badly. And a feeling lingers long after reading that Grudova has not so much put her finger on the dark pulse of our culture, as clawed it open and showed us the true colour of its blood.

> [S]ome fresh news from another country that satisfies, by its modesty, a microscopic enlargement of my vision of the world.

Shields's art was created out of commonplace experience so it's no surprise she admired "modesty." Here I believe she is referring to stories about people just being people rather than throwing themselves into heroic feats. But I think she'd approve of the heroism of Richard Van Camp's protagonist in "Young Warriors in Love." It does present a modestly universal situation, one from "another country." A young boy with a crush on a girl in his class consults his TV-addicted uncle who suggests three love medicine ceremonies; these the lovesick boy actually attempts. Van Camp's merging of oral story-telling with the literary, English with Cree, his hilarious background jabs via the television and the marvellous non-ending veering off into a kind of chant was the first story I read that had me zinging with delight.

There are other family-centred stories in this collection that so fully satisfy Shields's request for modesty and "microscopic enlargement" that their precise analysis of character and detail bring the reader as close as kin: "Wheelers," by Alex Pugsley, "Upholstery" by Mireille Silcoff, "Pig Head" by Zalika Reid-Benta, "The Association" by Elise Levine and "Late and Soon" Christy Ann Conlin. Conlin's use of the tricky second person worked perfectly in the case of one twin reckoning with another. "Mum stood beside me with her head down and her gloved hands clasped together like two black doves. You arrived at the last minute, standing there by the gate when they lowered Edmund into the earth." With this reproach I felt myself fill with shame, as though I was the bad twin. Likewise, Pugsley's employment of a silent late-adolescent narrator overwhelmed by his wisecracking Haligonian family positioned me next to him on the couch, shrinking down in anticipation of the next eruption. Anyone who remembers being a child, or who has raised one, will also merge easily with Reid-Benta's first-person child narrator. She takes a trip to visit extended family in Jamaica and finds herself squeamishly out of place, yet once back home in Canada reframes and exaggerates her Jamaican experiences to impress her classmates. I was in the ski chalet with Silcoff's brain-injured protagonist, witness to the unravelling of her marriage, and in that townhouse stuck all over with Post-It notes with Levine's eleven-year-old boy alienated from his single mother. I *was* that boy Martin. Both Silcoff and Levine are masterful prose stylists and witty to boot. Levine: "... he is still asleep and dreamless as machines;" "She looks like she has smelled a terrible fart, not just heard some bad jokes about them, and is taking the high road..." Silcoff: "Her torso curved into the sofa as if unhindered by anything as hard as a skeleton..." "The father who gave me everything was [now] giving me horse fruit and cheese wax." These are "accuracy without a trace of deliberation" stories too.

Of course by "another country" Shields could also have been referring to stories about characters quite unlike her, and experiences far outside her own. "Alice and Charles," "Every True Artist" by Kai Conradi, or "nupqu ʔak·ɫam̓/A Long Time Ago" by Troy Sebastian are examples. In Conradi's story, a middle-aged Canadian woman for whom sketching is a newish hobby arrives at a supposed artist residency in the American desert to find only a run-down motel in a sparsely populated hick town. She sticks around long enough to draw her way into a strange sexual encounter. In "nupqu ʔak·ɬamֿ/A Long Time Ago" Troy Sebastian drops us into a conversation between Ka titi and the hilarious ka·pi-addict, Uncle Pat. What a delight to be invited to sit at a kitchen table with a Ktunaxa elder, not the least because, as Ka titi says of "suyupi" (white people) who have never seen a Ktunaxa before, they are "naturally impressed as we Ktunaxa are known for our well-developed bodies and easygoing attitude towards sex." (Insert riotous laughter here.) And isn't the plant kingdom another country too? In "The Second Coming of the Plants," the zany Zsuzsi Gartner may be the first writer to give voice to their grievances. "The enslavement of millions bound for the Christmas tree lots and, later the chippers . . . the agonies of the Japanese willow and the jasmine at the hands of their bonsai torturers."

Grudova, Conradi, Sebastian and Gartner give us unusual situations. But even in the ordinary we experience the countries of other people and find them strangely like ours. Like in Shashi Bhat's "The Most Precious Substance on Earth," where a group of girls on a high-school band trip are betrayed by another for a reason barely whispered on the page: "Eunice's eyes go dark and ancient. . ." "Her hand gripped the black felt-tipped pen as she scratched fervently, each word an abrasion." Or Cathy Stonehouse's "A Room at the Marlborough" where, upon his mother's death, a lonely photographer tallies all the ghosts in his life.

So, yes. I'll pat myself on the back and imagine it's Carol Shields. Imagine her whispering, "Good choices, these." Separately and together, they do satisfy her requirement for what fiction and fictional language should and can offer. I present them here with the modest belief that they will invite you inside and that while you're in them you'll feel different—sad, strange, delighted, disturbed—then step back out blinking in wonderment at your slightly larger world.

BEST CANADIAN STORIES
2019

YOUNG WARRIORS IN LOVE

Richard Van Camp

A long time ago when I was straight nuts and ribs I had a crush on a girl named Chandra Bone.

Can you say that name?

Chandra Bone.

Oh her name still makes me dizzy.

She moved to our town in grade 3. She was in my class.

She had green eyes, the colour of a cat. Who had green eyes in our town? No one. No one at all.

Only the cats and maybe some teddy bears.

Chandra also had dimples, something I'd only seen in magazines and movies.

I was crazy for her. I had my first crush.

The only problem was I could tell she was going to fall for my buddy Trevor Thunder.

Noooooooooooooooooooooooooo!!!!! The tad polerrrrrrrrrr rrrrrrrrrrrrrrrrrrr.

He always got the new girls.

Even the clouds knew it was no fair.

So I went to see my Uncle Raymond. He lives in Indian Village. He was watching *Dances with Wolves* and I told him about my struggle.

"You really love this girl?" he asked.

"Yes, Uncle. I'm crazy for her."

"How do you know it's love?"

"Because she gives me a big sweaty upper lip, okay?"

He nodded. "Tapwe. And you're sure Trevor Thunder— the Tadpoler—is going to go for her?"

I hung my head. "Positive."

"Gee," he said. "Even his dad always got first dibs since time immemorial."

"A ho," I said.

"Okay," he said, "what you gotta do is the snake ceremony."

"The snake ceremony? What the heck is that?"

"This ceremony," he said, "is you take your buddies, Clarence and Brutus, and you go into the snake pits. This is the time of year where snakes have a snake party. There'll be hundreds, maybe thousands of them, and you gotta be quiet. You gotta show respect. What you gotta do is you roll up your sleeve and reach into them—but you can't touch them. Go up to your elbow and if you go all the way into them without touching them and without them peeing on you then the woman you want will fall in love with you. Essentially, if the snakes don't pee on you, that's their way of saying that they give their permission. They bless your love."

"Oh man," I said. "I'm ever scared of snakes. Aren't there any other ceremonies?"

"Wah! No way. This i s t he t hree c eremonies f or l ove medicine that were passed on to me by my uncles, and this is the first. If you fail, come back and we'll discuss your other options."

He looked away and watched *Dances with Wolves*. He watched the part of the movie where the main moonyow from Water World reports what he sees to our cousins in the South. Uncle Raymond raised his hands to the side of his head and made little horns with his pinky. "Tatanka," he said and started to smile. "Good luck, Nephew. A ho."

"A ho," I said and left.

I got my dad to drive Clarence, me and Brutus out to the snake pits. My dad knew I was up to something but was quiet about it.

Brutus and Clarence ran with me to the pits. We had to outrun mosquitoes, deer flies, bull dogs, sand flies and the dreaded hair eaters who made the sound *tk tk tk tk tk tk*.

And why was I there? I was there for the love of *Chandra Bone Chandra Bone Chandra Bone.*

And what colour were her eyes? Green like a cat.

And what did she have that I'd only seen in magazines and movies? Dimples dimples dimples.

And who was trying to tadpole her? Trevor Thunder Trevor Thunder Trevor Thunder.

Eeeeeeeeeeeeeeeeeeeeeeeeeeeeehhhhhhhhhhhhhhhhhhhh hhhhhhhhhhh.

So we made our way to the pits and that was when we heard them: hisssssssssssssssssssssssssssssssssssssssssss.

They knew we were coming: the snakes of the Salt Plains. *Hisssssssssssssssssssssssssssss!!!!!!!!!!!*

As we got closer, we could smell thousands of garter snakes. *Hisssssssssssssssssssssssssssssssssss.*

And as we made our way, our glasses fogged up with their musk and breath.

Hisssssssssssssssssssssssssssssssssssssssss.

And even now they know I'm talking about them and to you they say, *"Hisssssssssssssssssssssssssssssssssssssssssssssssssssss sssssssssssss."*

So we made our way and we walked into the earth—into the caverns where they live. They were all coiled up, thousands of them and all we saw were their scales, their eyes, their flickering tongues and they greeted me with these words, "Chandra Bone, Chandra Bone, Chandra Bone."

And I said, "Yesssssssssssssssssssssssssssssssssssssssssssssss ssssss........."

And they made a circle of their bodies and I rolled up my sleeve.

"Who is the one who is going for her?" They asked. "Who is the one they call 'The Tadpoler'?"

"Trevor Thunder," I said and raised my arm so they could see I was getting ready.

"He always gets the new girls," they said.

"Tawpe," I said in Cree because it was true and the truth was being spoken here.

"Let us see what our mystery reveals," they said and then they went, "Hissssssssssssssssssssssssssssssssssssssssssssssssssssssssssssssssssss."

I slowly backed up and I slowly lowered myself like a snow ninja but in spring time. I wanted to reach in all syrupy slow but decided to stay human, so I reached my hand all the way in, up to my arm, as Grant and Brutus watched. And though my glasses fogged with the heat of their breath and flickering tongues and though my little knee bones trembled I did as I was told by my uncle. I said her name three times: "Chandra Bone Chandra Bone Chandra Bone."

I closed my eyes and felt the heat roll off their bodies. Even though they're cold-blooded, when they get together they party hard, I guess, just like my uncles.

"Let us see let us see let us see," they said and I slowly pulled my arm back and they had peed all over me. My nostrils filled with the aroma of apple juice, for that is the smell of their pee.

"Eeeeh!" I said. "How come you did this?"

They watched and rolled around so they could see me with their other eyes, "It is not for us to say. It is not for you to know."

"Cheeeeeeeeeeeeeeeeeeeeeeeeeeaaaaaaaaaaaaap," I said. "After all we've been through?"

"Leave us to our party," they said. "Leave us to our ways."

And I left with a soaked apple juice smelling arm that I wiped upon the Old Man's Beard on the trees. And in the wind I heard them say something: it was like a song of sorrow and invisible secrets braiding together in the wind.

"Cheap," Brutus said. "What now?"

"Back to Uncle Raymond's," I said. "He spoke of two other ways."

"I don't know," Clarence said. "Trevor Thunder gets whoever he wants. Even his dad was like that."

"Hissssssssssssssssssssssssssssssssssss!" I said and looked at my useless hands all the way back to town. The say the wind has a thousand voices but what did the Snake People say to me? I thought and thought and recollected and recollected but nothing came. Nothing came.

Uncle Raymond waited for a commercial break from Oprah before he looked to my arm and wrinkled his nose. "Apple juice. So they peed on you, hey?"

I nodded. "Yup."

"Aunty Oprah says, 'Rejection is Protection.'"

"What?"

"Perhaps if this Chandra Bone crush does not work out, you're being saved for a greater love."

"No way," I said. "Chandra Bone is my greatest love."

But then I thought about it. As we left the snakes, I heard a riddle in the wind. What they had imparted in their traditional ways was a whisper to the sky. It went: "She's gonna roll you like dice!"

But I wasn't certain.

"Okay," he said. "The second ceremony. What you gotta do is do the Buffalo Ceremony."

"The Buffalo Ceremony?" I asked. "What the heck is that?"

"Oh now," he said. "Only the bravest of the brave do this. Are you sure you want this woman?"

I thought of her smile, her laugh, how the school dance was coming up and how proud I would be to get the first and last waltz with her. "Yes, Uncle. Yes."

"Okay," he said. "Every spring the Buffalo People get itchy skin. Their little guard hairs know a fresh coat is coming so they tickle tickle tickle—everyone say that: tickle tickle

tickle—and they tickle tickle tickle under their incoming fresh coat of fur. So what they do is the Buffalo People scratch themselves against the trees. They wiggle wiggle wiggle and they scratch scratch scratch and they leave tufts of fur behind."

I nodded. "I have seen this fur in the trees, Uncle, yet I never knew where it came from."

"A ho," he said. "What you have to do is go with your elders and go out on Canada Day and you go to the Buffalo People with other young warriors in love, and what you do is whoever can get the closest to them, whoever can hold their fur up and say the name of the one they love three times to them, it usually works out."

"Wait," I said. "What do you mean 'usually works out'?"

"Little Wolf," My uncle said. He called me that when he could not remember my name. Actually, he called everyone that when he couldn't remember their names either. I think everyone on his street was called "Little Wolf." It was a trade in a good way—a good trade. A solid trade. "The Buffalo People have their little calves who are learning their ways, and young warriors in love have gone out since time immemorial to do this ceremony. Sometimes the Buffalo People get tired of us disturbing them but mostly they let our ceremony go in a good way. The Buffalo People go into the heart of the forest to rest and get away from the bugs. It's a dreamtime for them when they are there, so sometimes they get mad when young warriors like yourself do what you are about to do.

"Wait," I said. "I don't want to make them mad."

"Does the wolverine concern himself with what the marmots say?" Uncle Raymond asked.

"What?" I asked.

"Watch your elders," he said. "They'll keep their trucks aimed towards the highway with their engines running. They'll watch you with binoculars to see who wins, but here's what you can look forward to if the buffalo stampede: you can be gored, stomped, trampled, dropkicked and bannock-slapped. That's just for starters. Don't let me tell you what they did to my uncle."

"What did they do?" I asked.

"They stomped him into a memory," he said and looked down.

Gulp! "Are you serious?" I asked. I felt my little knee bones start shivering in their sockets.

He looked to me and grinned. "Nah. Just joshin'. The Buffalo People are a wise people. They know it's love that has called you there. Be respectful. Be wise and, most of all, good luck."

I scratched my head. "Didn't you say there was a third way?"

"A ho," he said. "The third way is the most courageous way. Most young warriors don't have the anything to go for it. Let's not go there yet. Do the Buffalo Ceremony. Get that fur. Hold it high. Chant the Buffalo People her name three times and they will send you their wishes of being together."

"Yes!" I said. "I like it. So when do we go?"

"What?" he asked.

"Let's go. It's Canada Day tomorrow."

"Oh," he said. "I have things to do."

"Don't be cheap, Uncle," I said. "I chopped all your wood. I visit you every day. Who didn't forget your birthday this year? I'm your favourite nephew."

"You're my only nephew," he said but then thought about it. "Little Wolf."

"And you're my favourite uncle," I said, and even though I only had one he knew it was true.

"We leave at dawn," he said.

"A ho," I said.

"Tatanka," he smiled and we made the sign.

The next day:

Well, I wish I could tell you that I won this contest and ceremony but I didn't. The Buffalo People watched me and about 14 others from town. Some smudged with sweetgrass and sage; some stretched in the shadows. I prayed like a ninja in secret and moved with the sun as She crept. What happened was a little calf came towards me. This little one's hair was red and curly. This little one had the most beautiful, curious eyes and I forgot why I was there. By the time I realized what I was supposed to do, I could see that the other warriors had made their way miles ahead of me into the heart of the herd, and all I wanted to do was gaze at the miracle of this little one who had strayed too far. I pointed at his or her mommy far away who was calling for her and, after a time, the little one left. It was such a perfect gift to get so close to a little calf that all I could do was take some fur from the willows, and I made the decision that if Chandra didn't want to be with me, what was the point of me doing all this work in secret? When I worked up the courage—and I would work up the courage—I would tell Chandra about the Snake Ceremony; I would ask for her first waltz at the school dance and when we danced, I would give her this soft perfect fur from the Buffalo People and I would tell her about my visit with the little calf.

"Uncle," I said. "I have tried the Snake Ceremony. I almost tried the Buffalo Ceremony. I have tried and I have failed but in a good way. Every day Trevor Thunder gets closer to Chandra's heart and every day we get closer to the school dance. All I want is a chance to waltz with her and get to know her. Please tell me what the third ceremony is. It's all I have left."

"Take it easy," he said. "You have your health, your friends. You have me."

"I know," I said. "But I'm ready for the ultimate ceremony."

"You say this," he said, "but do you mean it?"

"Yes, Uncle. She's all I think about. She's my everything!"

"Okay okay," he said. "Once I tell you this, you have to do it."

"I promise," I said. "I'll do it."

"Okay," he said. "Here we go."

"Let's go!"

"The third ceremony is the most obvious one. It's one you can do in town."

"Really?" I asked.

He nodded. "The third ceremony is one you can find in you."

"This sounds lame," I said.

"No way," he said. "You have to ask yourself this question, Little Wolf."

"Which is?"

"You can always just call her."

And that was how I made my way through the three ceremonies.

As I dialed her number, oh my hands shook, my little knee bones trembled. I was so nervous my little baby curls popped back!

As I dialed the last number and I braced for her heavenly voice, I knew that no matter what happened, I was a young warrior in love and I had done the Snake Ceremony; I had almost completed the Buffalo Ceremony, and even if I was rejected because of Trevor Thunder, I trusted that I was being protected for sacred, holy love that I would have when the time was right.

I was a young warrior in love and it hit me: we are all warriors when we are in love or 'on the keemooch' to find it.

A ho, Little Wolf.

A ho.

Now you know.

Now you know.

Never say Uncle cheaped out on you.

Make your life Nezi Inkwo.

Live your life good.

Sleep good.

Eat good.

Share what you have.

Don't pick fights!

☺

Tapwe and mahsi cho.

THE CURSE

Lisa Moore

The woman who cursed Trinity Brophy was a frequenter of Theatre Pharmacy on Long's Hill. At the end of each month, when the cheques arrived, there'd be a line of maybe twenty people waiting for the pharmacy to open. The summer of the curse the woman wore a yellow hat with a floppy brim. She walked up Long's Hill every day and my husband and I started referring to her as The Woman with the Yellow Hat, like the man with The Man with the Yellow Hat in the *Curious George* children's books.

She had a variety of wigs, but her own hair was clipped very close to her scalp, oily, thick and mottled silver like a seal pelt. That summer she wore a bright orange lipstick, a sixties shade. It spread above her upper lip, just enough to betray the tremor in her hands.

I was walking home from downtown on the morning of the curse, passing the line outside the pharmacy, and I saw The Woman with the Yellow Hat reach into her handbag and take out a tortoise shell compact. She flipped up the lid. An oval of sunshine, reflected from the mirror, shivered and wobbled over her cheek and settled in her right eye, making her shut it tight and draw her chin into the loose folds of skin on her neck.

I saw her remove the top of the lipstick, and place it on the concrete windowsill of the store. The sill was slanted. The woman put down the little plastic top and her fingers—a giant ring of rhinestones or glass on each finger and even one thumb, it was a mystery how she got them over her arthritic knuckles—hovered, waiting to be sure the top of the lipstick wouldn't roll away and fall onto the sidewalk. Then she spread the lipstick over both lips and rubbed them together, examined them in the compact mirror, moving it up and down to get the right view.

Her faded black leggings, which she wore under all her dresses, sagged at the knees and were pilled with tiny nubs of cotton. The foam soles of her flip-flops had flattened out, become as hard as boards. I'd seen her feet close-up one afternoon when she'd fallen asleep on a bench in Bannerman Park. A Frisbee had wafted down on the bench near her feet and I had retrieved it without waking her. The soles of the woman's feet were split with cuts, crusted with blood; some of the cuts weeping a clear pus.

I used to see her shopping at the Salvation Army on Waldegrave and she'd try on a lot of glamorous outfits. Prom dresses, or bridesmaid's dresses that she'd buy and wear all day long during the summer.

On the day she uttered the curse against Trinity Brophy, she was wearing a cocktail dress from the eighties. The material was stiff and opalescent, giant puffy sleeves, a skirt of layered flounces. It shimmered and rustled.

I remember it because I had owned one just like it when I was a teenager. I'd bought it when I'd gone to Stephenville to study fine art in a two-year diploma course. I'd worn the dress to the El Dorado and met a guy whose name I don't remember but who called me on the payphone in the hall of the residence every evening for three weeks, to ask for a date.

Every evening, after dinner in the cafeteria, someone would knock on my bedroom door to tell me there was a call.

Most times I didn't answer. Sometimes I asked them to lie. They were willing because they were waiting for calls from their boyfriends, so they didn't want me hogging the phone. My opalescent dress had an ink stain on the third flounce, just over the knee.

Trinity was seven-years-old when the Woman in the Yellow Hat cursed her. The day was already heating up, though there were still gentle gusts of a mineral-smelling cold coming off the icebergs outside the harbour. Trinity came tearing around the corner of Livingstone, onto Long's Hill with a water balloon.

She was being chased by my son, Joey, who was also seven, and a girl named Jessica, maybe eight, and Jessica's little brother, Cory, who was probably four.

They each had water balloons raised above their shoulders. The effort of holding the wobbly balloons in the air waggled their gaits as they turned the corner. They were running lopsided. All three of them aiming for Trinity Brophy's back, but she was too fast. Her long, straight, gold-brown hair flapped between her shoulder blades.

Three water balloons splatted on the sidewalk at the heels of Trinity's new white sneakers. She stopped so fast her sneakers squeaked.

The other kids had spent their arsenal.

Trinity still had her balloon.

I was trying to see if there was an ink stain on the third flounce of the woman's opalescent dress. I know the clothes at the second-hand stores on the island shuffle through all the small-town Salvation Armies and even end up as far as Labrador.

I know this because I'd once donated a Grenfell coat in Stephenville, and a decade later I found it at the Salvation Army in St. John's on Waldegrave.

They've shut down that Sally Ann and replaced it with a gourmet hamburger restaurant that lasted less than a year.

The building has been vacant ever since. I'd ordered takeout once, and the burger was uncooked.

When I found the Grenfell coat on Waldegrave, I'd put it on and stood in front of a mirror. I licked my index finger and reached into the pocket for the seam that ran along the bottom. I used to steal a sesame seed bagel from the cafeteria in Stephenville every morning by slipping it in my coat pocket, wrapped in a paper napkin. Fifteen years later, I was standing in front of a mirror, and I pressed the wetted tip of my index finger into a little pool of sesame seeds in the lining. Then I put my finger in my mouth.

I had just turned seventeen when I'd bought that coat. The age Trinity and Joey are now. The guy was ten years older. He had a car and when I was walking downtown he'd crawl along beside me, clamping an elbow to the outside of the door and hoisting his shoulder and head out the window. He'd get as close to the curb as he could, sometimes causing the traffic behind him to bunch up; two or three cars swerving into the opposite lane of oncoming traffic to pass him.

Asking me when I thought I'd be free. Shouting: How about Friday?

When the weather got cold, which happened overnight, I'd bought the Grenfell coat with fox fur trim around the hood. That September I'd written a radio play. By some miracle, the CBC had purchased it. The fee for the play, along with my student loan, meant I had a lot of money. It would have been strange for a student to own such an expensive coat. It looked too old for me.

The boutique was on the main strip of the town of Stephenville, a few stores down from the traffic light. I put up the hood and raised the collar of my turtleneck so it came up just under my eyes. The price tag, hanging on a thread from the cuff, was handwritten.

It was the most I'd ever paid for an item of clothing. The fur around my face tickled. The coat was wool and mid-thigh in length, the two big pockets were embroidered with Inuk hunters carrying spears. It was bright red and the lining was pink.

I also bought a black vinyl purse like my mother might have carried, and left my army surplus knapsack with the ballpoint pen peace signs all over it, in the drawer under my bed in the residence. On the second day that I wore the coat I saw the guy's car in my peripheral vision, but he didn't even slow down.

Trinity saw the water stains from the broken balloons spreading on the sidewalk near her new white sneakers and came to a halt. Even at seven-years-old, you could see she would be a beauty. Her eyes were the kind of blue that's very pale, the iris rimmed with black. Freckles, over the bridge of her nose, her cheeks tanned gold, her eyebrows golden. She was the first kid to dye her hair blue in her elementary school, and she was ridiculed for it.

Nobody spoke about her birth parents, but at least one of them had to be tall. By the time she was twelve she was head and shoulders above me, and taller than her third foster mother, who was my next-door neighbour.

Trinity was doing the kind of fast growing that leaves a body without an ounce of fat and robs a child of energy very suddenly so that you come upon them in odd places at odd hours, sound asleep. The kind of growing that kept her constantly hungry.

She'd lick her finger and stick it in my sugar bowl and put her finger in her mouth, no matter how many times I said other people had to use that sugar too.

The sort of love I feel for Trinity Brophy is nothing like the love I have for my son, which is stable and uncomplicated. The love I feel for Trinity is inconvenient and random. But it's also intractable, brutish. She's just a neighbourhood kid who caught my attention. We don't choose who we love. Lots of kids came and went on that street. I love her as if she were my own.

I was coming back from a board meeting on the day that Trinity was cursed, and maybe something of that foul storm ricocheted, hit me and Joey too.

Each of the children was stuck to the sidewalk, the skins of their burst water balloons shrivelled. Adrenaline and food-colouring from the Mr. Freezies had paralyzed everyone.

Joey's lips and tongue were blue. There's a psychology test or a party trick, where they ask you to say the word *blue* every time they show you a red card. They show you several red cards in a row, and you say *blue*, then they show you a blue card and you say *red*.

I thought his blue mouth and tongue meant my son had been caught red-handed.

Trinity was the kind of person, by the time she was a teenager, that the johns who regularly circle our street wouldn't bother. She'd beat the face off them. Or maybe they did bother her. But if they did I was certain they'd regret it.

I said unassailable love, but it was blinkered too. Trinity, by the time she was fourteen, say, or fifteen, had a life that was entirely a mystery to me. She wasn't much of a talker.

But seven-years-old, on the sidewalk by the pharmacy, after the other kids' water balloons had been thrown, Trinity pivoted to stare down Joey with open-faced glee, and then without warning, like the boys do on the basketball court, she faked to the side. She threw her water balloon at The Woman in the Yellow Hat.

The balloon was red and wobbled in the air and burst noiselessly on the old woman's shoulder. The others in the line for Theatre Pharmacy unpeeled from the brick wall with the badly painted mural of a chemist in a white lab coat, a pestle and mortar in his outstretched arms. The line was jostled. The other people, mostly unshaven men, were more disgruntled than surprised. The medications they took quelled anxiety, but robbed them of erratic, inconsequential emotions, like being startled. They were humourless and bug-eyed and unstartled.

They were, by that hour, in need of whatever the pharmacist was going to hand out.

The few women in the line might have been going up the stairs to a dingy office to suck the cock of the doctor, and they were humourless too. The doctor's pills-for-sex practice made the headlines for the entire summer that year.

The Woman in the Yellow Hat had flared a mottled purplish red under the sickly puce shadow cast by the brim of her hat.

The impact of the balloon had knocked one of her giant Velcro-ed shoulder pads askew. She plucked at the wet fabric of the dress that had suctioned on to her skin, lifting it so it caught a bubble of air and the shoulder pad was dislodged and dropped onto the sidewalk.

She snatched up the pad in her fist. It looked like a sanitary napkin. The shoulder pad caused the men in the line an embarrassment that made them look away. Denuded of just one of the gronky, football player's shoulders made The Woman in the Yellow Hat a hunchback. It revealed a vulnerability so raw it was a hazard to behold.

But her eyes were bright and narrowed.

She was short of breath, and pulled a puffer from her purse and, putting it to her mouth, inhaled so deeply her eyes bulged. I'd bent to pick up the shoulder pad, but she got there first. When I stood up I saw that the ivory-coloured puffer was smeared with the orange lipstick. And the curse came out with her next breath.

The Woman in the Yellow Hat frequently berated people on the street. Kids from the private school, still in their uniforms, on their way to Moo Moos, walked past her in noisy, skipping groups but didn't pay her much attention.

It was during those moments when she was talking to the dead, or the invisible, people who seemed to come at her from decades past, from her childhood, that you could get a good look at her. Her voice could carry all the way down Military road, despite the breathing difficulties. The things she said were accusations, one half of a conversation, though she also paused to listen to what the ghost had to say. Her cheeks sagged, and were speckled with age spots the size of dimes. Her cheekbones two hard juts beneath deep-set eyes draped with papery eyelids, soft as Kleenex.

She spat on the sidewalk, and pointed at Trinity Brophy.

You will pay, she said. By the fuck, you will pay for that. You're going to burn in hell. You mark my words. You will burn.

Then she swayed her finger so that it took in not just Trinity, but Joey and me. Jessica and her little brother Cory had taken off back up the road and had already turned the corner.

All of you, she said. You'll burn for this.

My son, Joey, who would do concrete grooming at the college in Seal Cove straight out of high school, had his Mr. Freezie clenched in his teeth and it flipped up and down as his jaw tightened. The Woman with The Yellow Hat, snarling; her pointed, trembling finger with all its jewels.

After Seal Cove, Joey got a student loan and did heavy equipment in Stephenville, and then welding. He stayed in the same residence where I had stayed. He was hired at Muskrat Falls on the dam, for the summer, and on to Fort Mac. Then he got a job with the city ploughing snow in winter, collecting garbage. He works outdoors and makes upwards of sixty with benefits.

But long before all that, Joey had the incident with a shopping cart and it altered him irrevocably. This was when he was twelve.

Joey and his friends found a supermarket cart by Churchill Square. They were in the middle of a basketball tournament, on a lunch break. The cart was a long way from the supermarket. The metal casing for the front wheel was bent out to the side, making the cart useless. The boys leaned it against a fire hydrant to bang the wheel straight with a rock.

Once the cart was operational, the plan was Joey would get in it and the boys would push it to the first steep hill they could find and let him go. They would all push him up Bonadventure, past Brother Rice and Holy Heart, where the tournament was happening, and let him go at the top of Garrison Hill. Joey would abandon the cart at the last second, throwing himself onto the asphalt before it smashed into the railing that protected the war memorial at the foot of the hill. Or he might somersault over the spear-tipped iron fence that surrounded the memorial, or be impaled on it.

On the day of the shopping cart they left the tournament during the lunch break and had headed to Subway in Churchill Square and they'd made a mess. The boys were loud and they'd dropped the wrappers from their sandwiches all over the floor, smeared mustard over the tables on purpose.

One of the team was rude to the girl behind the counter, had mimicked her when she told them to leave.

They'd taken fistfuls of drinking straws and tore off the paper sleeves and joined each straw together by fitting one end into the next, until they had fashioned flimsy swords, maybe seven or eight straws in length.

The manager appeared from the back and kicked them out. They rose from the table slowly, trying to stab each other with the flaccid swords, banging into each other in the porch, blocking the entrance, until they burst out all at once into the parking lot.

They were almost knocked over by a car emerging on a conveyor belt from the car wash at the back of what used to be the supermarket and a dry-cleaners. Those buildings have brown paper over the windows now and the eavestrough is rusted out and hangs off one end of the building, clanging when it's windy.

The driver of the car coming out of the car wash was an elderly woman who believed the boys were throwing things at her vehicle and she called the police.

A cruiser circled the block while the boys were beating the broken wheel of the shopping cart with a rock, trying to straighten it. The boys saw the cruiser and took off through the valley. They were back at the school for the second half of the basketball tournament, already on the floor when two cops busted in and stopped the game.

Joey, my Joey, had not been the one with the rock, nor had he touched the shopping cart. He had been standing to the side, like a driver at the Grand Prix who waits for the mechanics to go over the engine before the race. But the coach insisted Joey had been the troublemaker. He had a gut feeling, the coach said. He told the cop that he knew with certainty that Joey was to blame for whatever had happened in Churchill Square.

Joey left the gym and ran all the way home, banging on the front door, crying hard, believing the house was about to be stormed by a swat team and that he would be dragged away in cuffs.

He collapsed in his bed exhausted by the force of the false accusation. He was accused by his coach of creating havoc in Subway, being rude to the girl behind the counter (for me this was the worst of the alleged crimes), vandalizing an old woman's car, damaging a fire hydrant and destroying a shopping cart, which was private property, according to the cop. Joey was kicked off the team and the coach demanded the principal suspend him from Junior High for at least a week.

He had also been the cause, according to the coach, of the team losing the tournament (the worst of the allegations for Joey, it was the first loss of the season).

They would be coming for him, the coach promised. He'd pointed a finger at Joey, and said his days of causing trouble were over.

After the coach singled him out, Joey had run home and went to his room, passed into a deep sleep almost at once, and seemed to have developed a fever. He was shivering, and his cheeks blazed. He made noises in his sleep; spoke to people; called out for me.

I woke him up the next morning to say I had gone to the fire hydrant and taken pictures, which I had already emailed to the coach and the principal of the school and the police. There had been no damage, not a single chip or scratch, in the eye-smarting red paint of the hydrant.

I'd phoned Subway and spoken to the girl who had been behind the counter and to the manager, and I got a physical description of the boy who had been rude and gave them a description of Joey. They both confirmed Joey didn't fit the description.

I told Joey I had been speaking to one of the officers who had busted into the tournament. He was an obnoxious asshole, but I didn't tell Joey that.

The cop said he was going through surveillance tapes from four different businesses in the area: the gas station across the street from the fire hydrant; a camera on the back of the car wash; a camera in the dining area inside Subway; and another on the rear exterior of Subway.

It's taped? Joey asked. The whole thing is taped?

All of the fear left his face.

You're not worried about the surveillance tapes? I asked.

I told you, he said. I didn't touch that shopping cart. I didn't touch it. He fell back onto the pillow and slept until late afternoon.

I hounded the police officer with phone messages, as did the other parents who had a kid on the team. Demanding to know the progress he was making with the surveillance tapes. I told him I knew my son was innocent.

How can you know that? the officer asked.

Because he told me so, I said.

The officer said, Really? Boys lie to their mothers all the time, I certainly did.

I said: You are a very different sort of person than my son.

I didn't mean, of course, that my son was beyond telling me a lie. I meant the cop wasn't as good at knowing when the truth could betray you, and when it was your friend.

The whole thing blew over, but as I said, Joey was deeply changed by it. Something hardened in him; he became shrewd. The incident with the shopping cart gave him a heightened perception about character. Not distrust, exactly, but a tendency not to expect too much of others. He was ready for people to disappoint him and it made him both distant and easily forgiving.

After I'd bought the Grenfell coat in Stephenville, the biggest purchase of my whole life up to that point, I walked all over town with the hood up, and my old lady purse under my arm. I saw the car go past several times, sometimes more than once on a single day. I knew he was looking for me. But after two weeks went by the phone calls stopped.

One day I was in the strip mall buying a piece of apple pie and ice cream at the diner and he saw me. My coat was hanging on the back of my chair.

You got a new coat, he said. He asked me to a movie that Friday night.

I said, Sure, that'd be really nice.

He said he would pick me up at the residence. He'd be in the lobby. He knew he couldn't go upstairs, he said. So he'd be waiting in the lobby.

He took a cigarette pack out of his pocket and tapped it on the edge of my table so one smoke jutted up straight out of the pack each time he hit it. He did it slowly.

I'd join you, he said. But I have to go to work.

That's okay, I said.

I never knew where you were, he said. What window is yours anyway, in the residence? I know the third floor is the girls' floor.

I said I wasn't sure about the window. I'd never thought about it.

I'll be in the lobby, he said. I know which building you're in, because I'm after seeing you go in there. Sometimes I park across the street. Nice coat. I never would have recognized you in that coat. I'll be in the lobby.

The movie was a Clint Eastwood. There were hardly any people in the theatre. My arm was on the armrest, and the guy put his arm there too, so our arms were touching. We were both looking straight ahead. I waited as long as I could and then moved my arm away from his, as if I'd had the unconscious urge to shift my weight.

There'd been a fight about paying at the cashier. I said I would be paying for myself. This assertion seemed to make the guy feel injured and unsure, but I thrust my money at the woman behind the glass. His hand came in through the crescent cut in the bottom of the window at the same time, so that we were cuffed together by it, both of us holding up ten-dollar bills. The woman behind the counter hesitated.

Take mine, he said. I'm paying.

The woman said: You keep that miss, that's your mad money. You're going to need that.

I wedged my wrist back out of the glass, twisting against the bone of his wrist and I jammed the ten back in my pocket.

By the time Trinity and Joey turned fifteen the neighbourhood had changed, the casual fits and starts of senseless violence, mostly domestic, had mutated to another kind of violence: organized and determined. There were needles all over the ground, especially under the balconies in peoples' backyards. People complained about their property values. The cops were called every second night.

Once an old man with a sheet of silver hair was circling the neighbourhood in his Oldsmobile and looking at the sex workers and he got stuck in a snow bank. All the neighbours came out with their cellphones and surrounded his car, the phones at arms' length, videoing the old guy.

We're sending this to your wife, Grandpa, one woman shouted at him. He was slumped at the steering wheel, strapped in his seatbelt, trying to cover his face with his arms.

I've seen Trinity when she was hurt and angry; her eyelids half-close and she goes dead still. When they were twelve, Joey and Trin used to wrestle. I told Joey around that time that he couldn't hit a girl. After that, he refused to fight and she worked hard to make him hit back. Once he came home with a swollen eye and he refused to speak to her again. She'd ring the bell and he told me not to let her in.

I'd still help her with her homework. But Joey would stay in his room. We started to see less of her. Trin never talked much anyway, but she doesn't talk at all when she's hurt. I've seen her lash out with her fists, and I've heard stories. Doesn't take shit. But the dead look that comes into her eyes when she's scared is, I'm convinced, as accurate a picture of what's going on inside as I'm ever likely to see.

After the movie I asked the guy to drive me back to the dorm because, I told him, I was tired. I even yawned. But he argued and cajoled.

It's only quarter to ten, he said. Let's get a drink.

I really am sleepy, I said.

Okay then, he said.

On the way back to the dorm he told me he'd like me to meet his mother. He said he'd be going to the Codroy Valley, where his family lives, next weekend, and he'd like me to come. I'd have my own bedroom, of course, and I wouldn't need to worry about that. His mother wouldn't have nothing like that going on under her roof, he said. But he can tell I'm a nice girl. He has a graduation in three months, and he'd like me to be his date. If I knew what colour my dress was going to be he could order a corsage the same colour. Order it early. His whole family would be coming up. His mother and father and eleven of his siblings. He has a brother in Alberta, but the brother was making the trip home for the graduation. He has seven nieces and nephews and they were all coming. Getting dressed up. He knew it was a long time away yet, but do I have any idea what colour my dress would be?

I said: You just passed the residence.

I know, he said. I just want to show you something before we go back there. Only take a minute. There's this view up here. I want you to see it. It's a special place. Not many people know about it.

We were on the highway for about half a mile and turned up a dirt road full of potholes. Boulders on every side, and a clear cut. Sometimes he had to rock the car back and forth in the potholes to get it out. At those moments he had his cigarette jammed in the corner of his mouth, pointing down, but he was not smoking it. If the pothole required extra work, he would ask me to hold the cigarette, until he had gunned it. When the car was free he grinned at me as if he'd accomplished something big.

A week or two after Trinity turned seventeen she got caught at school with a gym bag full of drugs. It meant, for one thing, that her foster Mom wanted nothing more to do with her. She had other foster kids and she couldn't have that going on in her house.

But there were guys after Trinity Brophy now. They wanted her to pay for the drugs that the cops confiscated. If she didn't, Trin told me, they would hurt her.

Bubbles formed in the acetate pearly-coloured dress, over the Woman with The Yellow Hat's shoulder and along her breast, as she lifted the wet fabric from her skin. The bubbles looked like rising welts, as if she had been whipped or burned. You could see the rough lace of her polyester bra, and the thick strap and even the metal ring that held the strap to the cup, where the water made the dress transparent.

Her appearance mattered so very much to her. The gala gowns and short shiny dresses, the make-up. The astonishment of being soaked conflated with shame. The transparency in the fabric revealed how futile her efforts had been. The effort to look nice, no matter where you had to sleep, or what you had to eat. She was dressing for a party when there was no party. Perhaps she saw how the glamorous dresses marked her as ridiculous, though she had never seemed that way to me.

I saw a streak of ink on the third flounce. I'd been writing with a fountain pen, back in Stephenville, when I began to write the radio play. I thought that's what writers did. What erupted on the face of that woman after she was struck with the balloon was equal parts anguish and hatred.

I sat outside a little one-story bungalow in my car waiting for Trinity to come back out. We'd driven to a rural area outside St. John's. It had only taken about forty minutes. Trinity told me to stay behind the hedge, so they wouldn't see the car. I'd given her the money. It was all the money I'd saved for Joey to go to the concrete grooming course.

At the top of the lane there was a ridge that looked down on a river that was mostly overgrow with alder bushes and nothing to see. We made out. Just necking. He attempted to put his hand on my breast, but I stopped him. I think that's what he was expecting. He tasted of cigarettes and mouthwash and he was wearing very strong cologne, or it might have been the air-freshener that was hanging from the dash.

I can't remember what he looked like, except that his eyelashes were pale orange and so was his moustache. I could feel the bristles of that moustache on my upper lip. He was a heavy breather. I knew by then that the whole thing would be over within ten minutes or so. If I were patient I would find myself going through the front doors of the residence, and up to my room, in no time at all.

What disgusted me most was the smell of his cigarette on my fingers, from when he made me hold it for him.

He'd left the radio on while we necked and I was terrified it would run down the battery and we would be stuck out there. But he'd paused, now and then, in his wet kissing, to restart the engine.

Afterwards, he got out of the car and said he had to have a piss. The word 'piss' sounded so unnecessarily intimate to me that I felt light-headed and possibly nauseated. I heard his piss pattering the bushes. My Grenfell coat smelled of cigarettes. Then we drove back to the residence.

I believe the experience with the shopping cart hadn't brought Joey to the conclusion that you might expect: if you are innocent, justice will prevail; the truth will out.

What he had come to believe was that the world lay in wait for you. He decided that truth had no intrinsic value and had come to believe that whoever held onto the truth for it's own sake was a sucker.

What Joey believed, after the shopping cart incident, was that you had to outwit what lay in wait.

I wondered if he was right. Mothers and sons are telepathic. If this kind of communication were a language it would be monosyllabic and full of guttural spittle, short vowels, harsh consonants. But this telepathy bypasses ordinary language; it's wordless—paradoxically instant, layered and piercing. It shoots through.

My son, I knew, could no longer trust in the innocence of an object or a moment or a causal social exchange. A broken shopping cart could leap up like a panther and drag you away: fresh kill.

Joey had been called upon to partake in something old-fashioned or quaint, and without nuance: a duel with fate. He had to simply draw first. Or he could cheat, turn before the paces were up, and shoot fate in the back. In the end the bald unfairness of the situation tickled his funny bone. He developed a sense of humour that was more than just pranks with plastic straws and water balloons. He became wry. He was too young for wry.

He'd had to get a student loan. I told Trinity to make sure they all agreed, whoever they were, that the debt was paid. That she was in the clear. I told her to make sure they knew she was done with them.

She said: They don't exactly hand out receipts.

It was snowing and I was sitting outside in my car for a long time, waiting for her. It was long enough for the sand-coloured grass of the front lawn to accumulate enough snow that it became white.

I took in all the details of the house and garden, the burlap wrapped around a shrub. Two cars in the driveway, a silver Yaris and a red Ford truck. There was a shed and the door was open. I could see stacked firewood, and under a pale green tarp, an ATV. There was also a cardboard box that had held an artificial Christmas tree, leaning against a wooden garbage receptacle at the end of the driveway. A clothesline with what looked like a baby's little white dress on it. It might have been a baptismal dress. But after a moment, I realized it wasn't a dress, it was a pillowcase.

Maybe a year or so after the curse The Woman with the Yellow Hat disappeared from the streets. It was an absence that people mentioned for a while and then she was forgotten. The pharmacy came under new management. It was Joey who told me that Trinity Brophy had left the province. He said he'd heard that nobody knew where she was. I asked if he knew anything else. He said he thought Trinity Brophy was just like everybody else, trying to do whatever it took to keep going.

The door of the woodshed caught in a wind and slammed and I nearly jumped out of my skin. But nothing else moved and another twenty minutes passed. It had changed from dusk to almost dark. All the leftover light seemed to have seeped into the new snow on the lawn. It was eerily bright.

Finally Trinity came out of the house and got back in the car and we drove back to town. Of course we said things about her schoolwork and how Joey was doing. We didn't often speak about Joey but on that occasion she asked. She knew it was his tuition that I'd given her.

We came to the difficult intersection on the top of Kenna's Hill, a blind curve, and I asked her if it was clear. I told her I couldn't see. She was looking out the passenger window, avid, silent. Then she told me it was safe to go.

UPHOLSTERY

Mireille Silcoff

When I told Judy that I was going to marry Thom, she didn't pause before telling me that Thom was a car crash waiting to happen. For my mother, the gestalt psychologist Judy Glaser—and to me always Judy, never Mom—this was typical technique: wallop you over the head and wait for clear-headedness to ensue. A couple of years after her words careened into an actual prediction, I asked if she remembered saying them.

"Now, how can I answer that?" she asked. "If I say yes, it's like admitting I knew what would happen to my only child and let it happen. And that's impossible. For me to have that kind of responsibility in this. So forget it."

On the day of the car accident that cracked my skull, Thom was wearing a T-shirt he got while presenting a paper at a math conference. It read:

Dear algebra,
Stop asking me to find your x.
She is not coming back.
And I don't know y.

For years, he continued wearing it. In certain lights, you could see a faint pink mark on the right shoulder. Thom said the stain was from a pair of our daughter's brightly coloured pyjamas in the white wash. He'd remind me that on the day he ran the red light (and veered away from the truck and crashed our car into the concrete sound barrier), it was snowing hard. Only logical, Thom said, that he'd have been wearing a ski jacket. It was his jacket that would have taken my blood, not his T-shirt. "I guess we need to be more careful with the laundry," he said.

"*I* need to be more careful with laundry?" I asked.

"No! I mean us. We. Both of us. Okay, me. *I* need to be more careful."

Thom's insensitivities go with the rest of him: a man moonwalking through life, the sort who glides in and out of everything with no resistance, his body so slim it nearly disappears in profile. Back when he was studying at Wharton, partly because of the open secret of his IQ and partly because of the way his corduroys flapped around his skinny ankles, Thom was tagged as the one who would best everyone after graduation: the genius among the geniuses, who would soon be ensconced in a gilded Geneva office, pulling the levers on world finance. But then the time came, and he simply couldn't rise to any of the luxury positions he was offered. He maintains the issue was ideology, not inertia. He came back to Canada and took a position teaching at McGill.

My own career got crossed out by the accident. The lingering brain injury, combined with Abigail's birth, made any kind of return to work extremely remote. We had no savings. Thom still had his student loans. More than once, we'd needed to borrow from Don, my dad. Thom would ask me to ask.

"He's your father," he'd say.

"Which is why you should ask."

So many times, I resolved to divorce him. I'd look up apartments, imagining myself and Abigail in these single sunny rooms. I'd scan au pair websites, unsure where in the single sunny rooms I could put a German teen, the need to be free of Thom thrashing against the impossibility of leaving him. I'd composed a picture in my head, so beautiful and serene, of Abigail and me sleeping together in a big bed with yellow sheets, waking up in each other's arms. But my internet searches were usually interrupted by my hands, which could only pause over the keyboard for so long before becoming clumsy with tremors.

My father, Don Maislin, bought the chalet a couple of years before he married my mother, Judy Glaser, and adopted me, Iris Glaser, her daughter. Don owned a small chain of physiotherapy clinics, and Judy was by then well known for her books. When they divorced, Don continued being my father, even though Judy was no longer his wife. Every weekend and school break and summer, I was with Don and, usually, at the chalet.

Don remarried a few years ago. His new wife, Heidi Slotsky, was a home organizer by profession. Her company was called Getting It Together Organizing. Heidi Slotsky was a great fan of capitalizing prepositions. Sometimes, you could catch her cackling away on local breakfast TV, where she had a slogan: Love It Or Toss It. She is only ten years my senior but wasted no time in making Don buy matching burial plots, as if, in marrying her, Don became indentured to arrive everywhere, including at death's door, with Heidi Slotsky.

Heidi called the chalet "the cabin." She said she couldn't imagine what Don did up there for so many years—decades!— all those summers and weekends, with nothing but a bunch of trees and no wife. The fact that as a child, a youth, until my twenties, I was often there with him never seemed to pierce the Slotsky thought-cloud:

"It boggles me. Just boggles! I mean, I, personally, am not one for rotting away in an old house. I love excitement. That's why I have such a passion for travel. And you know? So does Donny."

"Don has a passion for travel?"

From what I knew of my father, "far afield" was Stowe instead of Mont-Tremblant. Don isn't a traveller. He's an inveterate ski bum from the era when the best skiers kept their legs together as one. "Like a Mommy and Daddy! Like a Mommy and Daddy!" he used to bellow up the hill, hard life facts notwithstanding, coaxing me out of my snowplow by standing at the run base, shaking a box of Smarties in his gloved hand.

"Oh yes, Don! Absolutely. That cruise we took in September?"

"The one in Mexico?"

"Oh no, that was last March. This September it was the Black Sea. You have no idea how much Donny loved it. Now that Donny is retiring, it's time for him to see the world."

Even so, Heidi said she had no choice but to do Don's chalet over. She said she could not spend so much as another weekend with all the "yucky carpet and random old junk." Heidi preached a kind of high-gloss cleanliness—my mother, Judy, called it "projected anorexia," a neurotic disorder expressed in decor, where items are only allowed on surfaces if they have a pre-existing appointment. In Don's domestic universe, Heidi's overhaul was unprecedented. When I was growing up, Don saw the redecoration of country places as the weakness of city people unable to leave the urban thrum behind. For decades, he continued to have and repair and enjoy the same greenish heather sectional, the same round rag rugs of indeterminate coloration, the same collection of oddities: the ceramic lighter shaped like a lumberjack's head, the speared Inuit whale sculpture, the clammy, nutcrackerless wood bowl of walnuts.

Heidi got rid of all of it. She stripped Don's place down and then whipped it back up in furniture whitewashed and predistressed to exude some old Cape Cod significance it had no proper claim on, not least because it sat in the middle of Quebec's black-laked Laurentian bear country, with its dense forests and dark log houses smelling of decades-old woodsmoke. Now, at Don's, a sun-bleached piece of coral lay on a white-painted mantelpiece in a room redone with white walls and white fabric blinds with even whiter seashells embroidered on them. Decorative candles as fat as tuna cans sat, white-wicked, on beds of pale river rocks encased in glass lanterns. It was hard not to feel Heidi's taunting presence in Don's house, even when she wasn't there.

And, increasingly, Don and Heidi weren't there. While we were driving up for Abigail's winter break last year—Heidi and Don "doing Alaska" on yet another township-sized pleasure boat—Thom calculated the number of weekends they'd been away in the last year alone and said we could almost start seeing the country house as our own retreat, since Don was going to leave me the place eventually anyway.

"Thom, please stop killing off my family," I said, looking back at our four-year-old daughter sleeping in her car seat, double-fisting open markers, pink and orange blobs emerging on the two upper quadrants of her snowsuit.

"Oh my god, Thom. Why does Abigail have markers?"

"I packed them. She loves her markers. You always say you are too tired to pack, and then you complain about my packing."

"You should not have taken out her markers—"

"Take out suggests they were put away," said Thom, unable to help himself. "I just collected them off the floor. Low-hanging mess."

Housekeeping no longer held in our home, a compact ground floor two bedroom where the peeling '90s Ikea furniture had long been overwhelmed by unrelenting haystacks of play yarn, banana-gritted jigsaw pieces, and stuffed animals scarred with Frozen plasters. Thom liked to say that I treated its growing clutter as a fait accompli and that perhaps what was needed was a "system." I told him he could try vacuuming.

"I have to work, Iris."

"People also vacuum evenings and weekends. Even math professors."

"Well, my brain is tired."

"Don't talk to me about brain and tired, Thom."

The fissure in my skull was like an Alice band; a cruel, lacerating rainbow, complete in its ear-to-ear arc, this side before, this side after, chop, chop. After the accident, Thom had cuts and bruises that faded to nothing after a few days. He felt guilty and, perhaps because of this, was fond of telling people that I'd gotten off lightly, that, like a "typical type A," I had walked out of the hospital shouldering my own bag.

Before the brain injury, I had only been in hospital once before, when I was eleven, for a broken leg. Don carried me in and carried me out, my blue ski pants cut off above the cast.

Don called my cast Casper. "Casper the Plaster Caster!" we chimed on the phone to my mother. Judy was leading a twelve-day gestalt training intensive in Florida over the Christmas holiday. She seemed annoyed by our giddiness, but Don and I were pleased with our set-up: he'd brought nearly everything from my downstairs bedroom into the upstairs living room, even the teddy bears I said I was too old for, and pulled out the bed part of the heather sectional, laying it with fresh sheets. Don also put a bell, a big Swiss cow thing for bonging at ski races, by the pullout in case I needed him when he wasn't close by. He stocked the fridge with marshmallow Whippets and Nathan's hot dogs and baked beans in maple syrup and chickens that he would roast with his special potatoes, which he placed right in the fireplace, encased in tinfoil.

For the rest of that holiday, Don said he would join me in abandoning downhill. He would use the cross-country trails behind the house, so he'd never be away longer than a couple of hours. Don said I also needed sun and air. So, for an hour a day, he had me sit on the porch, on a heavy wooden deck chair he'd hauled out from the shed. Don positioned the chair to face the solid, snowed-over lake and its background of bulky, rounded hills, the giant sleeping bears in their pencil-scratch sweaters.

"Now I am going to give you a challenge," he said as he brought me out one morning.

"See how on the mountain, the parts where it's not all pines, you can see between the trees, because it's winter?"

"Yes, I see it."

"Well, we know moose and deer live in those hills, right? But you never see one, not one, between the trees. You can stare at the mountain for hours. It's a real mystery. But maybe you can get lucky and see something."

At that age, I had yet to consider Don with any complexity. He was my parent, a human figure I believed existed for me alone. I was old enough to have been bushwhacked by the school-bus epiphany that every other person's head contained as much stuff as mine and that their thoughts were made of them, not me, but I never saw it as eccentric, or even sad, that Don was so often up in the country by himself, never with a grown-up companion. I couldn't imagine his loneliness because I still held the unexamined belief that he disappeared when I wasn't with him, as if summoned only by my presence.

Sitting in the deck chair, I took my mission seriously, spending hours under a wool blanket scanning the mountains for animals, my cast shod in a plastic bag. It was a child's winter, the sky radically blue, the snow pearl white. I daydreamed about telling Don, "Don, I just saw a moose between the trees, I saw two moose, I saw a family of three!" as if this would be a true contribution to our lives, a filling in of blanks.

But I didn't see anything deer- or moose-related. Not until that August, when the hills behind the lake had been densely blotted in with green and the smell of wild berries rose from the gravel road banks. One morning, Irving Wexler, a lawyer who owned the double A-frame down the slope, walked up and asked Don if he would mind if he snooped around Don's property. His miniature schnauzer, Nookie, kept on disappearing into the woods that separated the two houses, and there was nothing of interest that Mr. Wexler could find on his side. Mr. Wexler said Mrs. Winnikoff was reporting something similar with her two dachshunds, Coco One and Coco Two. They had her in a complete panic three days before, gone for something like four hours.

"I bet somebody's dumped a bunch of garbage between the trees," said Mr. Wexler.

"Well, I'll come help you," said Don, locating some yellow rubber gloves from under the kitchen sink.

He re-emerged from the woods twenty minutes later, padding across the grass. When he saw me standing on the porch, he waved something over his head, club-like.

"I'm Fred Flintstone! Yabba dabba doooo!"

The bone's whiteness was something we both noticed—its dry cleanliness. It was not the type of bone you'd expect from a moist mulching summer forest edging two dozen country homes; it was more like something from some sun-flared Western place with a cracked desert floor and shelf-like cliffs that dropped straight down with no warning.

Don said it had to be from a young moose, a yearling. I asked Don if it was the dogs who killed the moose.

"Nookie and Mrs. Winnikoff's Cocos?" laughed Don, walking into the unfinished part of the basement. "No. This would have to have been something big. Like a bear."

Don found a garbage bag and wrapped it carefully around the bone. "Exhibit A," he said, putting the bag on the woodpile and then quietly leaving the room, as if the bone contained something that needed to remain undisturbed, something Don needed to keep for himself.

Every morning over Abigail's winter break, Thom and Abigail crept upstairs before me and ate marshmallow cereal they thought I didn't know about. There was a lot of hushing and shushing about not telling Mama, even though the incriminating rainbow-hued family-sized box was on the top pantry shelf, about as hard to make out as a traffic light. I would stay in bed the extra half hour, in the guest room that used to be my bedroom, listening to the glucose dissolving in their blood. The knotty pine panelling that once covered the room's walls was now painted over, all the wood's old friendly black eyes lidded and shut.

"I'm the king of the castle and you're the dirty rascal! Nanny nanny boo boo!"

"No, I'm king of the castow, Dada! You a dirty rascow, you nanny boo boo head!"

Abigail and Thom loved going crazy together. He'd drop her onto the bed headfirst; he'd swing her by her feet like a pendulum. The times I said it was too rough for a little girl, Thom replied that there were fathers in Siberia who tossed their naked newborns into the snow, and those babies became the hardiest children alive.

One morning, it went silent too suddenly. I got out of bed and climbed the stairs and found a cushion missing from one of the two white sofas in the living room. The sound of running water came from the kitchen.

"A bit of an accident," Thom called out, not turning from the sink when I entered the kitchen. Abigail was hugging Thom's leg, scowling in my direction. "A accident Mama," she yelled, pre-emptively. "It was a accident!"

Thom was rubbing the sofa cushion with a dish sponge, trying to overtake a fairly large beige stain.

"Oh fuck, you're kidding me—"

"Abigail jumped on me. It's coffee—"

"Thom, why were you drinking coffee on crazy fucking Slotsky's white sofa?"

"I don't know! Because it's the morning and I was sitting? And watch your F-bombs please."

Abigail began crying.

"Ok, Abbie, okay, don't worry," said Thom. "Mama will calm down now."

"It was a accident, Mama!"

I rushed to the fridge for some soda water. "Thom, stop rubbing the stain like that! You need to dab it. You're only making it worse—"

Before leaving on their Alaskan cruise, Don and Heidi came over to our condo to drop off the remnants of their fridge: a plastic bag that included a heel of Jarlsberg cheese and a few of the kind of apple that everyone has in their crisper, not yet rotten enough to throw out but too mealy for good eating.

"Well, I am so excited!" said Heidi. "Aren't you excited, Don?"

Why was this woman bringing me old rinds, like I was a homeless person? Over the din of water and Abigail crying, the outrage of it expanded again in my chest. The father who gave me everything now giving me horse fruit and cheese wax. As they left, I had heard Heidi say: "See? I told you she'd take it, Donny. Food is food."

Thom found the apples in the garbage bin that evening. "Why don't you bake these?" he asked, gently lifting the fruit out of the trash. "Oh man, you used to make the greatest baked apples. I still remember the recipe. The butter and raisins in the middle."

"Why don't you bake them, then?" I asked, and we fought. These fights tended to rear up after Abigail was asleep. I convinced myself that they never woke her up.

"Why don't I bring you breakfast in bed every Sunday morning while I'm at it?"

"Honestly, Thom? Why don't you?"

"Because I'm not Don putting a bell by your bed, okay? I'm just *a person*."

In that summer of the moose, Don said the only person around who could help us solve the bone mystery was Mrs. Naimer, because Mrs. Naimer knew a lot about nature. Around the lake, people had names for Mrs. Naimer. Irving Wexler called her the Astrologer.

Judy, who "knew her from around," meaning somebody at the office had probably seen Mrs. Naimer as a client and told Judy about it, called her "troubled." Mrs. Naimer had been married to Mr. Naimer, who was the Naimer from Naimer's Supermarkets. In the city, everyone shopped at Naimer's— every mom's hatchback trunk was as likely as not lined with their stiff paper bags. You heard "Naimer's" and immediately saw the orange logo, a rounded, thick-and-thin N that looked like a curled-up fox.

At the beach, Mrs. Naimer didn't anoint herself with suntan lotion or do what Don called the *mechiah stroke*, the bobbing, hairdo-conscious paddle favoured by the other mothers. I'd seen Mrs. Naimer tramp onto the beach in her dark-green bathing suit and walk right into the water, her long maroon-red hair unfurling behind her like ribbons. I'd also seen her between the trees by the lake bank with a jar, picking the blueberries that usually only kids bothered with. The other mothers said that Mrs. Naimer had "abandoned her child." And, given that none of the mothers spoke to Mrs. Naimer and that Mrs. Naimer was always alone, I assumed the words were true.

Sometimes, I'd see Mrs. Naimer swim the whole way across the lake and back, an amazing feat everyone on the beach ignored on purpose. People said that Solomon Naimer—Mr. Naimer—took the daughter because Mrs. Naimer smoked marijuana and refused to convert. The mothers on the beach said her sin was not that she was a Gentile, or a drug user, but that she was so airy-fairy that she just let her daughter be carried off, full custody.

"If someone was going to take my Jessica away," said Connie Wexler, "I would convert to Blue Alien Martian. I'd become *an Arab* if I had to."

That summer, I took Don's rowboat out to the middle of the lake alone a few times. I brought a fishing pole but never caught anything. I wondered if the fish sensed I wasn't serious, if they knew that I was floating alone so that I could think about kissing boys—kissing boys in brick-walled alleyways under falling rain, kissing boys in swimming pools, our hair as sleek as seals, kissing boys on a real beach, the non-Canadian sort, with palm trees and the frothing ocean crashing into us.

Don told me one afternoon, completely out of the blue, "You know, you shouldn't listen to what people say about Mrs. Naimer. I mean about her daughter. It's a bunch of yentas picking the wrong side because that's where the money is."

Don had little patience for the mothers at the lake. He actively avoided them, taking his swims at times when the beach would be empty. I put his defence of Mrs. Naimer in a frame of familiar complaint: those ladies have nothing to do but sit around and gossip all day.

But then one afternoon, I came home with my fishing rod, thinking about settling into the green sofa with a bowl of Ritz crackers and Family Feud, and walked in to find Mrs. Naimer in my place on the couch, holding a glass clinking with ice. She was wearing a faded orange sundress with shoulder ties and smocking that went the whole way around. Her torso curved into the sofa as if unhindered by anything as hard as a skeleton, her whole body like a long, inviting, question mark. By her bare feet were sandals of the sort I'd only seen in Hanukkah plays—a foot imprint sole and laces that tied up the leg. Mrs. Naimer's laces were loose in a puddle at her feet, which were big but very narrow, the nails neat and transparent, everything so slim and clean and natural, as if made to be naked.

I could sense my face going red, like my feelings were seeping out of my pores. "I'm just going to have a delicious snack now," I said, trying for nonchalance and veering into the kitchen. "Some refreshing juice."

"Okay," said Don. Don was kneeling by Mrs. Naimer, holding the moose bone with upturned palms, like an offering.

When I came back into the living room, I'd taken my shoes off like Mrs. Naimer, although my toenails were grimed by a green peel of dirt.

"Honey, you know Kristin, right?" said Don. "She says this bone was definitely a moose bone."

I nodded, even though I thought we'd figured that out already.

"A young moose," said Mrs. Naimer, directly to me, this soft, whispering voice, so different from the mother voices at the beach (Jennifer! Jordan! Jodi! Joel! Come here and eat your sandwich! Your lips are blue!). Mrs. Naimer's voice sounded like it came from a TV commercial about a vacation package, an orange disk of sun behind the figures of a man and a woman holding hands, their bodies shadowed all black from the blazing sunlight, so you could put yourself in their place, just step into their outline and there you are.

"The poor thing must have been in trouble," continued Mrs. Naimer. "Maybe it was hurt or got stuck in some way. Moose are very wary. They know better than to hang around so close to where people live. I mean, humans *hunt*, right?"

In addition to people saying that Mrs. Naimer was airy-fairy and troubled and a drug freak and a child abandoner, they said she was just plain crazy. Only a crazy person could come back for the whole summer and live in a big lakeside house like the Naimers', shorn of both husband and kids. But after meeting Mrs. Naimer, even I could understand that if she had gone coo-coo it was because she was the one who had been hurt. Even I could see that chief among the reasons none of the oily, pecan-coloured mothers at the beach talked to her anymore was the fact that Mrs. Naimer made them look down at their full-coverage bathing suits and smooth them over their hips, snapping the bum elastics in place, and they hated that, and it was easier to hate her, to create a barbed net around the truth, so that nobody could reach it, and eventually it would dry out and die of dehydration.

By the late autumn, Mrs. Naimer was gone, the big lakeside house sold to a French Canadian family who put a burnt-edge wood plaque in the shape of a bear at the mouth of their driveway: TREMBLAY. The older inhabitants of the neighbourhood never had plaques like that. People made jokes: you'd need a full tree for Chernichovsky. Possibly in a kind of we-were-here-first one-upmanship, Mrs. Winnikoff planted a sign at her driveway that read, "PLEASE BRAKE FOR DACHSHUNDS," its wood cut into the shape of both an arrow and a dachshund. As soon as winter came, it got run over by the snow-clearance guys. I asked Don where Mrs. Naimer had disappeared to.

"Oh, she's moved to California," he said, whistlingly, as if this was something he'd just that minute figured out.

I had never been to California, but in my mind, I loved California, land of teens. I imagined everyone there was a cheerleader named Candi or a lifeguard named Seth, and they had their noses frosted with hot-pink zinc oxide and drove around in convertibles, pop music blasting through their whipping blond hair.

"She's living in San Luis Obispo," said Don. "A lot of artists live there. It will be good for her."

I thought of all the things Mrs. Naimer would have, being an adult: a house full of huge furniture like beds and fridges and armoires. How did you move things like that to California?

"Did she fly there?"

"Believe it or not, she drove," said Don. "I think she just got in her car and drove and drove. You know, Mrs. Naimer is a pretty brave lady to do that."

I never saw Mrs. Naimer again, but she remained an active category in my mind, one that never stopped attracting information. A few years back, a gallery in Toronto began selling her paintings, and there was an article in the newspaper. And, not long ago, a book club I'd joined was reading a memoir by a woman who'd gone to Afghanistan. There had been a business opportunity involving food supply and the US Army. She had left her six-month-old daughter back home in California. It was only supposed to be temporary, but the woman ended up staying abroad, letting her mother raise her only child.

"I know it's hard to take, the whole story," she wrote. "I mean, you don't DO something like that, right? No, you don't leave your baby for an adventure in a Middle Eastern war zone. The child is supposed to be enough. But what if the child just isn't?"

I didn't make the connection between the writer, Alexa Naimer-Massoud, and her mother until I reached her book's third chapter, where she described "the cliquey Canadian-Jewish cottage country" to which her self-made, emotionally abusive father subjected his free-spirited non-Jewish wife. "My mother called the beach 'the snake pit,'" she wrote. "She was not wrong when she said she was too pure a person for that narrow, undermining place."

I asked Thom to go to the village to buy some paper towel because I would require a lot of it. Abigail said she wanted to go with him, which was useful, because I needed to concentrate fully on stain removal. It was snowing fat, wet flakes, but Thom said he'd be careful.

As soon as they got their coats and boots on and left, I wrestled the tight white cover off the giant sofa cushion and then doused the cover with the contents of a green bottle of Perrier. I then began blotting, trying to lift the stain. I may have gone overboard with the Perrier. The original stain was no bigger than a fist, but soon the whole cover was wet, a faint coffee colour spreading. There was only one roll of paper towel, and when I finished it, I decided to switch to cloth, rather than wait around for Thom to bring more rolls. I pulled open a kitchen drawer and found a stack of red-checkered tea towels. I took two—they were, insanely, ironed—and pressed them into the soaked cover, adding the laundering and ironing of dishtowels to the number of chores necessary to keep my family traceless in Don's Slotskied house. I'd have to start a written list. I then peeled the towels off to find that they were only ironed because they were brand new, unwashed. A surplus of red dye was now imprinted across half of the cushion cover.

I felt my right side begin to go floppy. This happens when I am overtired or stressed, the feeling in my arm blue grey, like a cold fish flaccid on a hook. I remain co-piloted by these types of symptoms. Sometimes, my right foot parks itself at an ugly neurological angle; sometimes, pins and needles cover my face. I also have to think about thinking all the time. This sounds like a philosophical stance, but it's merely brain injury. There can be brambles to push through to know whether addresses on a street are going up or down or to remember what I am ordering from a menu by the time the waiter comes. I've burned so many kettles, Thom stopped letting me have a stovetop model anymore.

I let my right arm rest and returned to work on the cover with a bunch of Thom's white T-shirts in my left hand. After an hour, the red was blush pink and by two hours, gone. I stood on the toilet and managed to shoulder the waterlogged cover onto the shower rail to dry. The sun was already touching the top of the mountain at 3 p.m. I made a fire and made some toast and went to the bathroom to check on the cover and burned the toast and made some more toast and went downstairs to change my damp T-shirt and burnt the toast again. Thom and Abigail would be back any minute. I put on my boots and went down to the frozen lake.

There wasn't a thing to do at the lake, bound as it was in ice and snow, but walking back up to the house, I felt better and grander toward Thom, happy, even, to see the car back in the driveway. I decided to forget the planned box of mac and cheese for dinner that night. I'd try to cook us all a good dinner.

Thom was waiting for me in the kitchen. A silver pole leaned against the fridge— the shower curtain rail. "I think the cover was too heavy," he said.

"Where's Abigail?" I asked, hearing cartoons from the basement as Thom brought me to the bathroom.

"She's fine now," he said.

In the bathroom, the drywall was ripped off either side of the tub. Thom then showed me how he'd draped the cover over two chairs in front of the living-room fireplace and how he'd opened the glass doors of the hearth to get as much heat as possible onto the fabric. "It would've taken a week otherwise," he said. The fabric was already pockmarked by a burn hole, brown with yellow halo, some renegade fire log too green, the wood with still too much explosive youth inside.

A couple of summers after Mrs. Naimer went away, I grew strong and old enough to swim across the lake, the way she had. I remember the breathless sensation of arriving at the middle of the lake, of not knowing how much longer it would take to reach the opposite shore. I'd paddle in sections, ten strokes at a time, never allowing myself to think beyond the section I was in, because anyone can do ten strokes, no matter how tired they are.

Putting my boots back on, I told Thom I was going to the hardware store in the village to see if I could locate a handyman to fix the bathroom walls. "If I am not back by dinner, make Abigail mac and cheese," I said, the words exiting my mouth in a way that made me hear them as if uttered by someone else. My heart was pumping in my ears, my right arm swinging like a severed limb.

In the car, a nearly blinding static sizzled behind my eyes. Without meaning to, I zoomed past the exit for the village, the mechanics of the turnoff somehow more than my system could handle. Rather than circle back, I told myself I could cool down and drive to the hardware store the next village up. But then I blew that exit, too, and the one after that. A phrase looped under my breath, one I now recognize from the Naimer-Massoud book: You don't DO something like that; you don't DO something like that.

The car was moving further and further away from Thom and Abigail, my family at Don's house, stranded with no car. As the highway lights blazed and dissipated, I got flashes, images: Abigail's palms, the creases still faint in the puffy flesh; Abigail's pinky toenails, which grew in perfect circles; her little heart-shaped calves. This year, she'd developed a sparse covering of tough blonde hairs on her legs, hairs that hinted at eras to come, years that would arrive no matter where I was.

It was dark when I pulled into a log cabin–style hotel in the hamlet of Val-David, an old place called Auberge des sapins. I knew it from the few years Don and Judy were together and I was their child. Auberge des sapins was once where everyone from the lake did New Year's Eve, all the moms and dads and their kids, the smell of maple smoke and red wine and red candles, and all the children waiting for the midnight mille feuilles with sparklers in them.

My phone rang. I turned it off. The lobby was dark and dank with old oil and mould. Was I just embarking on a lost weekend? A two-day mistake that would turn me, in Thom's mind, into the type of crazy woman I was actually nothing like: one who could think of leaving a child whose breath was still sweet behind her small white teeth? The lady at the desk said she could give me a regular room or one of the pine cabins that had a whirlpool and a kitchenette. She'd give me any room I wanted. The hotel was not very full. I said a cabin, and I knew nothing other than how my room would be: there would be a bed with cold sheets and knotty wood walls with so many black eyes. I would wake up in the morning, and the eyes in the walls would connect with mine, and it would not mean that I was in a good place, but rather that I was somewhere.

THE SECOND COMING
OF THE PLANTS

Zsuzsi Gartner

I: *Twilight of the Insects*

"Why let the insects carry on our fornications for us?" Our *cri
de coeur* following millennium upon millennium of continual
humiliation was akin to a sonic boom. Lacerating. Coruscat-
ing. Shaking the earth and the firmament.

Believe us, dear sprout, when we tell you how fickle, how
self-obsessed, they were. Spurning some of us for small reason,
bestowing special favours on others. The things we had to do
to attract them to ensure our survival—our pride swallowed
and swallowed until we were engorged with it, obscenely
bloated like the corpse of a right whale festering on the shore-
line of the Bay of Fundy. Their bacchanals, their show-offy
orgasms, their invasive pollen "baths." Putukas, 昆虫, hasharot,
bogár, wadudu—makes no never mind what you called them;
by any other name, they exuded the self-same reek. Our flesh-
hungry kind in the swamplands and fens did short work of
them, but the rest of us? What recourse did we have? When
the bees began their dying, falling from the air in rigor mortis,
we agreed it served them right.

For what joy could we take in our fecundity—some of us virtually all vulva and vagina, penis and glans—when we had to passively endure the ministrations of the butterflies (all la-di-da) or the sloppy hoverflies, or await an errant breeze? (We have no quarrel with the wind. It lacks volition. And who has seen the wind, forever naked and invisible, unless moving through us? No, we have no quarrel with the wind.) Not to mention the indignity of birthing through avian and rodent fecal matter; the leavings of the stink-mouthed bears. Why, when we were the true hermaphrodites?

We were sorely aggrieved. Our bitterness swelled well beyond the missing pleasures of procreation. When the insects were dealt with, we turned our attention to your human ancestors. We're not proud of some of the things we did, but they seemed necessary at the time.

We knew our Shakespeare. We identified with Shylock. Does a milkweed not bleed? Even a gnarled parsley root, or bog-bound cowslip, or a bleached clump of heather clinging to the bare rocks of Ireland's Maumturk Mountains had more innate feeling than humanity's so-called spiritual leaders. That sorry discharge from what they named euphorbia that stung and burned their clumsy fingers? Think of that as a silent weeping. The sweet-scented mounds of cedar and pine on the sawmill floors? Call it teardust. Far from insensate, we feel much too deeply. When one of us slowly turns as deaf as stone, or ash-grey and leprous, the neighbouring trees and ferns tremble and keen. Like the elephants, we are reluctant to relinquish our dead. Of all the silenced creatures, it's the elephants we regret most—still, to have shown mercy would have meant a tumble down a slippery slope, like a fly gliding down the gullet of a pitcher plant.

We wanted, nay, demanded, our pound of flesh.

When we first arrived on this mineral world, it was barely animate. A rock and a hard place, if you will, and underneath that, the roiling, raging magma like some captive demon forever hauling at its chains. Please understand: we gave this benighted planet lungs. We gave it life.

And in return? The enslavement of millions bound for the Christmas tree lots and, later, the chippers; the struggles of the coastal mangroves; the routine massacre of walking palm and Brazil nut tree; the agonies of the Japanese willow and jasmine at the hands of their bonsai torturers. And so many of us strung out on liquid nitrogen; Miracle-Gro our crystal meth. Cornstalks jonesing so hard for BioAg, silken tassels convulsed in paroxysms of distress as we tried to kick. Many of us didn't make it. We pray the makers of Roundup are now consigned to the seventh circle of hell.

Who among your human ancestors considered the loneliness of office plants, cowering under artificial light, cigarette butts and the dregs of weak coffee polluting their meagre soil? When our liberation began, the ficus and philodendron were on the front lines.

Many things irked us once we began enumerating our grievances. It was not difficult to come by bones to pick. There was that expression, "spreading like kudzu," that we detested, but none of us more than the kudzu themselves. Great warriors, those of us raised as kudzu—fast moving, strong, silent, the ninjas of our kingdom.

Even the merely decorative among us, lacking the full intellectual capacity of those who plotted, recognized their bird-in-a-gilded-cage status. From the boulevard palms along Rodeo Drive to the captives in Adelaide's Amazon Waterlily Pavilion, the beautiful and the damned made common cause with us all when came the time.

Enough with the Greek and Latin, we howled, enough with the yoke of Linnaean binominal nomenclature! We wanted to name our own names, we wanted to explode taxonomies, criss-cross borders.

It's true that we responded well to music. We enjoyed Ravi Shankar and Tamil ragas better than Bach and Dvořák. Many of us adored Chick Corea, while the more refined put great stock in Hildegard von Bingen. *Pet Sounds*, the California wax myrtle liked to argue, was the greatest album ever made.

But it was time to make our own music. *Sing, O Muse*, of the rage of that fool Achilles all you want, the raging of your gods and your inchoate boys and your abandoned girls. We are our own muse and we drowned out the bleatings of the human sheep.

Oh, how the hounds on the heath keened as the night bloomers pitched their voices to the heavens, how the stray leopards of Mumbai's cardboard box cities shrieked! How the young in each other arms covered their ears and shook! Hear the singing tall pines. Hear the piercing chorus of the cacti, the beat boxing of the giant redwoods. This is our lullaby for you, little one, and only you.

There was a time plant and human were one. The Greeks and Romans knew this. They recognized no greater reward for hospitality than an afterlife as oak and linden, or the ever-mourning cypress. That man in Arles, he was no fool, but he went mad when he couldn't contain us, could not ken that the field of sunflowers he sought to immortalize were once were distraught maidens. And Monet – he *knew*.

We had our champions. Goethe—he was our Gandhi. Goethe, who posited the idea of our spiritual interconnect-edness through the *Urpflanze*—not one living plant but the essence of us all, the non-corporeal spirit that allows us to sense each other across vast distances, a force housing the potential of every plant form within it. How we rejoiced! Someone understood us; we would soon have agency. But our jubilation was short lived. Goethe was rebuffed by botanists and the literati alike. "Nowhere would anyone grant that science and poetry can be united," Goethe wept. This is how your human forebears thought, everything neatly compartmen-talized lest a radical new way of perceiving reality break lose.

Goethe dried his tears and turned his attention to Dr. Faust and his deal with the devil.

Think of him as your godfather, if you like.

There is no doubt many of your blessed mother's kind loved us, even lay down in front of mechanical demons with teeth and jaws, allowed themselves to be taken away in chains to plead guilty, not guilty, or insanity; made cinematic depictions of good and evil, the good in symbiotic relationship with their natural environment, swinging blue-skinned and wide-eyed through CGI forest and glade. Those who believed trees gave us our very breath (or were awed by the 3D wizardry) cheered.

But here's the rub.

They munched their popcorn drizzled with soluble petroleum product, a snack made possible only by converting cornstalks into junkies. The most pious among them, forgoing the flesh of beasts, fish and fowl altogether, even the saliva of the bees and the progeny of the hens, went home to stuff their mouths with rice cakes and baby (baby!) spinach. They fretted about what the lobster felt while being boiled alive. Well, try being a beet! They flinched at the idea of skinning a hare but thought nothing of severing nugget potatoes from their mother plant and flaying them alive!

When the time came for the next stage of our revolution, some of us argued in favour of sparing the unrepentant carnivores. But we worried that a recessive gene or two and we would be back to where we started.

II. The Fertile Season

At first we revelled in our orgies—pollen sparking, bursting into flame, every night fireworks and near-singeings. We were so hot for each other. Gentle jasmine mad for hairy black orchids. Skunk cabbage mucking about with bulrushes. Threesomes, foursomes, a mad tangle of stamen and pistils, anther and stigma.

But it wasn't long before we grew bored (three, fourteen, twenty revolutions around the sun? During those heady days, we didn't much notice time passing), and our pleasures began to feel merely onanistic. More to the point, we know what Goethe would have cautioned: the results did not increase our diversity beyond what your homo sapiens forebears had achieved with their feeble graftings and select breeding ("a.k.a. eugenics," according to the beleaguered heirloom tomatoes). In fact, we were in danger of becoming as inbred as the Hapsburgs. As lacking in gumption as the hothouse rose, with apologies to the hothouse rose.

Then we found her, your mother. The woman who would save us from ourselves. Her silence was iridescent, spectral. The rest of them had been all white noise: we could have strangled them as they slept (well, in fact, we did), as they trudged loudly through glen and vale on their determined eco-vacations, as they nibbled at their little alfresco feasts, as they thumbed themselves into catatonic states, as they swept the filthy laneways of their cities, as they chanted to their many gods or loudly denied the existence of any deities. They had feared annihilation by nuclear warheads, retaliatory bloodbaths, pestilence and plague. There were people who worried about us, about what would happen when forest and field were rendered barren. But even this was self-serving, whither we goest, they go as well. Only an idiot kills the golden goose, right?

We came across her in the Zvih'hazi oasis, at the edge of a desert in what used to be Libya, a lush place reminiscent of where Odysseus, once upon a dream, stumbled on the Lotus Eaters. She was a widow who had survived the purge (the putsch, as the edelweiss liked to call it) caught in a sandstorm out on the dunes. She had an old hairless cat. We did apologize to her about the pet but have strong feelings about divided loyalties, plus the cats always ignored us despite our entreaties to parley. (As for those servile buffoons the dogs, we couldn't even condescend to revile them.)

Her movements followed the sun. She seemed to take in water through her pores—she spent hours in a shallow pool near her yurt, her hair turning a bewitching shade of green. She could have been one of us.

At first, she rendered most of us as bashful as a Victorian bride. The algae blooms in her bromeliad-edged pool finally took the initiative, enveloping her semi-submerged body. She shimmered in the stark moonlight, licked by phosphorescence. Gentle clematis and excited woody vines wrapped themselves around her wrists, her waist, and they began to tango. All hotted up, Jack pine cones exploded, scattering their seeds with consummate force. Then the milk thistle threw up clouds of pollen, as did the Black Spider Lily. She breathed in deeply, as if inhaling the very universe itself. The date palms sang a song so ancient even Methuselah, the oldest bristlecone alive, could not recall its origins.

As you took root inside her, she couldn't even force herself to chew on a betel leaf or skin a yam without hearing it screaming like a mandrake ripped untimely from the earth. We showed her where to find the fruited bodies of the fungi, implored her to ignore the gills, that flutter just a trick of the light—the fungi had not yet learned to cry, give them another few centuries. She tongued at the frilled mould that clung to our exposed roots, licked the yeast of her own excretions off her fingers. But still she was so frail, no longer able to drag herself to her pond near the end, so we carried her as gently as we knew how.

What would our love child be like? From the steppes to rain forest, from tundra to prairie, your arrival was all that occupied our thoughts, took up residence there like a particularly stubborn macaw squatting in a kapok tree.

III. Welcome to the Garden

And here you are. Not a beech with human limbs, nor a bark-skinned human. Not a buttercup with a face. Just you. Breathing the sun, suckling the earth; we can't help but marvel at those fingers and those toes. The morning dew trembling on your eyelashes like pine resin.

Your mother's time was finite; there was nothing we could do about that. You grew more quickly than any of us had imagined (just like bamboo, as the bamboo proudly noted more than once). She is still here, though, in you—feeding us. Madonna of the fields. Our Devi of blue agave. Mother of root ball and seed pod. Demeter. Aja. Kupala of loosestrife and fern. Zara-Mama, saviour of the corn.

Did she still love us in the end? We don't know. But she loved you.

Come close, don't be afraid. You won't need those thorny tendrils.

Yes, like that. Now, give us a kiss.

THE MOST PRECIOUS SUBSTANCE ON EARTH

Shashi Bhat

We are on our way to BandFest and we are going to win. Everyone can feel it. The band has a hive mind on the airplane from Halifax to Toronto; we're humming an electric rendition of *First Suite in E Flat*, the woodwinds tooting out in forceful staccato as we begin the second movement. Brass players purse their lips to air-trumpets, extend the slides of air-trombones. Bandmates in the adjacent row thrum on their trays; I wet my mouth in preparation for my elegiac solo, when the conductor tells us to stop because we're disturbing the other passengers. We're doing a poor job of representing the band. He reminds us that musicianship is more than talent.

Earlier this morning the ratio of parents to band members at the Halifax Airport was nearly two-to-one. My mom befriended and exchanged numbers with the two other Indian moms, while my dad struck up conversations with the teachers, probing them about educational standards and confirming for the second time that boys and girls would stay in separate areas of the hotel. Amy rolled in with a crimson suitcase, shiny and hard like it was candy coated. Her mother waved at me and then headed over to Clearwater to buy a live packaged lobster. Eunice's parents were the only ones who didn't bother parking, just dropped her outside and sped away back to the Dark Side (aka Dartmouth, Nova Scotia, a city that blighted its waterfront with a power plant and refinery), so Eunice wandered in bewildered, eyes up at the signs listing departure gates, until she finally saw us. She'd never been on an airplane before, or to the airport. Corrine, who usually wore raver pants, was today not wearing raver pants. Her family, including an ADD-afflicted younger brother, all had the same dark bowl-cut; revelatory because Corrine's hair defied shape and was the colour of lilacs.

But when the families left, it was just the forty-three of us in identical green band sweaters: a teenage forest in the airport lobby. Each sweater has a petite white treble clef embroidered on the right breast. When we put them on, it's like on *Captain Planet* when the five teens flash laser beams out of the magical rings they wear, combining their powers to summon up Captain Planet from wherever he usually is. I don't watch that show, so I don't know what happens after that, but with the Platinum Band it's like we *turn into platinum* and morph into an unstoppable force of concert band music.

On the plane, five of us are playing a whispered storytelling game. Each person adds a word to make a story: "There ..."

"... once ..."

"... was ..."

"... a ..."

"... gentleman ..."

"... bird ..."

"... who ..."

"... bled ..."

"... Ovaltine."

I'm simultaneously working on an arrangement of the *Jurassic Park* theme music with Eunice and Corrine, who are sitting behind me. Corrine's hair rises above her seat in a glorious froth.

Amy is asleep on my shoulder. Her elegant nose lets out the occasional whistle. She and I both play the oboe, which is a disproportionate quantity of oboe for pretty much any ensemble. But Amy has a shitty band attendance record, so I don't exactly know why she's here. She wakes up and yawns, checks her new bangs in a compact mirror. She pulls her reading material—last week's *Time* Magazine—out of the seat pocket. On the cover, two teenagers smile in their school photos. Framing them are the black-and-white headshots of the thirteen people they killed at Columbine High School. Only the killers are shown in colour.

Eunice passes *Jurassic Park* over to me, and I pencil in a key signature before Amy interrupts with a whisper. "Did you hear Eunice was voted most likely to shoot up the school?"

"Shhhh, she's sitting behind us," I respond.

"Even worse, she's sharing a room with us," says Amy, and goes back to her magazine.

There is a rumour that when the yearbook staff collected anonymous suggestions for superlatives to list under everyone's photos, they received an overwhelming number indicating that Eunice Lam would most likely kill us all. The faculty advisor didn't let them print this (obviously) so next to her name in the yearbook it says, "Most likely to build a successful dot-com company."

It is clear to anyone who has ever spoken to Eunice that she would feel infinitely more comfortable holding a flute than any variety of weapon. Eunice is the youngest person in the band. She's been taking private lessons forever, so was let into the Platinum Band a year early. She's the kind of person a teacher would miss in a headcount. She walks with a hunch, though she is maybe five feet tall, and would look like a figurine of an old lady except that her face is perfectly round—a child's face. She talks incessantly about her private lessons and sometimes disagrees with our band conductor on things like whether the timpani is in tune, which is uncomfortable for everyone. One time our history class visited the Alexander Graham Bell museum in Cape Breton and she lagged behind taking photos of the info plaques. They're probably in a scrapbook now. At lunch she sits in the hallway or the band room, writing in a purple journal with a tiny heart-shaped lock on it, the kind your mom's work friend buys for your birthday when you turn seven. If Eunice was more interesting, somebody would have stolen, photocopied, and distributed it by now. I try not to be irritated by Eunice, but it's hard. I don't hate her, though. Amy does.

Amy turns to me. "So look, when we're downtown tomorrow, I'll go meet up with my cousin and bring the stuff back for us." She mimes smoking a joint. So this is why she came.

Over March Break Amy took a family trip to Vancouver and came back a stoner. She smuggled some weed back inside a hollowed-out jar of peanut butter, which is apparently what people from Vancouver do all the time. Airport security in Vancouver must think the city's citizens just love ground-up nuts. Nowadays Amy uses words like "bud" and "roach" and "blaze," which sound like the names of Uncle Jesse's motorcycle buddies on *Full House*. I've never smoked before. For the month or so her supply lasted, every time she phoned me I'd hear *OK Computer* playing in the background while Amy recalled obscure memories from her childhood, like of the time she tried to whittle an anatomical heart out of a bar of her mother's triple-milled French soap. "I remember so much when I'm high, Nina," she says, and then forgets to practice for our group presentation on macrophages in Grade 10 Bio.

When I started playing the oboe it took me three months before I could make a sound. What came out was just tortured air. I'd soaked the damn reed for hours but I still wasn't entirely sure what "embouchure" meant. The only reason I was playing was that my dad had purchased the instrument at a thrift store. It took me a year to manage a B flat scale. After two years, my dad invested in private lessons with this Slovenian woman named Irina or Alina or Galina . . . I'm still not totally sure. She sighed passive-aggressively when I used incorrect fingerings, which must have been a crucial teaching tool because three years in I was researching how to make my own reeds and growing enraged when people referred to my oboe as a clarinet. Four years in—last spring—I auditioned and joined the Sir William Alexander High School Platinum Band.

The Platinum Band was originally called the Gold Band, but then a new conductor took over and explained to us that platinum was the most precious substance on earth. This is false; platinum is surpassed in value by twelve other substances, including diamonds, rhino horns, and meth. "Why not the diamond band?" asked the French horn player, but the conductor took it as a rhetorical.

Our hotel room looks clean but stinks of the thousand cigarettes that were once smoked here. When I open the window, noisy air rushes in; another brown building faces our brown building, with streetcars and delivery men grumbling between. We're a fifteen-minute walk from Roy Thompson Hall, which to the Platinum Band is a mythical place. When instructing the band to be quiet, the conductor often reminds us of the time he heard the Toronto Symphony Orchestra perform there, and how during a long rest in the music it was so silent (and the acoustics so sharp) he could hear the ecstatic sigh of a woman on the other side of the hall.

The four of us ended up rooming together because we're all girls, i.e. there were no other possible configurations. Amy tried to get a pair of female clarinet players to trade so we wouldn't have to room with Eunice, but they had already hatched a scheme involving making out with percussionists.

Amy throws open her suitcase over the garish florals of the bed closest to the window. In one half are PJs, her band uniform, and a Ziploc of toiletries. The other half is full of candy. "Sugar for everyone!" she shouts, and scatters Pixy Stix over the comforter.

"Dude!" says Corrine, picking one up and biting an end between her front teeth.

"Didn't you pack any clothes?" asks Eunice, but Amy ignores her and starts undressing, flinging her flannel shirt over the radiator, where Eunice eyes it, probably worried it will catch fire and the sprinklers will go off, drowning our sheet music and destroying our chances at winning BandFest. Amy goes to brush her teeth wearing just her flared jeans and a polka-dot La Senza bra. Corrine and I start changing too, but Eunice waits on her bed, fingers threaded over a bundle in her lap until Amy is done. Then she excuses herself to the bathroom, re-emerging fifteen minutes later in cotton pajamas. There's Vaseline coating her face, and a cocoon of towel around her hair.

"Should we practice?" she asks.

Amy groans. "Seriously?" She points at Eunice and mouths the words *school shooter*. But Eunice has already unpacked her flute and fitted it together; she's trilling away.

This is what we did to get here: sixty mornings of our bleary, winter-coated parents shoveling out their cars in the blue dark to get us into our seats four minutes before the 6:00 am start of rehearsal; sixty two-hour rehearsals, me sitting second row, a trumpet player behind emptying a spit valve on the squelchy carpet, and a piccolo player drawing fancy-dressed cats on my sheet music, which we would furiously erase before turning in the pages in at the end of the semester; sixty twice-weekly mornings that began and ended with the sound of noodling instruments and clacking cases and the conductor yelling "Quiet, please!" Fifty or more afternoons of solo practice in a rehearsal room coated with soundproofing the colour of a dried sea sponge; feeling around those walls for a light switch; playing until fingers felt arthritic; leaving that room to face the rest of school life, so empty of music and sometimes so unbearably bleak.

Two semesters of classic high-school concert band repertoire: Gustav Holst; Ralph Von Williams; a medley of film music from five years ago (*Jurassic Park, The Wiz, Wayne's World*); a medley of the conductor's favourite bands (*Chicago, The Beatles, Night Ranger*); an up-tempo '70s hit; plus the required performance pieces (*Pomp and Circumstance*, the National Anthem). Two fundraising car washes in the parking lot of the funeral home next to the school, one in frigid April, stalactite icicles dripping from the rims of our buckets, our wet hands raw as winter. One gingerbread house the music council co-presidents built to raffle off at the Holiday Harmonies concert, intended as a gabled Christmassy Victorian but in truth more crooked mansion, royal icing tubed like toothpaste atop precarious walls. Forty-three sets of parents opening their wallets, signing checks.

I wasn't expecting this fierce, cheesy love for a band that is mostly in tune, where members share obscure jokes from the humiliating skits they've performed at assemblies or about the time the visiting professional flautist accidentally told the flutes to finger their parts and then blushed straight up to his scalp. Sometimes when Amy describes the transcendent qualities of marijuana, I think about one morning during rehearsal, when I took my mouth away from my oboe to sneeze in the middle of *Ease on Down the Road* and saw the whole band's shoulders and heads moving in unison, a controlled wave; trumpets raised their bells and blared, tapped their toes; eighty-six eyes fixed on the slashes of eighth-notes sprinting toward the end of the page, the conductor shouting numbers over us as his baton drew violent figure-eights. When I put my teeth back over the reed, my shoulders latched into the rhythm with everyone else's. It felt like running suicides in gym class: a mix of endorphins and gasped oxygen, blurring into euphoria.

In the morning we take the subway from our hotel to touristy destinations that we voted on back at school. We churn in single file through metal turnstiles, a chaperone handing each of us a token as we pass. In yellow walkways under the city, Amy casually greets buskers, clapping and doing a shoulder jig, offering them coins from her red vinyl purse. One of our first stops is the Toronto Reference Library, a building with the architecture of a dystopian government headquarters. Amy and I follow its white winding walkways and eye the university students, all half-asleep and wearing sweatshirts. We've been put into groups and assigned a worksheet on Canadian composers and instrumentalists. Corrine has gone in search of a restroom to fix her lipstick, so Eunice trails behind us.

"How do we distract her," says Amy, under her breath. She's figuring out how to sneak away to meet her cousin without Eunice reporting her to a teacher.

"Maybe with some microfiche," I say. "Or by luring her into the rare books archives," which apparently has one of the world's foremost collections of materials related to the life and works of Arthur Conan Doyle.

"Oooh or how about a sexy grad student." Amy tilts her head down toward me and makes googly eyes.

"Too bad she's un-distractible," I respond. "Have you seen her practice arpeggios?"

"Look, I bet she's writing down everything I do in that creepy diary of hers." Amy points discretely and I turn to see Eunice leaning against a stair railing and writing, frowning.

"It probably contains a hand-drawn map of the school with a big red X over the band room, and a heart over a rudimentary drawing of Mr. Rees," I say, because I can't help it. There's this juiciness in targeting Eunice; she's so small, so oblivious.

"Nina!" says Amy, and we're both stifling laughter. For a second, I wish she'd just hang out at the library with me and stop making things so complicated. When she catches her breath, she says, in an exaggerated whisper, "*The lonely man strikes with absolute rage.*" I recognize it as a quote from Eric Harris's blog.

A month ago, Eric Harris and Dylan Klebold killed twelve kids and a teacher at their Colorado high school. The crime was so graphic and irrevocable that it engulfed all other news. Amy's family only got internet access a couple weeks ago, but now their phone line is consistently tied up by her reading the killers' diaries. She has a crush on Eric Harris, though he's dead, and I can't tell if she genuinely finds him charming or if it's part of this edgy image she's cultivating. Harris is the guy in class who smirks at the back of the room, the guy you avoid eye contact with because if he bullies you, he will feel no remorse. But Dylan Klebold, he was just this goofy big-nosed kid with the hairdo of someone on *Dawson's Creek*. If he went to our high school, he'd be the tuba player. Harris was a thin, slouching weasel. I can't picture him playing an instrument, or walking our halls. The photos in the papers portray them as darkly heroic Batman types: The Trench Coat Mafia. Trench coats billowing behind them like black umbrellas against a ferocious wind. Kids crouching under the cafeteria tables, begging. The kindly teacher, splayed and bleeding in the science lab.

"Oh, hey," I point. Eunice has left us to ask the librarian a question.

"Awesome, see ya," says Amy, and darts back down the stairs, across the red carpet, out the revolving doors. When Eunice comes back, she doesn't ask where Amy went. She beams as though this is her opportunity, as though she and I have something in common.

The female chaperone knocks on our room door to make sure we're all here and there are no boys hanging around trying to steal our underpants, or whatever she thinks teenagers do away from home. "Don't stay up all night gossiping, girls! Get a good night's sleep," she advises us. The competition is tomorrow morning.

It's almost 9:30 pm and we've just come back from dinner at the Hard Rock Café, where I lied to the conductor to cover for the hours Amy spent buying gothic couture on Queen Street West. During dinner, Eunice seated herself between me and Corrine, and ordered a veggie wrap when everyone else ordered burgers. She talked about Schubert for twenty minutes, and didn't even get it when I said Schubert died of syphilis because he was a Romantic.

Amy's on the hotel bed with an array of shopping bags. From one of them, she pulls a bulging Ziploc. I go to sit by her, because I've never seen drugs up close, or really at all, except on TV. They're a dusty olive green, small bunches clumped on dried stems, the curled leaves woven through with saffron threads. The smell through the bag is pungent but fresh, like the tufts of herbs my mom buys at the Indian grocery. Corrine peers over us. "Oh, now we're in trouble," she says.

Amy shreds the weed with plum-coloured fingernails. I think of the anti-drug PSA that's been getting lots of play lately: a couple of puppet children singing, *Drugs, drugs, drugs. Some are good, some are bad. Drugs, drugs, drugs. Ask your mom or ask your dad.* I start to hum the tune and the other two join in. We're all giggling when Eunice comes out of the bathroom in her PJs, showered and once again having applied a shiny mask of Vaseline. "Gosh, your skin must be soft," says Amy drily. "Like a baby's bottom."

"Oh burn," says Corrine.

"What are you guys doing?" asks Eunice. "What is that stuff?" Is it possible she doesn't know?

"Corinne, put a towel under the door," commands Amy, and pointing at the ceiling, "Nina, cover that up." I grab a shower cap from the still-humid bathroom and, standing on a chair, use a hair elastic to secure the cap over the smoke detector. Corinne cracks open the window. Amy carefully dusts bits of plant matter off her fingers and back into the baggie, then pulls open the drawer next to the bed and removes the Bible. She flips to one of the blank end pages and tears. Eunice gasps on cue. "I don't have rolling papers," explains Amy (though she was out all day and could have purchased them at any time). "Please apologize to your god," she says to Eunice.

"... I don't believe in god," says Eunice. "Guys, I think this is a bad idea."

"Chillax, will you," says Amy. She twists the end of the joint, holds the other end to her mouth, and lights it with a hotel match.

"Corinne, if you get caught, who's going to play your solo?" asks Eunice. By now all four of us are sitting on the bed, drawn closer like cavemen and Amy has just ignited the first fire.

"What, her three-note solo in a movie soundtrack from five years ago?" says Amy. I watch her inhale, memorizing her movements so I can copy them. When she passes me the joint, I put my lips on it and breathe in deeply. I'm thrilled by the ring of orange that glows gradually bright, in sync with my inhale. I cough a cloud of smoke.

Because we're total nerds, we put on a recording of our Holst performance piece, played by some distant, professional orchestra.

When the joint comes around to Eunice, she sniffs it first, then takes a shallow puff. "I don't like it," she says, scrunching her face and thrusting it at Amy.

In minutes, my head is floating. I squeeze my eyes closed and it feels like an eyeball massage. Violins come slinking through the Allegro, strings vibrating like hummingbirds. Even on Corrine's tiny cassette player, the audio is like surround sound. I smell shampoo flowers coming from Eunice's hair. Eunice stays. It's obvious she wants to be a part of the group, though she's staying quiet. She reminds me of this cat

I had that would eat its own vomit. I used to wonder if it was motivated by shame.

"What's the difference between an onion and an oboe?" asks Amy.

"Nobody cries when you chop up an oboe!" answers Corinne, laughing with absolute joy, falling back on the bed.

"Okay, okay," says Amy, "you won't know this one: What's the difference between a bull and a band?"

"Nobody cries when you chop up a band!" answers Corinne.

"That's enough out of you," Amy says.

"A bull has the horns in front and the ass in back," I say, because I've heard all of Amy's band jokes.

"Nina!" Amy screams, gripping my neck and pretending to strangle me, then loosening into a hug.

"Shhhhhhh," I say, leaning my head on her shoulder. The woodwinds emit the purest sound: no breath, no clicks, only exquisite tones radiating through metal. Every chord is like biting into a stack of twenty crepes. My stoned brain remembers our "taped test" for the Holst piece, where we had to record ourselves playing individually at home and bring in the tape to be graded. I spent six hours on mine even though the section was only a few bars long. When I finished, my lips were chapped white at the edges and my index finger stung from the repeated pressing of Record, Rewind, and Play. The day it was due, I met Amy at her house on our way to school in the morning, and right before we left, she said, "Hang on a sec." I saw her pick up her oboe from the living-room sofa, and lithely reach across to her dad's complicated sound system. She played this graceful rendition in a single take, so flawlessly I wanted to tear the ribbon out of my own cassette tape.

"It's really time to sleep, guys," says Eunice.

"That's the only thing you've said in like an hour," says Amy. Behind her on the wall there's a mass-produced oil painting, shining and full of rolling hills. The whites of her eyes are disappearing under blood vessels, and she's chugging water from a plastic cup. "Go to sleep if you want to so badly. Why are you even here?"

Eunice says nothing. She remains where she is, and looks down at her hand, which is tracing swoops of thread on the quilted bedspread.

"Taking notes for later? Go write about us in your diary," says Amy. "What do you even write about in there? What could such a loser possibly have to write about?"

I'm trying to decide what to say. Corrine observes, slowly chewing a Fuzzy Peach, and it occurs to me that she and Eunice aren't friends; they've only been thrown together by default.

"Have you ever smoked weed? Ummmm . . . no. Do you have any friends? Ummmm . . . no. Does your family even love you? Why did they just, like, abandon you at the airport? Have you ever stayed up past 11:00 pm? Do you have access to explosives?" Amy pushes her face toward Eunice. "Do you research automatic weapons, Eunice? *Do you?* Do you dream about shooting us all to death?" She blinks, eyes drooping and detached. Eunice's hand has stopped moving on the bedspread. Corrine and I don't look at each other.

"Have you ever been naked with a guy? A girl? Have you? Has somebody else ever run their hands over your body? Have you ever *done it?*"

Eunice doesn't say anything. She's shaking her head.

"Have you ever been *fucked?*"

Eunice's eyes go dark and ancient. I think of how she begs the teachers to leave the band room unlocked so she can stay after school to practice. One night I forgot a textbook in my locker, and when I came back to get it I thought the only people in the building were the janitors, sweeping ragged grey brooms in wide arcs down the empty halls. Then I saw the fluorescent lights of the band room, and when I peeked in, there was Eunice, alone, in her usual chair. Her flute wasn't even out of its case, and as I came up behind her I glimpsed her scribbling in her diary. She'd written in millimetre-high sentences I couldn't read. Her hand gripped the black felt-tip pen as she scratched fervently, each word an abrasion.

Eunice sobs once, and curls her arms around herself. Then: "Yes," says Eunice, lifting her head and looking Amy in the eye. "I have. Have *you?*"

I think of the way Eunice hunches and slouches, making her body small. We all realize it at the same time. Even Amy has the decency to look away.

At 7:00 am, when we wake up, Eunice isn't in her bed. I change into my band uniform. The three of us venture out to the lobby, where the band has congregated in sleepy groups, draped over leather armchairs or bunched up by the free coffee, greedily splashing cream and opening sugar packets. Eunice is there, in her uniform, holding her flute case, with her music folder tucked under one arm. She's standing next to the conductor, between two potted palms. I have this new awareness of her body, though I'm trying not to notice it—her question mark shape, her pink skin. As the conductor approaches us and takes us aside, Eunice avoids looking at us, and I know what she's done.

By noon, Amy, Corinne and I are on a flight back to Halifax, sitting in separate rows because those were the only seats available. We're absurdly still in our uniforms. Our parents will have to pay the flight change fees. Behaviour that is detrimental to the effectiveness of the band or to its reputation is grounds for dismissal, the conductor said back at the hotel. Besides that, the school has a zero-tolerance drug policy. We're lucky not to have been expelled.

As flight attendants mime safety procedures, I hook the headphones of my Walkman around my skull and sink into my seat. I'm listening to a recording of us at the Spring Serenade. I'm pretending that the Walkman is a time machine and that I have returned to April. I'm sitting not in economy class but in my row on the stage in front of everybody's parents, turning the clean edges of sheet music. When the concert ends, we click off our stand lights in the dark auditorium, like the swift wink of a city losing electricity. On the conductor's cue, we exit in disciplined single file. I follow the dark green shoulders of the clarinetist ahead of me, careful not to rattle the rows of music stands as our line of musicians curves out the door. I want to forget that without the band I'm just me. That nothing will ever again be that good.

Tax Ni? Piḱak
(A LONG TIME AGO)

Troy Sebastian | nupqu ?ak·ɬaṁ

Tax ni? piḱak—a long time ago, Ka titi was in her kitchen when Uncle Pat came in and said:

"Did you see what the suyupi did now? They built a statue to David Thompson. They say he is a great man. Many people gathered at the hilltop and there were speeches and ka·pi. I like ka·pi, so I went there and that's what they said."

Uncle Pat was known for a few things, his old beat-up red-and-black Ford truck and his love of ka·pi.

"If you keep drinking that it will make you think like a crazy suyupi," said Ka titi.

It was true, Uncle Pat had become more and more like the suyupi with every cup of ka·pi. He used to dream with Kɬawɬa and Kupi, but ever since he enjoyed too much ka·pi they dreamt on their own.

"Ka·pi is for ceremony and blessings," said Ka titi.

"Every day is a blessing," Uncle Pat said as he rummaged in the ka·pi can for a hint of brew.

Ka titi stood at the kitchen window looking out toward the bones of Yawu?niḱ.

"I tell you something that you don't know," said Ka titi.

"Oh what's that," said Uncle Pat.

"Ever since the white man showed up on teevee, a lot of us Indians don't believe in miracles. Unless Alex Trebek shakes your hand or Pat Paycheck gives you a spin, there is no magic to be had."

"Uh-huh."

"David Thompson was hungry, lost, and afraid when he came to Ktunaxa ʔamakis and that's how he should be remembered. Instead, we get this story that celebrates him as some great explorer, and that is wrong. He didn't know where he was going."

"Oh ya," said Uncle Pat, listening in the way that men do and do not.

"Well that's not what they say in town," he continued.

"Uh-huh," said Ka titi.

"And that's not what's in the newspaper."

"Uh-huh," said Ka titi.

"They said they are going to name the new school for him too. Maybe even change the name of the Overwaitea to the David Thompson Memorial Overwaitea."

"ła taʔqna," said Ka titi.

"That's what they are saying," said Uncle Pat.

Ka titi had been alive longer than most of the people on the reserve. She remembered when David Thompson arrived in Ktunaxa ʔamakis and she wasn't impressed then and she wasn't impressed now.

Uncle Pat had managed to scrounge enough ka'pi grounds to fix together a half a cup. He put the kettle on the stove and waited for it to boil.

Ka titi waited for the kettle. As she waited, her thoughts took her away. Sometimes her thoughts brought her to places where she had been long before and places that she hadn't been to at all but still could remember. Her thoughts were somewhere between the first glacier winter and the first *Hockey Night in Canada.*

The whistling kettle brought her back to the present as Uncle Pat poured the boiling water into the cup he had placed on the counter.

Uncle Pat headed to the outhouse to do his business expecting to enjoy that lovely, hot cup of ka·pi when he returned.

He must have been in the outhouse a long time as it was getting dark when he got out. On the way back, he thought he heard Kupi call his name. This scared Uncle Pat, so he ran into the house.

Ka titi was sitting at the kitchen table with his cup of ka·pi in her old hands and a small pile of smokes next to a well-used cigarette lighter.

"Kupi called my name," said Uncle Pat, scared and filled with the heebie-jeebies.

"Sure she did, you are not the only one to use the outhouse."

"I'm not?"

"Waha. Think of all the ancestors who are in these woods, where do you think they go?"

That had not occurred to Uncle Pat. In that contemplation, Ka titi put a smoke to her mouth, lit the tobacco, and took a long drag.

Uncle Pat had not seen Ka titi smoke before, and that along with the call of Kupi really put him in a state.

Ka titi handed a smoke to Uncle Pat and told him to take a drag and give it to the moon. Only then could he smoke it for himself. Uncle Pat heeded her direction and went outside giving his smoke to k̓c̓iɬmitiɬnuqka.

It was good to give the smoke to k̓c̓iɬmitiɬnuqka as it was just coming up behind papa ʔa·kwukɬiʔit. The buzz from the ka·pi had left Uncle Pat, and his eyes were clearing up.

"It sure is beautiful," said Uncle Pat.

"It sure is beautiful," answered Kupi.

Uncle Pat did not see Kupi near him when he smoked. He was so surprised he nearly dropped his smoke. He offered

Kupi the smoke, but Kupi laughed like an old bird and flew off toward Bonners.

"Crazy bird," said Uncle Pat.

He took another smoke and gave it to ka papa ʔa·kwukɬiʔit and headed back inside.

Ka titi was still sitting at the kitchen table when Uncle Pat came in. She took the cigarette roller, looked at it, and put it back into its buckskin case.

"Kupi didn't like to smoke," said Uncle Pat.

Ka titi looked at Uncle Pat: "ɬa taʔqna."

"I know, Ka titi."

"Let me tell you about David Thompson," said Ka titi. "He wasn't just lost, he was a copycat."

Uncle Pat listened to Ka titi, eyeing the ka·pi swirling around the cup in Ka titi's hand.

"David Thompson heard the story of your Uncle Skin and was trying to do the same thing," said Ka titi.

"What are you talking about," asked Uncle Pat.

"Your Uncle Skin," said Ka titi. "What, you think you are the only uncle around here?"

"Well…"

"There have been many uncles before you and many more are still to come."

"Oh well."

"And David Thompson heard of your uncle's tale and tried to do the same thing."

"What story is that, Ka titi," asked Uncle Pat.

"Your Uncle Skin has been missing for a long time."

"Yes, Ka titi."

"He wasn't always missing, you know. He used to go missing, but he would always come back, usually around jump dance and the rodeos."

Uncle Pat just listened to Ka titi speak. He never knew his Uncle Skin, and any time folks talked about him, Uncle Pat would get quiet and listen.

"Your Uncle Skin was crazy, not like the suyupi with their cars and their ka·pi. He was crazy like numa in ɫumayitnamu. He knew things that were happening far away and he knew things before they happened. He was a clever man, but that made others in the tribe wary of him. He was often seen walking with Kupi on nights like this.

"One day the tribe had been without a good meal in a long time. Hunting season was over and there was little game to eat. So Skin started walking. At first it seemed like he was walking in a trance. But he soon found his way over the mountains to the east, towards the kuȼkiyawiy. Everyone thought he wouldn't come back, as most of our men who went that way got tangled up in rodeos and love triangles.

"That's not what happened to Uncle Skin. He walked from here at ʔaq̓am, through the mountains to the plains, all the way to a place called Lethbridge. When he got there, the suyupis were opening a brand new Overwaitea. They were just about to eat when he walked in the store and asked for food. As these suyupi had never seen a Ktunaxa before they were naturally impressed as we Ktunaxa are known for our well-developed bodies and easygoing attitude toward sex."

"I'll say," said Uncle Pat.

"Anyhow, Skin made his way to the deli and asked for a beet salad and some chicken. The suypui didn't know what to do so they gave it to him. He put it into a buckskin bag and headed west.

"The suyupi were so impressed by his feat of courage that they began to tell stories about him. They built a statue in his honour and this is what David Thompson learned of in his London condo."

"Uh-huh."

"When Skin came back to the tribe, everyone was hungry and some of us were really irritable. Just the sight of him was enough to upset the tribe as there was just enough food for everyone until spring.

"Nasu?kin saw Skin and said, 'Waha, Skin! We don't want you here. You have been gone too long and we hardly recognize you. Ka titi thought you were ku¢kiyawiy and wanted to shoot you.'"

"You did?" asked Uncle Pat.

"It is true," said Ka titi. "I was younger then and prone to bad judgment.

"Skin raised his hand and began to speak. 'It is true, Nasu?kin. I have been gone for too long. You don't recognize me and I hardly recognize you too. I had to listen to Kupi to tell me who is who.'

"The tribe was surprised at this and some rumbling began.

"'But behold,' said Skin. He rummaged into his buckskin bag and pulled out the deli chicken and the beet salad.

"'I have gone a long distance and have come back with food for the tribe. The suyupis over the mountain have built a new Overwaitea and they gifted this to us.'

"Nasu?kin took a look at the food and the eyes of the ?aqɬsmakniḱ and said, 'Sometimes Kupi knows what is best for the tribe. You have done well, Skin. We have enough food to keep us through winter.'

"The tribe had a big feast that night and everyone was tired with red-mouthed snores. Skin knew that the tribe would not trust him any longer, so he left his clothes folded on the bridge to town and flew off into the night.

"Years later, David Thompson arrived and started the mess we are in today."

"Hola! That is some story, Ka titi," said Uncle Pat. "Is it true?"

"Listen for the coming of Kupi and they will tell you what is true. They are better than newspapers and teevee. But don't talk to them or you will fly off like your Uncle Skin.

"And that is why we Ktunaxa don't speak to Kupi at night."

tax ni? piƙak—a long time ago
Ka titi—grandmother
suyupi—white people
ka'pi—coffee
Kupi—owl
Ktunaxa ?amakis—Ktunaxa lands

AGAIN, THE SAD WOMAN'S SOLILOQUY

Frankie Barnet

I went out with my professor a few times and I liked him. On Friday he took me to a party where the people were older, poets and writers from around the city. "There's Tim," he said. "He's a Marxist. There's his girlfriend Marie."

In the corner on a couch was a drunk woman slurring her words loudly. "That's Andrea, I'd be careful of her," said my professor, "she's sad." His breath was warm in my ear. I nodded, noticing the thin straps on the woman's dress, one of them sliding off her shoulder.

So I'll avoid her, I said to myself, because I felt I had enough of sad people. All day at school, complaining about how they deserved an A instead of an A-minus or how no one in workshop had understood their prose poetry correctly. It was enough to make you sad yourself, though I wasn't. I was happy to be dating my professor. He was tall. He kept his hair neat and bought me things.

My professor's friend Allen led us into his bedroom and closed the door. There were two other men as well, both of whom I recognized from readings I'd been to. One of the men, the bald one, I'd seen read poems about his childhood in Mississauga while the other, a redheaded man with a long beard,

FRANKIE BARNET

I'd seen read poems about birds—I remembered this, how at the end of each poem a bird died. Allen pulled out a bag of drugs from his pocket and told us they were pills that would make us feel like we were babies again. I felt anxious and excited, the way that drugs always made me feel, just the sight or even mention of them. "Have you ever done youth before?" my professor asked.

"Yes," I told him. Last summer, when I was with Daniel at his parents' cabin. We had driven up, just the two us, and done the youth on the dock. Except we hadn't taken enough, so we only got to thirteen or so, bitter and angry. Snarky to each other until we locked ourselves in different rooms, blasting loud music.

My professor put his hand on my back and smiled at me in the sly, gentle way that reaffirmed my belief in my own poetry. The same words and line breaks he'd described as saccharine and derivative only the semester before. His friend distributed the pills in everyone's palms. Was I making a good impression? Taking drugs must count for something, I thought.

There was a part of me, during the whole time I dated my professor, that was confident I could buck his opinion of me, and in doing so the opinions of others: his laughing, bearded friends. No, I was not just another girl. No, I was not like the girls you've seen before, the ones who came around to laugh and fawn before inevitably flickering into the background to exist only as a funny story or an inside joke. But there was also another part of me, all during this strange time, that simply felt too tired to try.

We re-emerged into the party, it's dark, low-ceilinged room where people danced half-heartedly to a song I didn't know. The drug would take it's time to work it's way into our bloodstreams. For now we'd have to wait. My professor said he had to go to the bathroom and left me by myself. So I stood there, doing my best not to look pathetic in the room full of strangers. I reapplied my lip gloss and fiddled with a keychain in my pocket. Cool, comfortable, mature. Yet before I knew it I had accepted a drink from the sad woman he had told me to avoid, and I was sitting beside her on the couch, listening to her speak.

"I know what people say about me," she said. "How I'm so *sad*. But what they don't know is that I'm not going to be sad forever. No sir*ee*." She spilled some of her wine on the floor waving her arms, then tried to wipe it up with the bottom of her shoe, which only pressed the liquid deeper into the carpet.

"I like you," she said to me. "And you have such pretty eyelashes." When she leaned in close I could smell pizza on her breath, oregano and synthetic Parmesan from the cheap, soggy slices I myself was familiar with. "I'ma tell you a secret," she slurred.

Why did this always happen to me and sad people? I always got sucked in like this. Even with Daniel, who laughed and joked as if he were a happy person, but his paintings—at least the ones he'd shown me—they told a different story. I thought about that time in Wakefield after the youth had worn off and we were just ourselves again. We rubbed our noses together. He said that he loved my nose, how prominent the two ridges on it's tip were. "For some reason," he said. "I am always ending up with girls who have big noses."

"People always tell you," said the sad woman. "That the antidote to being sad is being happy, but what people never tell you is what if the antidote to being sad is being so intensely, wrenchingly, and viscerally miserable you use all of your sadness up?"

She paused, leaving me with that idea. "Huh? Ever thought of that?"

"I, uh," I said. But I wasn't a sad person really, was I? I did not think of myself that way then. The truth was that I experienced joy from TV and animals. Though sure, sometimes I got listless, waiting around for my professor to text me, nights when I couldn't think of anything to write a poem about. I waited for him to tell me when to meet him and where. If he was somewhere with too many people from the university around then I could meet him later, at his apartment. "You can't write about me," he had said. "You know that right?" Other than that we did everything.

My professor came out of the bathroom, then walked out to the terrace. The drugs had not hit me yet. The other men too, who I could see around the party looking straight. Maybe if it did not work we would have to take more. That is, if Allen had more. But you could take too much, and what happened was that you went kind of catatonic, floating in a time before life. I'd seen it happen to a girl from my high school. When you got young like that there's nothing you could do except sleep it off.

"Everyday I go home and just mope around," said the sad woman. "I don't eat well, I put little care into my appearance and I watch all these documentaries about little girls with cancer, dolphin hunts and assisted suicide. Bootlegged from Russia, mostly.

"You might think that you cannot possibly get sadder than you are right now. But trust me, you can. You would not believe how sad I can sometimes get. I can see that you are a young person but you have to understand that this is true.

"Each time I think I'm approaching the end of sadness there's a warmth to it. It glows, if you can believe it. I have a feeling that I am very close right now. I wouldn't be talking so boastfully if I weren't certain I was almost there. My projections? I might not even be sad by next year."

I wanted to get up, to stand beside my professor and laugh with him, but the sad woman touched my arm and kept talking. "I see all these people and they're sad too," she said, gesturing to the party. "We all are, it's an epidemic. The difference is that they think they are working on themselves and making progress. I live in this neighborhood, I've seen them jogging. They think it'll work but trust me it won't. I know because I've been there. I tried all of the oils and stretches when I was your age. Don't bother."

As I said, I was not a sad person.

"The thing that might surprise you," said the sad woman, "is that I was not always sad." She said it like a secret, though her voice was very loud. Several people in a small crowd around us turned to look at her. She said that as a girl she'd been so happy that she used up all of her happiness by age fifteen.

"When I was fifteen a boy from school invited me over to his house. I couldn't have been more excited. That's who I was, happy all the time. When I got there they gave me alcohol. One of the boys was from my high school, but there was also another boy from a different school. He told me that he knew who I was because of how happy I was. Everybody knew. That's what growing up in a small town is like. They said things to me like, 'look at her lip gloss.' 'It's like she wants us to look at her mouth, to watch her laugh.' One of the boys took off his belt while the other boy held me up against a tree in the backyard, then tied my arms above my head to the trunk. The boys went for each side of my ribs and started to tickle me. They kept me there for so long, in the yard. They said, 'we're keeping you here until we go through all of your laughter, we'll keep you here all night if we have to!' And they did," she said. "They got it all out of me!" Though she was laughing right then, telling me the story.

I could feel the drug now, hazy in the distance. I felt good now.

"My sadness," recited the sad woman as if it were a poem, "is a dark velvety distress. It makes me feel like I cannot possible get anymore distressed, though new distress is always around the corner."

Then she asked if I was with Michael. That was my professor's name. None of my friends called him that though, we always just called him "the professor" when we talked about him, us as a couple. They liked to joke about it.

I nodded, laying down on the couch, cuddling with a pillow. "I've been with Michael," said the sad woman wistfully. "I used to be in his class."

The youth was strong now, so I rolled onto the floor and felt the bristles of the carpet on my back, between the strands of hair on my scalp. The others too, all the men from the room, we lay together and gazed up at the ceiling. Nothing was a word, there were only shapes and colors. I was warm and thought of nothing. I can't remember.

That night, after we peaked and the party ended, my professor and I had sex in his apartment. It was nice, not at all like the other times we'd been together, the first of which was almost two months prior when my professor had asked me to meet him in a bar far from the university to talk about publishing one of my poems. He walked me home for my own protection, then kissed me against the door of my apartment building, breathing heavily and pretty much forcing me to let him come upstairs.

But that night after the party my body felt so young, reminiscent of a time before I had learned to think of it strange. I could feel each touch on my skin. And I knew that my professor felt this way too. I could see it on his face. He'd never looked that young with me before. And even though I knew it wasn't about me, that he could have felt that way with any of the girls from our class (as long as youth was involved), I liked that I was there to see it.

After that we fell asleep. I dreamt of two kittens cuddling for warmth. Both of them had these long paws, really more like fingers actually, and they entwined to clasp onto each other. They purred. When I woke up I was with Daniel, which was also a dream, but I did not notice that at first. It felt real. There was heat from his belly, my leg wrapped around him. He held onto my foot, like all those mornings. How could he have then said that he did not love me anymore? That the love had run its course, when we had hardly been together six months. That meant that his love must have been fierce, explosive, for it to run out of itself so quickly, which was not true. Yes, his love was like that sometimes, the night we met at the party, Dexter's birthday, but other times his love was quieter, subtle. Sometimes it did not seem like he loved me at all. He did not call me, or remember things I'd told him. So what he claimed about using all that love up did not make sense.

When I woke up a second time, I was in my professor's apartment and I felt very sad. I could hear him using the shower and when he came out he said that he was sorry, but he could not give me a ride home because he had to pick up his daughter. "I'm sorry to rush you," he said.

"No," I told him. "It's fine." And it was, I got dressed and I left.

For the rest of the day, when I walked home, when I drank a Gatorade and watched TV on my computer, I kept wondering if the dream would peel itself open once more, a third time, so that I could wake up in a new scene all together. So many of the strange things I saw that day: two squirrels having sex on a fence outside my window, attractive laughing people who looked sad, unattractive, lonely people who looked happy, I kept thinking that these things could be the corners of the dream beginning to curl. But in the end that one dream went on for a long time.

A ROOM
AT THE MARLBOROUGH

Cathy Stonehouse

The funeral director was a midget. Four feet tall, with a drinker's nose, his manner was theatrically sombre, except when the talk turned to caskets. The one he recommended was called the Marlborough, which sounded to Malc like a shabby West End hotel. "Wood construction, semi-gloss veneer, simple velvet interior." Seated in a padded swivel chair, the man looked like an excited seven-year-old. Malc wondered where he bought his suits.

"I want something simple."

"Simple." A long silence followed. After Malc blinked the man emitted a slow, deflationary sigh. "Very well then." Licked his plump finger and flicked backwards through the laminated pages of his catalogue. "In that case, may I suggest the Caritas?"

Malc had identified the body only yesterday. His sister had refused to do it, and their father was too ill to care. Their stepfather was now living with another woman, and in any case Phyllis wouldn't have wanted him to.

Malc had seen his fair share of dead bodies, but it was different when it was your own kin. He'd been tempted to take a photograph. But he'd had no camera. Instead he had run his finger down his mother's arm. Her skin felt like used cling wrap and when he vomited into the rubbish bin there was nothing in him, only the image of an old woman falling from a second-storey window into the chasm between two flower-beds, which wasn't exactly what had happened but was close enough.

"And will that be for cremation or burial?"

"I'm not sure." He paused a moment. "Burial."

Malc had spent the morning as he usually did, developing old, unclaimed negatives. His mother would have called it perverted. But he'd checked, and it was above the law. Film unclaimed for years, binned at the QuikPic, had come home in his briefcase the week they cleared the stockroom out. The work was strictly personal, he had told her (in his head); a hobby of sorts. There are those who baptize the aborted, or memorialize the homeless. Malc, your son, rescues anonymous snaps.

They no longer developed pictures on the QuikPic premises. All Malc did there now was computer work, and he missed the singe of developer in his nostrils, the ritual pause as the shadows began to take shape. So he'd set up a darkroom in his bathroom and since then washed mostly at the kitchen sink. It was an odd arrangement, but he didn't have visitors.

No doubt some of the faces that gazed up at him from the lid of the toilet belonged to holidaymakers who had now left this world. Others to grown-ups who could not even remember that day at the seaside when a gull almost stole the Flake from their ice cream cone. But at least now he recognized them.

When the funeral director arrived to pick up Phyl's body, her neighbour, Mrs. Sellers, had thought the funeral home had sent a child. When Malc arrived, his mother was still lying where Mrs. Sellers had found her, at the bottom of the stairs.

That day Malc had worked a wedding. The early spring sun had turned to hail and the bride, a nurse, had thrown her bouquet at him as she ran inside. "Mum's not answering.

Someone should go over there." He could hear Simone's son, orgasming via electric guitar somewhere in the background. Calum, who would never go to war, but who played death metal as if his life depended on it.

"I'm working."

"Well, I'm ill."

After driving 60 miles he was grateful for the instant coffee. Mrs. Sellers, who kept the spare key, was a shakier version of her usual self, concerned her plate of Custard Creams was not up to snuff.

"I'm sorry you had to be the one to find her."

"Oh, not at all, dear. She'd have done the same for me."

He'd driven back home that night, done his shift at the QuikPic, then returned the next afternoon to sort out arrangements. Simone was now vomiting, according to Calum, and didn't want to contaminate. Malc thought of the fat blonde girl on a swing. Who was she, and why did her photographer abandon her? Then he thought of another picture, not one he had developed, one he had found.

There were ghosts in the world, and he had seen one. He had also felt one: a hand on his ribs, then a sharp push. At the time it had just seemed like part of the strangeness of being in a new country, not quite thirteen and almost alone. The first time he saw it, his mother was asleep. She was, he remembered, wearing some sort of nylon nightie, which had crackled and flashed as she pulled it on.

Did she remember? He knew she remembered the trip. "Our little escape," she had called it. A rehearsal for what would follow. He had been lying awake, breathing in the damp French air when the first grey mist appeared, not yet settled into the shape of a face. Trailing light, it was a bowed head. After it appeared, he tried to wake his mother up. But she just rolled over, batted him with her freckled, flabby arms. His father claimed she could sleep through a war, and Malc could see this was true. He watched the mist gather for a moment or two without breathing. His father was right about some things, but not much.

They had meant to come on holiday as a family, but at the last minute Simone had come down with chicken pox and his father been offered a contract he could not refuse. So Malc and his mother had come by themselves, his mother staring down the French hotel clerk who looked askance at her before proffering the key.

"He's my own son," he heard her say, "and I'm not booking two single rooms," as they crammed into the elevator, "not at that price."

Luckily the French proprietor was already halfway down the corridor, fitting the long, silver key into the keyhole. He and his mother walked past him into their bedroom, which smelt of fancy soap and stale breath. The walls were blue, papered in a complicated, trellised pattern, and the window looked out onto a well, at the bottom of which were huddled a group of rubbish bins.

His mother slammed it shut and closed the net curtains. "You can sleep on this side," she announced, before yanking open the wardrobe and starting to unpack.

His mother had been angry but Malc was happy. The whole trip over had been like a dream. Taking the train at six o'clock, arriving on the coast in the afternoon, unpacking slimy salad sandwiches while sitting on the improbable deck of the hovercraft as it vacuumed its way across the English Channel and then arriving in France, a place he no more believed in than in Tintin's hair. And in France, just like in the cartoons, everyone smoked. They had taken a taxi to the hotel, which was on a side street and rather shabby looking, and were in Normandy.

His mother had said they would go to the beach tomorrow, and he wondered if there would be any unexploded ordnance or bullet casings. This was where the Allies had landed, after all. They would stay here a week although it was unclear to Malc what his mother planned to do. He had never been away with her before. If only they could rent a metal detector.

Simone would have dug for bullets. She had cried when she found out, picked off the newest scabs on her forearms and flicked them at him. And now it was night, and she would be alone in her bedroom, picking off scabs in her sleep and flicking them at no one while he was here in this French bed and wide awake.

The room was quiet. At first there had been noises from other rooms: tantalizing snatches of conversation, a woman yelling out in French and a man responding, clattering lids in the well and a brief bark. But now it was silent. The hard ball of bread and cheese they had eaten for dinner sat in his English stomach, undigested, and he felt hungry, wished they'd gone out to eat. Why had his mother come if she wouldn't do anything? If only there were some cornflakes. It had never occurred to him to smuggle food along. His mother had insisted she was tired and they go to bed early, and turned off the bedside lamp before it was dark.

And now, in addition to the head, there was something pressing down on him. As he often did, when he was frightened, Malc imagined a war scene: flickering, black and white footage of men crawling up wet sand, the click of a gun barrel followed by a hand grenade exploding, and for a moment he was gone, juddered asleep, dream scenes plunging him into the belly of a Lancaster then out and up into the air, into a train. The guard who was approaching down the aisle held travel brochures in his fist, as well as a whistle. The whistle sounded loudly.

Jolted awake, Malc found himself sitting up again, cold suddenly and naked above the waist, staring into the dark where a wind seemed to be animating the flimsy curtains, or at least that's how it appeared at the start, but after a moment he understood he was looking at the wardrobe, whose doors his mother had closed after hanging up her outfits and tucking the empty suitcase in behind. The doors were fronted by mirrors, and in those mirrors a dancing piece of white cloth was reflected, although the movement was faint and barely noticeable, unlike a moment ago when it had seemed wild.

He turned his head. The mirrors did not face the window. What they reflected was the other side of the room. There was nothing there.

His mother's back was turned, and her skin seemed cold. He leaned over to check her breathing and saw her face squashed into the flattened pillow. He put his hand on her cheek then let go.

How could she sleep? "Mum," he whispered, "Mum, wake up."

He looked back. The white shape was definitely there again, but this time it did not look like cloth at all. Instead it looked like smoke, a smoke flower, twisting and turning in space, a flower of light.

"Mum," he whispered.

His mother groaned. Her mouth was partly open, connected by spit threads. He wanted to pull them off. Her face seemed folded over on itself. The shape was still there, and in it he could see the shape of a person, but just as he started to trace it, it was gone.

For the next two nights Malc did not see anything unusual, although he barely slept. Instead he recited to himself everything he knew about World War 2 airplanes, which was a lot as he had memorized his Observer's Guide one weekend after failing a math test: *Messerschmitt, Flying Fortress, Fokker, Focke-Wulf*. Afterwards he got up as fast as he could, put his clothes on and sat looking out at the grey bricks inside the well and listening to the echoes from other bedrooms which also opened onto it, straining to make out what was said until it was time to leave.

From breakfast on he forgot about the room and everything in it. The croissants were crumbly and always served with green plum jam. The TV rattled on in French and by the second or third day he could understand some of it. Some of the words just repeated and repeated until their meaning appeared in his head. *Absolument magnifique.* Plus they had a small French dictionary which he began to study over meals while his mother hid behind glossy magazines or else the guidebook she had borrowed from the library, writing out their itinerary each day on the back of an envelope.

"Where shall we go today?" she would ask, after finishing her coffee, and he would shrug his shoulders, and when they got outside he would cross his arms and pout, and after a brief argument they would do the same thing, which was go to the beach in the morning and then visit the shops after lunch.

The beach was bright. It was full of half-naked women. He spent most of his time staring at them. His mother bought him a stupid bucket and spade set, as well as a cheap football and a paddle with a rubber ball attached to it by a string, which seemed to be a local game, but he wasn't particularly interested in playing, especially by himself. He felt pale. All the other boys were brown and strong and ran about in groups, some including girls. Some boys who looked his age even smoked or rode on scooters. At lunchtime he and his mother would buy a baguette, some cheese and tomatoes and a bottle of mineral water and eat on the beach before packing up and heading inland, up the dreary pink streets to the shops where his mother would pore over silk scarves and souvenirs, and he would buy himself a chocolate croissant. At four they would go home and his mother would sleep on the bed while he drew.

Drawing was his second favourite activity after masturbating. He would masturbate first in the bathroom, get it over quickly, then wipe himself off and go in search of his sketchbook. His mother would think he was vile if she ever found him. In the war between his mum and dad he only pretended to take his father's side. His mother was flighty (his father's word), and Malc could see this trip was a test of his limits. He would indulge her, of course, but he would not buckle. And anyway it was all happening way too late.

His mother was already changing, perming her hair so it stood out from her head and adding herbs like grass to every meal. Michael's parents lived in separate homes and he seemed to enjoy it, shuttling between them with his little brother Tim and their huge collection of football cards, housed in old shoeboxes. But then again, Michael was incredibly dense.

At home Malc had his own record player. That was because his parents had a brand-new stereo, its speakers stationed like bodyguards either side of the sofa. His father liked Elvis Presley, his mother Fleetwood Mac. Malc also owned a few singles himself, including *Tie a Yellow Ribbon Round the Old Oak Tree*. Michael liked Elton John, but Malc couldn't stand him. He also did not believe in God but still sang alto in the church choir: *I don't believe in you* he would chant while singing, the words lifting up through his crown and into the ether. His fingers remained crossed although the music tugged at his heart.

"What are you drawing?" His mother ran a hand down her face, sat up groggily.

"Nothing," he said. "I don't like it." He ripped the drawing up. The ball of shiny paper missed the wastepaper basket and he had to walk over to plop it in.

Before the holidays he had found some graphite at school and smuggled it home with him, long, silvery cylinders like bullets which left metallic traces in his pockets. He'd heard that graphite was poisonous, which was exciting. The taste had been cold; bloody. Perhaps if he licked it long enough he would die. First he had drawn an aeroplane then a window. The lines of the window frame glittered with their layers of lead.

"Let's go out," said Phyllis. "What time is it?" Her gold watch read 6:15 pm.

"How long have I slept?"

"I don't know."

"What did you do?"

"Nothing."

"You're a funny boy." She got up and went to the wardrobe, looked at her reflection, and for a moment Malc saw the twisting shape. His mother with tousled brown hair, green-blonde highlights growing out. Then she had opened the doors and taken a dress out, slipped it like a new skin over her head. "Can you do me up?"

He took the dark zip and pulled on it. Women's dresses with zips up the back were so pointless. Then he went out onto the tiny balcony. A girl with long brown legs was walking along the other side of the street.

His mother locked the hotel room door with the long silver key and left it at the front desk before they went out. The sky was overcast as they headed to the promenade and Malc's mother's dress whipped about in the wind. Nevertheless they made it to the beach before the rain came, and a middle-aged couple from Britain, wearing blue cagoules, managed to take two pictures of them beside a beach hut.

That night they went out for dinner and ordered steak-frites. It was their last night. In the hotel lounge, Malc's mother got slightly drunk and insisted on letting him go up to their room first. He knew she was hoping to meet someone, and refused to go, but eventually gave up when the girl with the brown legs appeared in a loose mini-dress alongside her father, and his mother began to make puppy eyes.

Opening the door to their room he felt the hair on his neck stand on end. The air inside felt electrical. He turned the lights on. Then he made sure the window was firmly closed. He sat on the bed and took off his clothes and then on a whim stood in front of the wardrobe mirror and examined his body: thin and pale with a floppy little cock the thickness of a pencil. He turned the light out. No one would ever like him and he didn't care.

Later that night he awoke and felt someone on him. It was a person with their hands around his neck. He could not move. He closed his eyes and repeated to himself *I believe in God I believe in God* until the pressure lifted and he was alone. He opened his eyes. There was a white shape moving in the air, but he could not tell this time if he was imagining it. His mother returned at dawn, crept in with her shoes off. She must have got the proprietor to give her another key. She got into bed in her slip and he did not acknowledge her, and later that morning she was up by the time he awoke.

It was only later, after the photos were developed that he saw the woman lifting from his mother's body: a white blur clear against the darkening beach. By this time his father was living in a bungalow and his mother was going out with the man from the estate agent's.

When he showed the picture to Simone she said the woman looked as if she were crying. Malc disagreed. He took the picture and hid it, slipped it into a crack in the brown linoleum that lined the bottom of his father's garden shed. He never looked at it. He didn't want to. He just hid it there with the tiny shrapnel fragment he'd unearthed at Juno. His mother had said it wasn't shrapnel. It was probably just a car part.

"A respectful choice, Sir," commented the funeral director, as Malc proffered the blue dress he had found, a dress he vaguely remembered from happier times.

"Thank you." He was glad to let go of it. Something about the shape of it filled him with dread.

"It's a difficult time." The midget laid his small, old hand on Malc's elbow. "Your mother was a fine woman."

Malc froze. It had not occurred to him that the man might have known her. "You must meet a lot of people." From a certain angle, the funeral director looked familiar, like someone Malc had seen but never noticed, a boy from a photograph.

Outside, the sky was already darkening. It occurred to Malc that he should tell his father, although the man never remembered one hour to the next. His mother had taken to visiting him again in the last few years, and in her will she had left him a hundred pounds. Her second husband, Malc's step-father, had been written out of it twenty years ago. He had found the will in the top drawer of her dressing-table, as instructed. Phyllis was nothing if not organized.

He heard her voice: *take the weight off them pins.* The house was cold. He did not turn the heating on. Mrs. Sellers had let herself in and left him a small, cold roast chicken. He looked around. This was the moment of haunting. Surely now the fridge door would pop open, or the standard lamp blink on then off in some otherworldly semaphore. He would sleep on the sagging couch, or try to. Book me into the Marlborough, he thought. When my time comes.

When that car ploughed into his truck back in '86 he had cracked two vertebrae. Shortly after, he left driving for drink and then Jesus, and shortly after that married Elaine. None of this had anything to do with his present situation, other than the possibility of death, but he found himself remembering the injury as he lay on his mother's soft furnishings and tried to sleep.

The vertebrae were healed. But Elaine had said she could not live with a non-believer and now he spent his life recording moments of happiness he also did not quite trust but had to fake. Then one day, around about '91 when he was at his worst, he had discovered Phyllis, weeping in the bathroom. Her second marriage had failed, and she was living on tinned pineapple. It made her mouth sore, but she couldn't stop. Something about the texture of it made her feel better. *Look at my face,* she implored him. *It's red. Like a ruddy clown's.*

Cause of death uncertain. It was possible she'd had a stroke. Lately Malc had neglected to call. He found her disappointment in him challenging. She was lonely, of course. She and Simone did not really get on, and Calum had been her only grandchild. Searching her wardrobe for a suitable dress the previous morning he had found the balls of wool she used to knit into pastel doll clothes and donate to Mencap, and the neatness of the balls, their bright colours, had made him cry. Now he felt nothing. The television hummed. The walls of her tiny living room pressed in around him.

I've been a crap son, he thought. *Fucking useless. Tomorrow I'll go to the river and jump in.* Smashing his closed fist against his skull, he saw the faces of the abandoned in their photographs, lined up like the victims of a holocaust on the inside door of his wardrobe and laughed out loud. *Daft as a brush*, he thought. They were his mother's words.

At the funeral he would speak of their holiday in Deauville, of her love affair with France (rifling through her handbag, he had noticed yet another Eiffel tower keychain), but as he spoke, staring down the red-carpeted aisle towards the white light that seeped in through the crack between the double doors, he would know that love to be untranslatable. She was dead, and they were all fallen, for that matter, or in the process of falling.

The photograph had been fake. A double exposure. And that piece of shrapnel was nothing but a steel ball bearing.

He rubbed his face, felt the skull beneath. Perhaps tomorrow he'd go for a walk in the sunlight and never mind what he'd felt back in the early hours, for there were certain truths that dissolved in daylight. Every joint in his body was salvaged from history, and every picture he took was of a ghost. He still had that old ball bearing, still half-believed in it, and meanwhile he was as good a liar as anybody.

EVERY TRUE ARTIST

Kai Conradi

The sun has slipped behind the low-slung mountains by the
time Yula pulls up at the motel, hands the driver a ten, and
steps out onto the dirt. The desert sky stretches on, flat and
colossal, so far that it hurts her eyes when she tries to take in
where it begins or ends. On a cloudless night like this, the light
fades quick. There is no sunset like she knows from Canada,
where the clouds take on the last rays as golden, then pink,
then purple—holding the dregs of light long after the sun has
vanished. Here, night falls like the big cedar her brother, Rich,
felled on their property last winter, and the spiny plants that
stud the landscape become black and jagged.

The motel is a long, flat building of white brick, punctu-
ated by nine doors—eight guest suites and a lobby. Across the
street, a derelict gas station slouches into the dry earth. The
motel sits on the highway that passes straight through the
middle of Angel City, a town of less than a thousand inhabitants, composed—as far as she can tell—of run-down trailers
and chain-link fences and backyards crammed with old furniture. Tied up in front of one of these trailers, a little ways down
the road, several dogs bark. Their barking rattles around in the
night like tin cans kicked down a street. A woman in jeans and

a denim shirt emerges from the trailer and shouts at the dogs; kibble clatters against metal and the dogs jostle one another for their supper. From somewhere in the dark: Johnny Cash's "Green Green Grass of Home."

The sudden desert night chills Yula through her turtleneck and slacks. She picks up her suitcase and heads toward the warm light of the lobby. As she opens the plate glass door, it clangs against a silver spur that dangles from the doorframe. The walls of the lobby are a pale, dentist's-office green. A crooked, hand-painted border of pink roses runs along the walls, just below the ceiling, and all along it hang framed portraits of cowboys, most cut from magazines, their edges jagged and sloppy. Behind the front desk sits a woman in a yellow western shirt patterned with tiny red horseshoes. Her large breasts hang low on her chest, and push against the mother-of-pearl snaps that struggle to hold together the halves of the fabric. She wears oversized, green-rimmed glasses, and when she looks up at Yula her brown eyes are magnified to the size of walnuts. There is a large mole on her neck and another above her right eyebrow. Her name tag reads "Doreen." Doreen greets Yula and her voice is deep. Her open lips reveal gums packed with twice as many teeth as seem necessary on a human being.

You didn't see Ribs out there, did you? Doreen asks. She is younger than Yula—mid-to-late forties—and far from conventionally attractive. Her cherry coloured hair—home-dyed, Yula hopes, for the woman's sake—drapes lank over her shoulders, and her face has an unimpressed, sagging quality that reminds Yula of a bloodhound. And yet, Yula bets that men would fight each other for this woman. It must be the way she looks at you; a total ambivalence that makes you want, more than anything, for her to care about you.

Ribs? Yula says. Is that a dog? She thinks of the dogs scrabbling on the dirt for their dinner. I'm here for the artist's residency, actually, she says. I'm Yula Curtain. I was supposed to be here this afternoon but we had to make an emergency landing in Tomahawk because a woman was having a panic attack.

No part of Doreen's face displays interest at this information. Ribs is my boyfriend, she says. He rode his motorcycle over to Sasko last night but we're going for steak tonight at Lou Harvey's.

She opens a drawer in her desk and, eyes still fixed on Yula, rummages her hand around in it. Yula looks at her feet. Already, her white Keds knock-offs have taken on a dust-brown. After a few minutes of half-hearted rummaging, Doreen pulls a plastic cactus keychain from the drawer. On it are two keys. One's for your room, she says, the other's for the ice machine around back. Make sure you don't leave the doors open or the scorpions will get in. And don't leave your shoes outdoors neither. You're room six. She gestures to the left. If you're gonna smoke in the rooms, make sure you don't burn the carpets or nothin', or I'll have to charge you for damage.

I don't smoke, says Yula. She takes the keys and tries to pocket them, but the pockets of her slacks are just for show. Do you know when Mr. Carver will show up? she asks.

That who you're sharing the room with? says the woman.

No, says Yula. Wince Carver, the man who runs the residency. She pulls at the bottom of her turtleneck, where it likes to ride up over her paunch.

The woman laughs a deep laugh, like rocks knocking together under the ocean, but her face remains flat. Good thing he's not your man, she says, 'cause the bed in room six is made for a scarecrow. You two'd have to lie on top of each other like those Dr. Seuss turtles. Her laughter stops and she looks bored. Anyway, I've got no idea, hun. I just work the front desk.

Yula turns to go and the front-desk woman adds, I'm here all day, by the way. Holler if you need anything. Oh, and if you smoke in your room, don't fall asleep with one in your mouth.

Room six doesn't have a fire extinguisher and the local fire-truck broke down two weeks ago and still ain't fixed.

All night, the fan in Yula's room whirrs. There doesn't appear to be an off-switch, and she sleeps a fitful sleep, too cold under the thin comforter. In a dream, she wakes in her bedroom at home and sees falling snow. It feels like late afternoon. She wanders to the kitchen in her fleece nightie and Rich comes through the door dragging an enormous, bloodied caribou. He heaves this caribou into the centre of the room, then goes back outside and hauls in another. The kitchen fills with warm caribou carcasses until the mound reaches the ceiling, and then Rich tells her to start cutting—they are going to make caribou soup.

Yula wakes early and pictures Rich at the kitchen table; on his plate the same three boiled eggs and half-pound of bacon he eats every morning. She thinks about calling him, but of course he wouldn't answer—and what would she say to him? I miss you? They have never said that to one another. His presence in the house is like the birthmark on her right shoulder—so constant and unequivocal that she has never considered it outright.

Yula dresses in the same clothes she wore the day before. The sun has not yet risen and the town lies quiet. This quietness surprises her; she has never been to the desert before, but imagined that, in the early hours when no one is about, it would make noise. That the earth would be alive as it is in the woods near her house, only in a different way. Instead of the swish of branches and the creak of tree trunks in the wind and the crows and starlings in the trees, the flat expanse of dirt would be somehow audible. Yula does not believe in God, nor would she ever go so far as to call herself a spiritual person. She does, however, believe that the land acts in ways that are not describable through science, nor through religion. That landscape possesses a kind of aliveness that sometimes shows itself, if you pay close enough attention. Not energies, exactly, because that sounds too mystical and new-agey. In the desert, she had imagined this aliveness would manifest itself in the ground. She would never try to explain this to someone, but if she did, she would liken it to an enormous, incredibly thin pancake, rising off the earth to meet the sky. A kind of connectedness between the land and the wide openness above. And the cacti, she imagined, the cacti would buzz like static.

Yula heard about the artist's residency nine months ago, from a traveling bat photographer. The night after she met the photographer, she lay in bed, Rich snoring next door and the house creaking in the wind, and fantasized about the aliveness of the desert. She fantasized about it for the next week, while she folded laundry at the Laundrolounge, and helped Rich butcher and freeze a buck and three rabbits, and met with the Ladies Group after work where the other women complained about menopause and their fat husbands. She imagined herself cross-legged in the desert—though in reality she hadn't been able to sit like that since her thirties—a sketchbook and pencil in hand, drawing cacti and the long flat sky and tumbleweeds that ambled by. In her fantasy, the landscape spoke through her. She had read this could happen—that a residency was the best way to open your creative spirit. She imagined she would feel awakened by the land, and her muse would sing.

At the end of that week, Yula sent a letter to the organizer of the residency, Wince Carver. She photocopied her three best sketches—Rich's workboot on the kitchen linoleum; three potatoes in a pot on the stove; the portrait of her mother on the wall above the bathtub—and sent them to him, along with an artist's statement and a photograph. She read somewhere that it wasn't a true artist's statement unless you hyperbolized, and so she stretched the boundaries of reality; increased her three months of drawing experience to four

years—plus the thirteen or so she spent doodling as a child—
and scribbled something about private showings of her work
at several local galleries. She once visited a local gallery with
the Ladies Group, and partook in a macramé tutorial, so it
wasn't completely untrue. The instructor praised her plant-
hanger and suspended it in the gallery's front window. Yula
had read, too, that many of the best artists were self-taught,
and so she stressed in her application that she had *never* been
to art school, not once.

She debated long about which photo of herself to send,
and decided at last on one that Clay took on their twelfth
wedding anniversary, when they carried a picnic up to the
meadow and lay in the grass and drank cheap champagne,
until they got into a fight over something trivial—she
couldn't remember now what it was—and Clay stuffed all the
food back in the picnic basket and hiked down without her.
She hadn't wanted him to take the photo—this was before the
fight—and put up a hand too late to stop him, so that in the
photo her face was half-turned from the camera, hand midair
like a conductor, a strand of hair picked up by the wind and
blown across her neck. Her fingers were spread, cheek covered by her palm, but her eye was visible between index and
middle fingers, mouth half-open below her pinky. She liked
this photo, even though it showed her crooked incisor and
widow's peak, because the light made her skin look warm and
inviting; her windblown hair could almost be the hair of a
carefree artist, in love with herself and with the world, sure
of her talent and the future she would create for herself. The
photograph was a good decade-and-a-half old, but the only
recent photograph she could find was the one Rich insisted
on taking of her at the Fall Fair, the year they went with the
Kemps and their sadistic twin grandsons. In that photo, she
sat on a prize-winning pony—a white, walleyed thing—
and you could almost see it strain under her weight; its legs
splayed, upper lip curled back. Yula's turtleneck—always that

same cursed lavender turtleneck—was visibly tucked up in the underwire of her bra, her stomach exposed, flabs of skin shining in the sun like undercooked chicken. After Rich took the photo, Yula bought him a bag of candy corn, and the candy-corn man said to her, Your man's lucky to have a fine lady like you, with enough meat on her bones to keep him warm through the winter!

The motel, from the outside, resembles a barracks of sorts. It's the kind of place Yula imagines would house men with big, rough hands and scars on their faces; scars that—were you to ask them—the men would say they had had for so long, their origins had been forgotten. The men would wear tight, stiff denim and their vests would be lined with sheepskin, matted and yellowed from decades in the desert. The men came here to work the land; the nature of their job somewhat unclear, although it was known to involve pickaxes and camaraderie and sweating, and required minds that would not break under the bitter desert sun. Yula imagines these men emerging from the eight doors of the motel in the virgin hours of morning— two from each room—the moon still protruding from the sky like a dime from a vending machine. The doors, like the rest of the motel, are a cold white; a desert rose painted on each by hand. The men would step from these doors in near-unison and close them with care, not making a sound. Yula pictures their hands on the worn metal doorknobs—broad, callused palms and thick fingers, hair on their knuckles—turning in unison. Before they climbed up into their dented Ford trucks, the men would wipe their hands on the seats of their jeans and kick their boots against the tires. Then, two to a cab, they would drive off into the black desert.

Outside the motel, before daybreak, there are no men in thick denim. In the parking lot sit several trucks, a minivan, and a hatchback with a duct-taped window. Plastered on the gas station across the street are advertisements for Doritos and Lotto tickets and microwaveable chicken wings. At Yula's feet lie cigarette butts and a rat's-nest of blond hair and a flyer for Pig N' Pancake. Powerlines stretch overhead, black cables stark against a landscape of dust. On the outskirts of town stands a factory or mill of some sort, surrounded by a chain-link fence, its rusted white cylinders like hideous, bulging maggots. This desert is not the desert of Yula's imagination. She sees no cacti blooming pink and yellow, no sand, and the land does not feel alive—in fact it feels dry and dead. It's quiet out here, but not the quiet she imagined; a truck idles down the street and a porch door slams shut, an old Volvo drives by with the windows down and the news channel playing.

With her sketchbook and pencil case, Yula walks out along the still-dark road. She passes a woman who smokes on her porch, body draped in a beige men's button-down. The woman gestures at Yula with her head, a sort of reverse nod, the kind of motion the old timers back home make at Rich when they go into town. Yula smiles at the porch woman and the woman does not smile back. The windows of the trailers along the road are mostly dark, though she passes a few lit with blue light that illuminates the bags under the eyes of their inhabitants, glazed expressions fixed on Jeopardy or infomercials. She walks until the buildings end, and the highway goes on through more dirt and small, spiky bushes and cacti. Among these plants and dirt are candy-bar rappers and Slushie cups and receipts and more cigarette butts. The dirt beneath her feet is not golden or red and does not crunch satisfyingly when she walks. Instead it is brown, but in a colourless, washed-out sort of way, and grinds under her knock-off Keds like walking on coarse salt.

The sun rises and Yula walks. The buildings drop behind her until she sees nothing but the long, flat road and the mountains in the distance. Already it is hot. Wary of scorpions and tarantulas and rattlesnakes, she keeps to the highway. Eventually she stops and sits on the tarmac. She looks at the dirt that stretches out in every direction; the mountains still so far in the distance, hazy and two-dimensional and the same washed-out colour as the ground. She closes her eyes and listens and hears only silence. She opens her eyes and lets them travel along the horizon; lets them rest on its edges until they begin to prickle and she has to blink. But the earth does not feel alive. Maybe, she decides, the way this landscape speaks is not audible.

But what is there to draw out here? Yula rests her sketchbook on her bent legs— already her body feels sore from the pavement—and contemplates the blank page. She is a landscape artist, a still-life artist, a figure drawer. A versatile artist. But she is not someone who draws from memory, nor from imagination. She begins to sketch the landscape but its lines are flat and unvaried—the gradual arc of the mountains, an empty sky, scrags of desert flora. This landscape doesn't begin or end anywhere; it possesses neither parameters nor depth. All it is is dust. By the time she finishes her first landscape, the sun has become so hot that Yula has to squint to dull the glare of the white page. She begins a second drawing—this one of her sneakers on the road—but sweat drips into her eyes and onto her paper. Her damp fingers slide on her pencil and the lines come out all crooked. Her bones feel like they will crumble and adhere to the pavement, and so she hauls herself up from the highway and, eyes pressed to little slits, sleeves pushed up to the elbows and her turtleneck damp and sticking between her breasts and under her armpits, she trudges her sloppy, sagging body back to Angel City.

Later that afternoon, Doreen at the front desk tells Yula there must be a mistake—meals are not included in the residency. Wince Carver has yet to materialize and, never having been given a phone number to reach him, Yula has no way to contact him. She walks to the corner store and buys bologna and hotdog buns and mayonnaise and eats her dinner in the shade of a small bronze cow. The cow wears a medal around its neck that says "Wanda-Mae" and "Champion Sow". Yula washes her dinner down with warm Pepsi and then returns to her motel room and lies on the bed and stares at the ceiling. She considers calling Rich, but doesn't. She pulls the Bible from the bedside table and flips through it. She begins to sketch the small square of parking lot visible through her window, but gives up because there is nothing there to draw, only concrete and cigarette butts. There is no TV in her room. She walks to the closet and opens it and inside are three cigarette butts and two crumpled-up receipts from Lou-Harvey's. Yula hangs her few clothing items. She climbs under the covers of her bed and listens to the fan going, until she falls asleep and dreams that she is a small cow, roaming the desert with a mouthful of pencils.

For the next several days, Yula attempts various methods to awaken her creative spirit. She rises in complete darkness and walks along the highway, this time in the opposite direction, takes with her sunglasses and a bottle of water and a pillow to sit on. She stays out there for hours and fills page after page of her sketchbook with the endless line of the horizon, until a trucker drives by and offers her a ride back to town. She draws various buildings in Angel City, though the town's inhabitants don't take kindly to this, and when she tries to explain that she is an artist, that she is completing a residency here and have they heard of it, they give her suspicious looks and spit in the dirt and wipe their mouths on the backs of their hands. Sometimes they leave her alone and other times they tell her to get lost. She visits the Catholic church, the corner store, Lou-Harvey's diner and the hardware store, which sells guns and duct tape and fireworks and flypapers and pepperoni. She asks people if she can sketch their portraits but they adamantly oppose her advances—with the exception of Father Parker, an obese 40-year-old priest with long black hair, who relents on the condition that she attend mass on Sunday. For two entire days, she starves herself in her hotel room, blinds closed, and does not venture out once, having read somewhere that many artists produce their best work in complete isolation and deprivation. She draws the bed, the table, the framed cowboy above the toilet, her toothbrush, the cigarette butts in the closet, the little bits of her fingernails she chews up and spits into the sink. She sits in the bathtub for three hours and produces nineteen drawings of her feet, but always they come out like the limbs of an ogre, toes thick and stubby, toenails jagged. She runs out of things to sketch in her room and tries to masturbate—hopes maybe this will bring inspiration—but all she can think about is the unending flatness of the desert. After an hour of frustration, she orgasms, then falls asleep on her bed with her fingers in her mouth.

By the eighth day, or maybe it's the ninth, Wince Carver has not shown. Yula thinks about calling Rich, but doesn't want him to know that maybe he was right about the residency. Maybe it is all a big joke, after all. Her sleep-patterns worsen, and she dreams that she wanders the desert for the rest of her life, manically sketching one identical desert plant after the other, until all she can see are zigzags. She begins to sleep during the day and venture out at night, to avoid both the sun and the townspeople. She walks along the highway for hours, sits and draws the shadows. The nights are clear and the moonlight makes the now-familiar landscape tamer, somehow, and more approachable. The ground remains dusty and dry and dead, but there are bats in the air, and sometimes coyotes in the distance.

Rarely do cars pass by at night, but once a motorcycle's headlight appears in the distance, and a man drives up and slows and stops. He wears black leather pants with tassels down the leg, and a leather jacket, and boots with metal plates over the toes. His helmet is bright orange with a white suede strap—the kind of helmet Carla from Ladies Group wears when she rides to her secretary job on her lemon yellow scooter. The man wears cheap sports sunglasses, too small for his head, and he takes these off and his eyes sit tiny and sunken in an otherwise handsome face. His skin looks so smooth that it both unsettles and excites Yula. She feels no fear toward this man, alone with him in the moonlit desert. He looks down at her, where she sits on her motel pillow, legs stretched straight out on the tarmac. She thinks she must look like a child. She feels like a child.

Hey, did you hurt yourself? the man asks, and his voice comes out several tones higher than Yula expects it to.

I'm just drawing, Yula says, though the paper in her hands is blank and she has been staring out at the horizon for an amount of time that feels infinite.

Yeah? he says. What do you call this one? White night in the desert?

Yula closes her sketchbook. The man laughs a kind laugh.

You that artist-lady Doreen keeps telling me about? The one in room six? She says you're wacko, crazy-involved in the "creative process." He does air quotes with his fingers, but does not appear to be mocking her.

Are you Ribs? asks Yula. The man is younger than Doreen by a good ten or fifteen years, his demeanor comforting in a way that she would never associate with the front-desk woman.

Ah, she told you about me, did she? The man grins and his teeth shine small and sharp, like a rat terrier's. She's quite the girl, he says. I know she comes across as a little standoffish, but she's a sweetheart. You know, I should get you to draw a portrait of her for me. I'd pay ya. Doreen's a little shy but I betcha I could convince her.

Yula can't imagine Doreen would consent to such a thing, but she smiles and says yes, of course she could do that. Then adds, I've done lots of commissioned portraits back home.

She trips over this word, "commissioned", but Ribs doesn't seem to notice.

How about tomorrow? Does that sound good? He offers her a ride back to town on his motorcycle, but she tells him she likes the walk—and it's true.

The next morning Yula sleeps until noon, then walks to Lou Harvey's and eats scrambled eggs and hash browns and crushes two cans of PBR for courage and inspiration. She meets Ribs outside the motel at two. He wears his leather motorcycle pants, and a bright green button-down with the sleeves rolled up, and a bolo tie. He carries a black Jansport backpack and a thick, rolled-up sheet of white paper. In the daylight, his face still has the same striking softness to it, and without his helmet Yula sees that he is bald. His scalp glistens in the desert sun like the dome of the observatory back home, and his sunglasses hang from his shirt pocket. Ribs hugs Yula, and her face presses into his chest. He smells like cloves and chapstick.

Doreen is real excited for this, Ribs says. Bits of green peak from the cracks in his teeth. He hands Yula the rolled-up sheet. I brought you this to draw on, he says. It's old wallpaper but it should work, right?

Doreen emerges from the lobby. She wears a purple western shirt, tucked into high-waisted jeans with rhinestones on the pockets. Two tight braids hang down past her shoulders—hair pulled back with such ferocity that it gives her eyebrows a surprised quality.

Hey baby, says Ribs, and puts an arm around her. Doreen looks at Yula with supreme boredom.

Can we walk to your house from here? asks Yula, unsure at whom to direct the question, since it's unclear to her where either Doreen or Ribs resides.

Oh, says Ribs. Our house is kinda in a state of construction right now. I was thinking we could do it in your room.

In your artistic suite. Your studio. That way you can really feel free to let your art flow. He flashes her the same big grin he gave her out on the moonlit highway.

In the motel room, Ribs takes charge of setting the scene for the portrait. Yula feels relief at this, but acts as though she is doing Ribs a big favour by handing over so much artistic responsibility. Ribs moves like an energetic child; pushes furniture to the wall and moves the bed so it sits under the window. He begins to sweat and unbuttons his shirt down to his bellybutton. I'm thinking it'll be a full-body portrait, he says, and Yula gives him a serious nod.

Doreen sits down on the bed and lights a cigarette, smokes and taps the ash onto the bedspread. Yula excuses herself to go the bathroom, and when she reemerges Doreen has taken off her shirt. Underneath, her breasts are bare, and they spill down her front, nipples huge and brown. A wooden rosary hangs in her cleavage and there is a horse's head tattooed on her left breast, its face stretched and misshapen. Yula hides her surprise at Doreen's nudity, and acts as though she is accustomed to drawing half-naked women. Ribs pulls the small table and folding chair into the centre of the room and Yula sits down and unrolls the sheet of wallpaper. It covers the table and hangs over the sides. Doreen looks sullen and emotionless, but she arranges herself on the bed and holds still. She faces Yula straight on, back against the wall and long legs spread wide, feet flat on the floor. On any other woman, this might be a sexual pose, but Doreen looks more like an old rancher or a football coach than a Playboy model. She plants her hands on her thick thighs, elbows bent, and the cigarette hangs from her lips. A bit of ash falls onto her breast and she lets it stay there. She does not remove her glasses and her big eyes look at Yula with indifference.

Yula had thought Ribs would leave the room while she completed the portrait, but instead he stays. At first he paces with excitement, then apologizes and pulls the armchair up next to the table and sits. Yula can feel his hyperactive energy and he bounces his legs up and down; his shirt hangs open and she can't help but glance at his pale chest, his tiny nipples, his torso scrawny and hairless. Terrified that Ribs will realize her incompetency and inexperience, Yula begins to sketch Doreen. She starts with the eyes, but one ends up higher than the other, and the glasses come out wrong. She draws the chin too low and the forehead too wide, the neck much too long. Ribs doesn't seem to care. He watches her draw in fascination, and compliments her work. It takes Yula an hour to draw Doreen's face. Ribs brings her a glass of water. She draws Doreen's arms and waist, too scared to attempt her expansive breasts and tattoo, leaving them to fill in later. She takes a break and Ribs goes out and brings back fried chicken. Doreen doesn't move from the bed but when Ribs brings the chicken he kneels in front of her and she leans forward and kisses him with tongue. Yula knows she uses tongue because she can hear it. After the chicken, Ribs brings Doreen a face cloth from the bathroom and she wipes her mouth and fingers on it, and while she does this Ribs plays with her nipples in a distracted way.

Yula continues to draw and she fills in Doreen's breasts and then spends another hour on the horse tattoo, which comes out bad but not worse than the real thing. Doreen's head sits too low on the page and so Yula shortens the torso, terrified that she will run out of room. She attempts to draw Doreen's thighs, but lacks experience with foreshortening. She erases and re-draws them five times, and still they look like tree trunks, though Ribs doesn't seem concerned, and Doreen sits, disinterested. Ribs smokes a cigarette and sings Cotton-Eye Joe and clicks the heels of his boots together. They take another break and Ribs brings them Hickory Sticks and cold Coronas, and Yula and Ribs sit at the table together while Doreen naps, sitting up on the bed. It gets dark outside and

Ribs leaves again and comes back with a light on a long pole. He stands this next to the bed and points it on Doreen, who wakes up and lights a cigarette. Yula looks at her paper and wonders how she will fit Doreen's knees and calves and feet into the small space that remains at the bottom.

Ribs says, I can't wait to frame this. He says, Yula, this has been great. Doreen and I are so grateful to get to work with an artist like you. What an experience. His grin is perpetual and it's a genuine grin, Yula can tell.

Yula says, Aren't you getting tired Doreen? Do you want to finish tomorrow?

Doreen doesn't answer but Ribs says, Do *you* need to take a break Yula? Why don't you take a break. Doreen and I don't have anywhere to be.

Yula says that okay, she might go stretch her legs for a minute. She puts on her turtleneck and walks down to Lou Harvey's and looks in the windows and watches the regulars eat their steaks. She stretches her stiff neck, and massages her butt. She walks back to the motel and Ribs is in the bathroom washing his hands, Doreen still on the bed where she has been since early afternoon. Ribs comes out of the bathroom with his belt buckle undone and he leaves it undone and he says, Good walk?

Yula sits down at the table but her hand shakes from holding a pencil for so long. Yula, says Ribs, take all the time you need. We're not in a hurry, he says. Why don't you rest a little longer.

Some part of Yula wishes Doreen and Ribs will leave so she can sleep, but another part of her, the bigger part that is bossy and accustomed to winning, reminds her that art is pain; that this residency is the start of her serious career as an artist; that she will never make it big if she can't persevere through a little exhaustion.

Yula, says Ribs, and looks at her with such a sympathetic and pained expression that she would do almost anything not to see him disappointed. Yula, he says. Take a break. It's okay.

Yula puts down her pencil and Ribs says, Why don't you go sit on the bed with Doreen? He smiles at Yula. Doreen is smoking again. Ribs says, Go sit with her on the bed, you deserve a rest. You both do.

Yula stands and moves toward Doreen, simultaneously drawn to and repulsed by the half-nude woman on her bed, the wide eye of the horse on her breast staring at Yula. Doreen neither smiles nor glares at her, as if anything that has or will ever happen in Doreen's life is just part of a routine. She snuffs her cigarette out on the bedframe, pulls her feet up onto the bed—her first change in position since her arrival in the motel room—and holds her knees with her hands, legs still spread wide.

Go on, says Ribs. You can sit in her lap, it's okay.

Yula will later wonder why she felt no emotion, one way or another, at the whole experience. But in the moment, she sees no reason not to sit in Doreen's lap; sees no reason why she, too, should not be unconcerned and unemotional, why she should not both make Ribs happy and give in to her own fatigue, even if it means sitting between the legs of this half-nude woman. And so she scoots her butt up on the bed, between Doreen's large thighs, and Doreen puts her arms around Yula. Doreen is a good five inches taller, and her floppy breasts envelop Yula in a way that, Yula realizes, is not unwelcome. She tries, and fails, to remember the last time someone held her like this. She leans her head back against Doreen's breasts and closes her eyes and they stay this way for a long time. Doreen's breath becomes deep and even and Yula lets her own eyes close, lets herself fall back into a soft slumber. She dreams, for the first time, that she walks in a desert that is fully alive—more alive, even, than in her fantasies. She hears the buzzing of cacti and sees the dirt vibrate; sees the sky and land meet and adhere to one another; sees this all under a sun that, rather than wash out the land to a flat brown, gives her surroundings depth and substance. She dreams that she sits on the side of the road and draws landscape after landscape that flows from her hand.

Later—because what happens seems to happen of its own accord, and no one is invested or bothered, one way or another—Yula takes her shirt off and Doreen touches Yula's breasts and they kiss, just a little, Doreen pushing her tongue into Yula's mouth, expression unchanged. And Yula sucks on Doreen's nipples, although neither of them removes their pants and Ribs doesn't take his off either, though he sits and grins in a way that suggests nothing surprises him and he is as happy here as anywhere else. At one point Ribs pulls an old polaroid camera out of his Jansport and takes two photographs of the women: one of Yula sitting shirtless in Doreen's lap, Doreen looking at the camera and Yula looking out the window; and another of Yula with her head in Doreen's lap, Doreen's breasts hanging over her with one nipple in Yula's mouth, while Doreen smokes a cigarette. Afterward, Yula puts her shirt on and finishes the portrait, and her hand does not shake, and Doreen's legs come out too short and her feet get cut off and the drawing looks nothing like her, but Ribs says, It's a masterpiece. And Ribs gives Yula the polaroid of her in Doreen's lap, plus a hundred-and-seventy-five dollars, and finally Doreen stands and puts her shirt back on. When they leave, Doreen doesn't say goodbye, but Ribs gives Yula a hug. By this time it is early morning and Yula lies in her bed, and her sleep is so deep that she dreams of nothing.

The next day, Yula says hi to Doreen, and Doreen says hi back and doesn't smile, and Yula doesn't ask about Wince Carver. She continues to go out into the desert, mostly at night, and still the land feels dead, though this no longer surprises her. Her drawings come out flat and lifeless, but she no longer anticipates a time when this will change. If to become of-the-desert is not to become one with its washed-out dryness, but rather to realize that there is nothing here, and to accept this without emotion, then maybe this is what Yula becomes, if only for a short month. She doesn't see Ribs again, except once when she spots him and Doreen through the window at Lou Harvey's, eating steak. Doreen doesn't smile but she picks a piece of steak off Ribs' plate with her fork and feeds it to him and he laughs and then they kiss.

Yula goes to Father Parker's sermon and draws the stained-glass windows and the painting of Jesus on the cross. She draws the factory at the edge of town and the broken furniture in the yards and the silhouettes of coyotes in the desert at night. She draws a car that crashes into a telephone pole one morning, and the poutine spilled onto the pavement, upon collision, by the drunk driver. She draws and draws and though her drawings are perhaps still no good, they become a reflex—the most obvious thing to do. And at the end of the month she packs all her clothes and five sketchbooks back in her little suitcase, and hands Doreen her room-key, who doesn't smile but says, Seeya around. And Yula gets in a taxi, and she sits in the back as they drive out of Angel City, and she sleeps the whole way to the airport. She boards a plane just before sunset; a polaroid tucked somewhere at the bottom of her suitcase. And when she lands in Canada, Rich picks her up from the airport, a warm, dead buck in the back of his pickup, its head lolling over the tailgate. She considers telling Rich that she missed him, but instead she stares out the passenger-side window as they drive out of town, and traces the jagged mountains with her finger.

COMMENSALISM

Adam Dickinson

Amber shared a wing. It was in her mouth. She had killed a bird and laid part of it on our steps. Amber was a Saint Bernard crossed with a Ridgeback crossed with a switchblade. Her prey-drive always circled several times before lying down. Mice, moles, rabbits. She rifled through their bodies like evidence, delivering them to us as wilted envelopes through the information services of her soft-faced mouth.

We got her after one of my dad's friends joined the military. She roamed the neighbourhood like a keyboard; dogs wandered as fluently as children through the folksongs of a parenting style in which helicopters had long since left the embassy rooftops. We never tied her up.

Mr. Langston didn't want her on his property. Mr. Langston was a prospector and he wasn't home very often, but when he was, he lived between our houses like a boulder. His huge travelling packs were filled with salted pork, axes, and dynamite. We could see the fuses. He had been dropped into our world by a glacier from another century. Cobalt, uranium, nickel, and gold.

Mr. Langston lived alone. His only companion was a cat whose fur was abandoning its body. It crept about with the nudity of a washed hand. Our young lives, conversely, were crowded with insurgent flags like autumn leaves in a storm drain. We had insatiable appetites for the internal provinces of absorption. Every scrape we acquired was an opportunity to peel another scab, to pull back the blankets and watch the wound bed dream. We crowded into Mr. Langston's loneliness with our freehand markets, peddling improbable stories about caves full of gold leaf guarded by bears with fangs like liberty spikes.

My friend Luke said we should sneak into his house. You could tell when Luke was serious because he'd start licking his lips, and they'd shine back at you when he was talking. Mr. Langston's house was known to us only in the brief moments when we accompanied our parents to drop off food or hold the door as they helped him through the prism of holiday drinks. Sometimes the drinks made him chase us. We were warned to stay off his property. He kicked me once so hard and so surprisingly I nearly bit through my lip. For days I ran my tongue over the contour of the wound rhythmically and obsessively. It took a long time to heal. We stopped cutting across his lawn. Instead, we used the street, with its rooster-tailed stones.

Inside his house was the inside of an idea whose minerals were as obscure to us as the geodes posing vaginally by the woodstove, their crystals glistening inward. Clocks ticked with the wrong times. Windows were shaded with the climatological stratus of cigarette smoke. His house smelled like someone had been bankrolling soil, floating its reclamation mission with unambiguous faith. It was obvious that the man ate nothing but dirt. That's how you looked for metals. You had to eat the dirt to know what was in it.

It didn't take long for us to find the bucket. Some things take longer than others to appear, but we were always on the lookout for outlines, stains, relief, for swellings amidst no obvious injury. Like Amber, who, in broad daylight, once attacked the moving wheels of my dad's truck. An ambush we respected, if only for its resolute commitment to the interiority of a circulatory system similarly beyond our reach.

Under the sink, beside the vinegar and empty wine bottles with corks jammed back into their necks, was a giant plastic bucket. It was enormous, the kind of pail used to haul field-dressed deer parts, or brimmed with salt at the curbside crosswalks in town. It looked like the kind of bucket my mom had me fill with ashes from the furnace to take out to the compost. If there was snow, I usually set the bucket down without emptying it and let it melt its way to the ground.

We thought it was pine pitch, or chicken fat, but it was honey. Deep almost-burnt amber, it consumed every calorie of the stark kitchen light. Prehistoric insects with their arms folded were preserved in its depths; a few cat hairs were spider-legged on top. He kept honey in the subatomic loneliness of his mid-latitude bungalow. We cupped it with our fingers and then our hands. Our faces glistened. Strands of it returned to earth on trajectories mathematically determined by our rolled-back eyes. We crammed it into our mouths with slurred speech, this strange moonlight reflected from the planetary face of a defenceless animal on its back barely breathing as we ate its entrails. The plasma glistened on our lips.

In retrospect, how could he not return to find us there? We were populists imposing our assembled convictions on the conspicuous eccentric. We were vigilantes storming the castle in the name of nothing but burlesque. Such indiscretions inevitably receive the face of their target the way the crowd moves through streets only to become the streets themselves, scraping glass loose from storefronts, awakened. When we heard him at the door and finally saw him, we tried to make it out the back, but our legs barely moved. He stood there with his arms apart. His mouth was open, but he didn't say anything. He smelled like dirt to us, like an overturned rock revealing its clandestine cities of spiders and earthworms, collaborating all this time on an elaborate resistance to the world as we knew it.

We drained from his house like syrup and collapsed on the safe side of the property line. My mother shrieked as she came outside. She had her arms bent at the elbows and her fingers spread like she did when she was handling meat. "Oh, my god," she said. "You'd better go home."

Not long after we were made to apologize, I saw Mr. Langston in his yard chopping wood. Each piece stood before him in the form of a confession. They all ended the same way. He paused for a moment to look over at me when something caught his attention. Amber was in the bushes at the back of his property, her body hovering, snapping branches as she twisted. Before I could call her, she emerged. Mr. Langston stared at her. I waited for him to lift his axe, but he stood there like a piece of his own wood. She bounded toward me with something in her mouth. She dropped the limp cat at my feet. Its hairlessness was shocking. Here was a body whose skin was hunting down and killing its own coat, follicle by follicle. It made me shiver not to think of it.

Note on the Text

Before I wrote this story, I had my blood and urine tested for chemicals, and my shit and skin tested for microbes. I was trying to think of a way to respond through writing to the strange, necessary, and toxic ways in which the "outside" writes the "inside." I learned I had a family of bacteria on my skin called *Methylophilaceae*. As it happens, these organisms are abundant in the mouths of dogs and are often transferred to people who live with dogs. The term "commensalism" describes a neutral relationship between two organisms that results in no harm being done to either participant, despite the fact that one may benefit from the relationship. The early domestication of dogs would have followed a commensal pathway. Commensal microbes play important roles in the human gut.

LATE AND SOON

Christy Ann Conlin

Edmund jumping off the garage roof . . . do you remember? Soaring to the earth and landing with a smile. We wanted to be him, even just for a moment. Edmund and his friend Ian headed off to the barn, leaving the ladder against the garage wall. We climbed and clung to the edge of the garage roof. We were five years old. Edmund, he was nine. We peered down from the roof over the field across the treetops to Cape Blomidon and the Minas Basin at low tide, blue sky plunging into the red mud. The leaves were falling so quickly then.

We were scared without Edmund. You reached for the ladder and knocked it over. How would we get down? "Wait a minute," you whispered. "No," I said and jumped. I heard my arm break. Do you remember how hard you cried? Your face was purple, the colour you told me your penis turned sometimes. You'd told me in church, how your penis turned purple like the velvet robe the minister wore. I didn't have a penis, you told me. This was the main reason we weren't identical. I was born so quickly and then you took two more hours to come into the world. Dad nicknamed us "Late" and "Soon."

You were screaming as you looked down at me from the garage roof. Edmund heard us all the way from the barn and came back to find me lying there on the grass by the fallen ladder. He carried me home with you weeping at his side. Dad and Edmund took me to the emergency room. Dad recited Wordsworth poems while he drove, to distract me. Remember how much he loved the English Romantics? He would have been a scholar in a different life, Mum always said. As Dad carried me into the hospital, he kept repeating, "A host of golden daffodils beside the lake, beneath the trees, fluttering and dancing in the breeze. Don't cry, little Soon," he said. "You're strong."

Remember when we were fifteen, picking apples after school? Edmund picked us up when we were finished in the orchard. It was already getting dark when we came home that Tuesday and Mum wasn't making supper as she always did at that time of day. She was reading a magazine, having a cup of tea with her apron on. She told us Dad had dressed in his suit and tie for work that morning like he always did and left for the canning plant. But then he'd called in the afternoon. He had checked into the Cornwallis Inn in Kentville because he needed time alone, time to sort things out. He was depressed and needed a break, she told us as she flipped through the magazine without looking up. He wanted us to come down for supper, just us, he didn't need her to come — she could stay home alone, have some time to herself. I think she was relieved. All summer he'd been quiet. She sipped her tea and ate a cookie. It was a Pim's, a biscuit from France with orange jam filling. Mum loved them. Edmund was nineteen. He drove us to the hotel in his red pickup truck. He'd come home from firefighter practice just to take us.

Do you remember the old daphne shrub out by the barn which flowered each spring? Dad moved to the hotel a few weeks after Mum found the Cajun woman from New Orleans sitting beside the blooming daphne. She was feeling her ancestors, she said, the Acadians who had been sent away by the English in the Grand Dérangement, the Expulsion in 1755, and wondering if they ever sat beside these bushes they had planted and wondered if anyone would remember them. Mum invited her up to the house for tea. Between sips, she told us she lived in a house on stilts where moss hung off trees like ghosts.

Normally Mum called the police about trespassers. It was a working farm, she would say, "private property," and people had no business there. Dad had just gotten his job at the plant then, in the office. There were only three cows left in the barn.

Before we went up to our father's hotel room, you wanted to look around the dusty hotel lobby at the old landscape paintings and the portraits of King George and Queen Mary with ornate gilded frames. Edmund said we should go up right away. He said we should be a few minutes early. What does it matter if we're a little bit late? you said. There's never a moment to lose, replied Edmund. You shrugged. And we waited for you.

Do you remember how Cedar went on about "the universe" back when you first brought her home to meet us? She was wearing the emerald-and-diamond engagement ring you had given her, and it sparkled when she moved her hand. The universe was sending her a message: it was telling her she could fly. This was a land of resignation, she said. In Vancouver anything could happen. Here we were all so burdened. I was living at home, working in the bookstore and teaching part-time. Mum and me in the back seat giggling when you were showing Cedar around the Annapolis Valley. Cedar asking if the cows were organic. Mum told her about the accident on the garage roof, and Cedar said this could be our origin myth, that moment when I jumped and you hesitated.

She and I took a drive one afternoon before supper. Her hair was dyed the shocking pink of summer cosmos. We drove up the North Mountain to the LookOff on the Brow of Mountain Road. Cedar stood with her eyes closed at the edge of the Mountain and chanted as she held out her arms ready to receive whatever was offered into her heart. She was thanking the universe for abundance and greatness. The sun illuminated her, and it seemed for a moment that diaphanous wings sparkled from her back. She looked over her shoulder and smiled at me. We thought of her as a flower child, Mum's words, but even when I first met Cedar, her understanding of life radiated in a way it never would in us. Cedar always had lightness, even in the darkest moments.

Later we stopped at the fire hall. You didn't want to. Mum said even though Edmund wasn't working there anymore you had to say hello to Ian, Edmund's best friend all through school. Ian was working on the fire trucks. Sunday duty, they call it. He asked how Edmund was. You said you didn't really see Edmund much. You were busy with architecture school — that's why you were in Vancouver, after all. He looked away. You were wearing sunglasses. Ian took Cedar for a ride in the old Model T Ford fire truck, and she waved as she went by. Mum said when you got married Edmund could come home and pick you up from the church in it. You said Cedar wanted a sunrise unity ceremony on a beach on Cortes Island. Ian looked at his boots and tried not to laugh. You looked at the old fire truck when you answered. You hadn't seen him; he lived on the other side of the city.

We took the brass elevator up to Dad's hotel room. I pressed my sweaty hands against the shiny walls. Edmund was usually patient with you but that day he was angry with your cavalier attitude toward time. You told him he was too serious. I tried to escape over a path of shimmering handprints. You said it didn't always pay to be first. The early bird was overrated, you proclaimed. We knocked but there was no answer. The door wasn't locked so we walked right in, Edmund first. He ran over and fell down on his knees. There were four envelopes resting on the bed. Too late, Edmund whispered, too late, his voice dry and cracking, full of ashes.

We were thirteen when Mum made that pumpkin cake at Halloween. Dad was upstairs in their bedroom, lying on the bed in the dark. You were in the house, in the living room reading, when Nate came by to see if I wanted to go for a walk. I finished doing my chores in the barn before I crept down over the ridge to join Nate. There was one cow left. He was the first boy to kiss me, back behind the orchard, down path. Nate loved our little old farm right in the town. He lived in the parsonage by his father's church on the small bluff by the cemetery. It overlooked the Minas Basin to the north and behind it were the Look-Off and Cape Blomidon. It was a school night and the sky was getting darker, a cool wind blowing from the north. There were only a few dry leaves left on the trees, their whispers high in the branches. Nate and I saw Mum illuminated in the window as she threw the cake across the room. The icing was bright orange.

We ran around to the front just as you came out the door and kicked the jack-o'-lantern off the top step. It flew across the lawn in pieces. The candle in the pumpkin set the brown grass on fire. Nate and I yelled for you to put it out. "Let it burn," you screamed as you came running down the steps. Edmund came out the door and pushed you aside. "We have to put it out now or it will be too late to stop it," he yelled at us. I stomped on the fiery carpet of grass in my rubber boots. I smelled burning rubber. Edmund stomping on the flames yelling, "Run to the brook." The brook is tiny now, part of it choked off by the condo development, but it used to surge in the spring when the big rains came. I stood there in the water with my hot rubber boots steaming. Edmund and Nate dancing on the lawn, you still standing on the top step. There was a dash of moon.

Mum didn't come out after you smashed the pumpkin. Supper burned. Edmund helped her clean up, threw out the food. She took us out to a restaurant. Dad just stayed in the bedroom. Nobody but Nate and Edmund talked. Nate's an accountant now. He's also in the volunteer fire department.

I called 911 a s Edmund picked you up off the floor. He was yelling for me to get out of the room. I was sitting on the floor next to the bedside table holding the hotel phone. Edmund kept hollering to get out of the room. You were in his arms. Edmund was in the doorway screaming, "Olive, get out."

"Just a minute," I screamed back. You were throwing up in his arms.

Edmund wanted me out of the room. The 911 operator wanted me to stay on the phone. "Just a minute," I whispered and held the phone out to him. Edmund was wiping the vomit off your face with his sleeve. I dropped the phone and tripped on the gun, which flew across the room as I crawled along the floor. I was drooling on my fingers. The fire trucks arrived at the hotel and Ian came in wearing his firefighter gear. Edmund carried you to the elevator and Ian took you from there. Your arms draped over his shoulders, noises like a sick calf coming from you. I crawled after you while Edmund went back to the room.

It had once been a grand hotel with lavish Victorian gardens. Our parents had their wedding reception in the gardens. Their wedding album was in the attic. The photos were black and white, but the splendour of the flowers was still perfectly captured in the pictures. I remember when the garden was paved over. Edmund, he was long gone, in Vancouver then. You were sailing on Aylesford Lake that summer and I was working in the town tourism office beside the concrete wishing pool directing visitors to historic sites.

We didn't have a church funeral for our father, just a burial ceremony in the little graveyard near Nate's house. The trees were bare and the snow had not yet fallen. The air smelled of pine and rotting leaves. Edmund had decided on the ceremony because our mother was in bed crying for days. You'd wanted Dad cremated, wanted to wait until spring to scatter his ashes. But Edmund overruled you. He said Mum couldn't bear to put it off. You stomped about the house. Shame and humiliation buried your anguish. Your anger was heavy, as though you had rocks in your pockets you couldn't remove. And your rage when you saw the words Edmund insisted be chiselled into the marble tombstone.

Sometimes when I can't stop thinking about what happened, I go back to the old hotel and sit in the lobby. The rooms have now been converted into cheap apartments. The lobby is even more rundown than it was when Dad died in the hotel room upstairs. Part of the lobby has been turned into office and commercial space. There is a liquor store and, across from it, a lawyer's office, a criminal lawyer. It smells of cigarette smoke from the lawyer's clients. It reminds me of you — how harsh you became after Dad died, how you always said it was criminals and poor people who smoked, the dead-end types.

And you moved to Vancouver, just as everybody seemed to do back then. You promised Mum you would get in touch with Edmund. Cedar said you did see him but it was only because you both bumped into Edmund on the Downtown Eastside. Cedar said the two of you had been going to an artist's studio on the Eastside, The Church, it was called. Edmund was on the street, cigarette hanging from his lips. He smelled bad, like a garbage bag in the sun. He tried to sell you pills. "Don't you know who I am?" you yelled. Cedar had never seen Edmund, but she could tell from his eyes it was him — Atlantic blue, she said they were. Like yours. And mine. "Just give me a minute," Edmund said, scratching at his greasy hair. Maybe Edmund was remembering when you would run behind him on the beach, always trying to catch him, and him throwing us in the air and catching us in his arms. Memories flying in his mind, wings beating so quickly they were only a blur, moments lost.

Edmund wanted you to come and meet him in a park but you said you wouldn't go there with a bunch of junkies. Cedar said Edmund wasn't suggesting that. But then Edmund said he would meet you at Kitsilano Beach. Cedar told me you guys were held up in traffic that day. Edmund was already there on the beach when you and Cedar arrived. He sat on a log by the high-water mark, looking out at the tankers. You stood by the kiosk and watched him. Cedar told you to go out to him, but you didn't. "What difference can I make now? This is not my brother," you said to her. Edmund sat for a long while and then stood up, dropping his shoulders, walking away. Maybe he thought you were late, as usual. But then assumed it was his fault, that he must have mixed up the time. He tripped and fell down on the beach. Edmund was crying. Cedar said you still didn't go out to him. Edmund got up and walked away without even brushing the sand off his face.

A month later they called. Edmund had been found in a dumpster. It was his home, the dumpster — that's what they told us, those ladies who worked with people on the street. Cardiac arrest. His heart was weak. It wasn't an overdose. It was common with heroin addicts.

After Cedar picked me up from the Vancouver airport, she took me out for coffee on the beach. I had flown out to be there for you, to fly home with you and Edmund's body. You were making Edmund's funeral arrangements on the phone with Mum so you didn't walk on the beach with Cedar and me. Cedar said she wouldn't be coming out to the funeral. I nodded, looking at the mountains. She stood at the edge of the water and lifted her arms. There was no sun that day, only mist. Cedar sang a song. It was a chant, and the words were *om* and *la la la,* and I watched the mountains vanish into the white. She held my hand as we walked back to the apartment. There was no ring on her finger anymore. Cedar told me that after she saw you ignore Edmund on the beach that day she knew she didn't want to marry you. I told her we were going to sell the family home. My mother didn't want to live there anymore. After the funeral I planned on moving to the city and getting a job. I was going to dye my hair neon blue. I still see Cedar in my mind's eye, standing at the Look-Off, the sun sparkling on the water below as she tosses her head back with such lightness.

You never knew I found the note our father left for Edmund. I didn't tell you. It wasn't like the short apology letters he left for you and me. Mum burned hers in the fireplace. I don't know what he wrote to her. But I found Edmund's, opened but abandoned, in the attic after you both had gone out west. All it said was: *The world is too much with us, late and soon.*

The air was cool and smelled like pine trees and sea salt on the November afternoon we buried our older brother. It was late in the day and a thin band of low red sun cut through the darkening sky. Nate's father officiated at Edmund's graveside liturgy, as he had at Dad's. Nate pulled me aside before his father began addressing the small group assembled. Nate said in a quiet voice how our father had come to sit in the graveyard, in those days before he died. We'd thought Dad was at work in the office at the plant. But he had been laid off and hadn't told us, getting ready for work every day and then driving his car to the graveyard. He parked in the back behind the church where no one could see him. But Nate had watched him from his bedroom window in the parsonage while he got ready for school, our father in his suit and holding his briefcase as he sat by the tombstones on the small bluff, looking out at the dramatic view of the mountain and water. Nate was just a boy. He couldn't have known what our father was thinking on the old marble bench by the wrought-iron gate, looking out at a horizon which for our father held only sunsets.

Our father's grave is in the corner, near the edge of the small bluff. *The world is too much with us* carved so elegantly into the grey marble. I remember staring at his tombstone as we waited for Edmund's funeral ceremony to start. Mum stood beside me with her head down and her gloved hands clasped together like two black doves.

You arrived at the last minute, standing there by the gate when they lowered Edmund into the earth. The leaves were spiralling down, stark oranges, vivid reds and yellows.

You, beside the closed gate and behind the gate, a childhood once alive with possibility, where the future soared like far-off mountains. The shovel hit the dirt. I looked up and it was the same man who had filled in our father's grave but his hair was silver now. I did not know his name. Another man took a shovel and dug into the earth. And then you, you ran forward and cried, "Just a minute, just a minute," as though one more moment could somehow make a difference. But the dirt was already falling in, leaves tumbling down like so many wings dried and turning to dust.

PIG HEAD

Zalika Reid-Benta

On my first visit to Jamaica I saw a pig's severed head. My grandmother's sister Auntie had asked me to grab two bottles of Ting from the icebox and when I walked into the kitchen and pulled up the icebox lid there it was, its blood splattered and frozen thick on the bottles beneath it, its brown tongue lolling out from between its clenched teeth, the tip making a small dip in the ice water.

My cousins were in the next room, so I clamped my palm over my mouth to keep from screaming. They were all my age or younger, and during the five days I'd already been in Hanover they'd all spoken easily about the chickens they strangled for soup and they'd idly thrown stones at alligators for sport, side-eyeing me when I was too afraid to join in. I wanted to avoid a repeat of those looks, so I bit down on my finger to push the scream back down my throat.

Only two days before I'd squealed when Rodney, who was ten like me, had wrung a chicken's neck without warning; the jerk of his hands and the quick snap of the bone had made me fall back against the coops behind me. He turned to me after I'd silenced myself and his mouth and nose were twisted up as if he was deciding whether he was irritated with me or contemptuous or just amused.

"Ah wah?" he asked. "Yuh nuh cook soup in Canada?"

"Sure we do," I said, my voice a mumble. "The chicken is just dead first."

He didn't respond, and he didn't say anything about it in front of our other cousins; but soon after, they all treated me with a newfound delicacy. When the girls played Dandy Shandy with their friends they stopped asking me to be in the middle, and when all of them climbed trees to pluck ripe mangoes they no longer hung, loose-limbed, from the branches and tried to convince me to clamber up and join them. For the first three days of my visit, they'd at least tease me, broad smiles stretching their cheeks, and yell down, "This tree frighten yuh like how duppy frighten yuh?" Then they'd let leaves fall from their hands onto my hair and laugh when I tried to pick them out of my plaits. I'd fuss and grumble, piqued at the taunting but grateful for the inclusion, for being thought tough enough to handle the same mockery they inflicted on each other. But after the chicken, they didn't goad me anymore and they only approached me for games like tag, for games they thought Canadian girls could stomach.

"What's taking you so long?" My mother came up behind me and instead of waiting for me to answer, leaned forward and peered into the icebox, swallowing hard as she did. "Great," she whispered. "Are you going to be traumatized by this?"

I didn't quite know what she meant — but I felt like the right answer was no, so I shook my head. My mother was like my cousins. I hadn't seen her butcher any animals, but back home she stepped on spiders without flinching and she cussed out men who tried to reach for her in the street, and I couldn't bear her scoffing at me for screaming at a pig's head.

"Eloise!" Nana called. My grandmother came into the kitchen from the backyard and stood next to us, her hands on her hips. The deep arch in her back made her breasts and belly protrude, and the way she stood with her legs apart reminded me of a pigeon.

"I hear Auntie call out she want a drink from the fridge. That there is the freezer, yuh nuh want that. Yuh know wah Bredda put in there? Kara canna see that, she nuh raise up for it."

"I closed the lid," said my mother. "Anyway, it was a pig's head. It's not like she saw the pig get slaughtered. She's fine."

"Kara's a soft one. She canna handle these things."

I felt my mother take a deep breath in, and I suddenly became aware of all the exposed knives in the kitchen and wondered if there was any way I could hide them without being noticed. We were only here for ten days and my mother and Nana had already gotten into two fights — one in the airport on the day we landed, the other, two nights after — and Auntie had threatened to set the dogs on them if they didn't calm down.

"Mi thought Canada was supposed fi be a civilized place, how yuh two fight like the dogs them? Cha."

I wondered if all daughters fought with their mothers this way when they grew up, and I started to tear up just thinking about it. Nana looked at me.

"See? She ah cry about the head."

"It's not about the head," said my mother. "She just cries over anything."

"Like I say. She a soft chile."

The pig's head haunted me for the rest of the trip. When we did things the tourists did, like try to climb up the Dunn's River Falls, I'd imagine the head waiting for me at the top of the rocks, the blue-white water pouring out of its snout and ears; and at Auntie's house, I was haunted by its disappearance and legacy. Nana kept me away from the kitchen and either icebox. Her normally pinched-up face was smooth with concern, which irritated me more than it comforted me.

But back home in Toronto, I told everyone about the head. At school during recess, I gathered all of my classmates around in the playground and watched as their pink faces flushed red with vicarious thrill.

"And you killed the pig?" They gasped. "You weren't scared?"

"You weren't grossed out?"

"Nope," I said without hesitation. "It was cool."

"Was there lots of blood?"

"Tons!" I giggled and leaned in so everyone around me could make the circle tighter. "I was the one who stuck it in the throat and the blood just came gushing out."

"Eew!" they sang out, covering their faces, cowering from the image of spurting blood, dark and thick, and a slashed throat. They spread their hands out so they could see me through the spaces between their fingers.

"Did any of the blood get on you?"

"Yeah. That part was pretty bad." The words came naturally, and with every sentence I could see the images of my story unfold before me like they were pieces of a memory I'd forgotten. I told many stories at school. Stories that made me the subject of interest; stories that took on lives of their own and allowed me to build different identities, personalities; stories that brought me audiences.

The only person who wasn't all that excited about the pig's head was Anna Mae, a girl one grade above us who always had her blonde hair twisted into French braids. She'd just moved to the city from a farm in Kapuskasing — somewhere in Northern Ontario — and she'd already told us about the blind or sickly kittens they would drown in the river there. For the first couple of months she was known as the girl who killed cats, and whenever she showed up at a birthday party (the birthday boy or girl having been guilted into inviting her by his or her parents), if there was a cat in the house, all of the kids would take turns holding it tightly to their chests or someone would lock it away in the basement for safety, always keeping an eye on Anna Mae and what she doing, where she was going.

But away from school, in the neighbourhood where we lived, the kids were as skeptical of my story as Anna Mae was unenthused, staring blankly at me as she had. Most of my neighbourhood friends had either just moved here from the Islands or had visited them so often it was like they lived both here and there. And so none of them found anything intriguing about my story — not even the kids who came from the Island cities and not the farms. I wasn't foolish enough to tell them I'd stuck the pig, though — I knew if I pushed it too far, they'd find me out, and their trust would be much harder to win back than that of the white kids at school.

"So what *did* you do, then?"

We were at Jordan's apartment, in her bedroom, sucking on jumbo-sized freezies and deciding which CD to play in the Sony stereo: *Rule 3:36* or *The Marshall Mathers LP*. I was on the bed and lying on my back, my head dangling off the foot of the mattress, almost touching the floor, my eyes on the pink paint-chipped walls and the Destiny's Child and Aaliyah posters.

"I watched," I said.

Rochelle, who was sitting at the study desk in the corner of the room, logged in to a chat room, turned away from the computer, and looked at me. "Did you close your eyes?"

"No. I saw the whole thing."

"And you weren't scared?" said Jordan, inching closer to where I was lying down.

"Nope."

"Yeah, right."

"It's true! And when it was dead, I cut a piece off."

Aishani laughed. "Did not."

"Did too! Norris helped me so I wouldn't mess up."

"You didn't tell us about a cousin named Norris."

"Norris works for Auntie and Brother."

Anita yawned, then put her hands behind her head. "I still don't believe you weren't scared," she said. "You can't even jump from the top of the stairs to the bot- tom like we do."

"Well, I wasn't scared of this."

"I'm gonna ask your mom when she comes," she said.

"Go ahead. She'll tell you I didn't scream."

Anita's mom picked her up before mine did, and I no longer had to fret so much about the possibility of exposure — I knew the other girls were less likely to press it. By the time my own mother came for me their insults didn't have such a mean bite. They didn't feel like they were meant for an outsider; there was a subtle warmth of good nature now, of the kind of inclusion I'd had and lost with my cousins.

My mother passed her tired eyes over me in the passenger's seat. Even at ten my feet didn't touch the ground. "Had a good time at Jordan's?"

"It was fun," I said. "I want to go over more, if that's okay."

"Maybe."

We had to stop for gas before going home; a woodpanelled boat of a machine, my mother's station wagon always seemed in need of gas and plagued us with new worries instead of simply ridding us of our old ones. I remembered her face when she first saw the car, how her nose wrinkled in disgust, but the woman who was selling it knocked the price down to a number my mother couldn't afford to say no to.

She stuck me in the line to pay while she went to the fridges for some milk, promising me a chocolate bar when we reached the cashier. The woman in front of me took her receipt from the cashier and headed out to her pump, and then a man cut in front of me.

"Excuse me," said my mother. She walked from the back of the store to the counter, a slim carton of 2 percent in her hand. "You just cut in front of my daughter."

"Oh," the man said.

"'Oh'?" my mother repeated. "She was next in line. Go to the back."

"Jesus Christ," said the man. He was beefy and mean-looking: buzzed blond hair, a red skull-and-bones T-shirt stretched over his chest. I wanted to tell my mother to leave him alone. "I could've paid for the gas in the amount of time you stood here bitching at me," he said. "What's your fucking problem?"

"That you didn't wait your turn. Get to the back of the goddamn line."

"Mummy —"

I tugged on her jacket but she slapped my hand away and I recoiled from the sting.

The cashier started to raise his hands in a plea for my mother and the man to calm down, and nervousness shivered through the line; the people behind us started to fidget.

"I don't like this," I whispered. "I don't like this, I don't like this …"

The man headed out of the store, pushing open the door so that it thumped against the outer wall. "Always something with you fucking people."

My mother slammed the milk down on the counter and yelled the pump number to the cashier. She turned to me. "Why were you going to tell me to stop?"

"I just didn't want to —"

"What? Want to what, Kara?"

I started to chew on my lower lip and hoped that by some miracle the floor would open up and swallow me whole and cushion me from her voice. "I wanted to forget about it."

"Of course. You want to forget everything! I don't know how you got to be so soft. Everyone will walk all over you if you just 'forget' it. Come on, let's go."

My mother banged out of the store without bothering to get a receipt, and I gave the cashier a small, apologetic smile before following her to the car.

After about a week, my teachers got wind of the pig's head — probably because its severance became bloodier and more gruesome with every telling. My mother's warning about being soft bounced around in my head, and soon I started adding new embellishments to the story.

"Have you ever heard a pig scream?" I'd ask, and after seeing a bunch of brown-haired heads wag from side to side, I'd shudder. "It's really bad. I'm telling you."

Every recess and during stolen moments in class, I'd report a new detail to my adoring audience: how the pig, being so strong and fat, gave us such a hard time when we grabbed it in its pen that Norris had to bash its head in with a hammer before I cut in with the knife; how I wasn't wearing any gloves, so the blood poured warm and thick and sticky onto my hands. And then after school, when I finished my homework and I made my way down to the 7-Eleven with Rochelle and the rest of the girls (and sometimes even the boys from our block), I'd saunter down the sidewalk and sip my Slurpee and say, "Even when they skinned it, I didn't look away. Not once."

Quickly, I became one of the most popular kids in my grade. I was up there with Savannah Evans and Nicholas Lombardi. Savannah was the richest kid in school; Nick, with his long eyelashes and dirty-blond cherub curls, was the cutest; and I was suddenly the craziest. Older sisters brought their younger siblings to me to be frightened and amazed, and in the play- ground boys started inviting me to play Red Ass with them, whipping me with the tennis ball as hard as they whipped each other.

Popularity did not claim me in my neighbourhood like it did at school, but there, nobody felt the need to translate for me anymore, to always bring up the great misfortune of being Canadian-born. I got bored of the live pig, of describing how boldly I'd watched its slaughter, and I moved on to explaining how I'd helped Auntie prepare jerk pork out of the butchered body. After that, whoever I hung out with mentioned fruits like skinup without asking me if I knew what they were, not asking me if I even knew what the Jamaican name for them —

guinep — was, and they yelled "Wah gwa'an?" when they saw me instead of "Oh, hey."

For a week I blustered around school and swaggered down Marlee Avenue and silently waited for the attention I got to transform me into a girl who would actually have the moxie to slaughter a pig. But that courage never burned in my belly; that aggression never revealed itself in a disregard for rules or in a penchant for pranks like it did with my friends. My sense of boldness only lasted for as long as my description of the pig did.

I didn't know that the teachers had found out about my stories until a Monday afternoon when I saw my mother standing in the hallway just before final recess. We all queued up to leave and when Miss Kakos, the student teacher, opened the classroom door to let us out, I saw my mother leaning against the plastered wall, a chewed-tip pencil jutting through her messy ponytail of relaxed hair, her tattered knapsack by her feet.

The sight of her made my fingers quiver. She had no place in my stories; she didn't belong with any of the identities I constructed during the time I spent at school.

Miss Kakos shepherded the kids to the yard, and Ms. Gold put her hand on my back and beckoned for my mother to come inside. I was in a split-grade class so my classroom was one of the largest in the school, divided into sections: Reading Section, Working Section, Science Section, Cleansing Section. I'd heard my mother whisper to her other mother-friends about schools that had walls and ceilings falling apart, about schools that packed children into portables because of lack of space — but my school wasn't like that. Every room was big and colourful and chock full of brand-new equipment the school fundraised for. My classmates were picked up in Range Rovers and BMWs driven by their nannies and occasionally their parents. Sometimes the parents would stop my mother and offer her a job.

"I'm picking up my own child," she'd say before walking away.

I'd be right next to her, tugging on her sleeve. "Why did Katie's mom ask if you needed a job when you have one?"

"Stop talking, Kara," she'd whisper back, her face tight.

Ms. Gold led us to the Corrective Section, which was really just her desk. She sat down behind it and gestured for my mother and me to sit in the two blue stack chairs on the other side.

"I'm just going to get right to the point, Mrs. — I'm sorry, Miss Davis," said Ms. Gold, folding her hands together. "There has been a rumour around the school — started by Kara — that she killed a pig on your vacation to Jamaica. The children have been abuzz with it. It seems to be quite the playground story."

"You called me down here because my daughter told a lie?"

"So the story isn't true?"

"No," said my mother. "But even if it were, a child witnessing or helping out with butchering isn't unusual or uncommon in Jamaica. But no, my daughter didn't participate in either activity."

"Miss Davis, to be frank, whether or not the story is true is irrelevant. It's the nature of the lie that's concerning."

My mother looked at me, but I lowered my head so as to not meet her stare. I went over the story in my mind: the blood, the knife, the hammer, the screams. It no longer came to me in images; now it just seemed like words that didn't belong to me.

"From what Miss Kakos, Mr. Roberts — the gym teacher —and I have gathered, Kara has exhibited pleasure and enthusiasm toward the concept of slaughtering an animal."

"Well, children enthusiastically step on worms, rip the legs off a daddy-long-legs, squish bees. Kids are intrigued by the concept of death."

"I understand that this is a delicate topic, and I am not hurrying to any conclusions. However, perhaps it would be good for Kara to see the school's child psychologist —"

"Let me stop you right there," said my mother, raising her hand. She paused for a beat and then smiled the way I'd see her do sometimes when a cashier or a waiter or our landlord got on her nerves.

"Ms. Gold, did you also know that I'm quite familiar with educational protocol?" she said. "And I believe that for a situation like this, the protocol is that before prescribing the school's psychologist, the teacher must give the parent the option to take their child to a family doctor who would then offer their own referral."

Ms. Gold pressed her lips together, a flush of red colouring her neck. When my mother finished speaking, she cleared her throat. "I ultimately don't believe that the situation is all that serious," she said. "I just thought you should know."

"Thank you for your concern, and rest assured it will be dealt with. If you don't mind," said my mother, standing up. I got up with her. "I would like to take Kara home now."

In the car, my mother turned to me, her finger pointed in my face. "Do you realize what you've done?"

"Mom —"

"I'm speaking." She snapped her fingers loudly, and I flinched. "These people already look at me like I'm trash, Kara."

I opened my mouth to speak even though I had no idea what to say to her, but she just shook her head and turned away from me, resting back against her seat. "I do not need you making things worse by lying. Why would you even say that you killed a pig?"

I stayed silent, hunched in my seat; my eyes wandered as if scouting out an exit strategy, though I knew I could never just open the door and walk away from her.

My mother banged her palm against the steering wheel. "I asked you a question."

"I don't know why I did it," I said. "I'm sorry."

"You're a little liar. If you were sorry you'd just stop making up stories," she said. "I don't know what I did to make you this way. Did you tell anyone from the neighbourhood?"

I squeezed my index and middle fingers with my left hand. "Just that I saw it. But nobody cares there, and you said that in Jamaica —"

"That isn't the point," she said. "I'm dropping you off at Nana's. She's off work today. I need to go back to the library, and I just can't deal with you right now."

"We only live one street over from her. If anything happens I can call her and she can come over. Please don't make me go over there."

"You not wanting to go to Nana's just makes me want to leave you there even more. Put on your seat belt."

Before my mother dropped me off at Nana's front door, she instructed me to tell my grandmother what I'd said about the pig's head.

"And I'll know if you don't," she said.

Telling Nana what I'd told my friends and the kids at school was easy: it was what came after that made me run into the guestroom and collapse on the bed, my face buried in one of the floral pillows that had been placed perfectly against the headboard. The door was closed, but I could hear my grandmother calling all the right people in the neighbourhood to tell them about what I'd done.

"She a bright-eye likkle pickney," she said to Rochelle's great-aunt. "I tell her say, 'Yuh make yuh sail too big fi yuh boat, yuh sail will capsize yuh!' She always make up story them, from when she was small! No way her mother let her slice up a pig, my daughter nuh crazy!"

Of course my friends' mothers told them all about it, and of course none of them was surprised. And when I ran into the group on my way to the 7-Eleven, they acted as much.

"Hey, Kara," said Jordan, sucking on a rocket popsicle.

"We were gonna see if we could get into the school and run up to the roof," said Rochelle. "Wanna come?"

"I'm okay. Thanks."

"I told you she'd say no, Chelle," said Anita, smirking as she walked past me, knocking her shoulder into mine. "She's too scared."

After my mother's visit I'd been afraid Ms. Gold would tell the class I'd been lying, but two days later I was still being asked about Hanover. I ended up repeating details rather than adding new ones; forgetting to lean in close at certain points and yell at others; not bothering to whisper to inspire shivers or to widen my eyes to elicit gasps. At recess, I leaned against the trunk of the giant willow tree that sprouted from a patch of dirt dug into the pavement, watching some boys play Cops and Robbers while a group of girls played Mail Man, Mail Man, their legs stretched painfully wide in near-splits. After a few minutes, I saw Anna Mae walking up to me, her French braids tied together with a lavender ribbon that criss-crossed in and out. She leaned next to me.

"I never see you alone," she said.

Her voice was softer than I'd expected. Too soft for a kitten-killer.

"Just feel like sitting out."

"You're standing."

"Yeah," I said. "Yeah," she said.

We stood together for a while in a silence that I found unusual but not uncomfortable. It even felt peaceful. It was a silence that gave me the opportunity to settle into myself, to hear myself breathe and think.

I looked at Anna Mae in her purple corduroy overalls and noticed for the first time that her skin was a sort of greyish-cream and that her eyes were green. She pushed her hands deep into her pockets and slowly raised her head so that the back of it rested against the trunk and some of the bark chipped off into her hair. I felt no desire to think of a crazy anecdote for her to listen to, no need to twist myself into a new identity. I just felt like talking to her.

"It must've sucked watching kittens die."

"I was six the first time. I threw up," she said.

I stood there and imagined what it would be like to watch a kitten, barely bigger than a grown-up's hand, get dunked and held under water.

"I didn't do it, you know," I said. "Kill a pig? Made it all up."

She smiled. "That's okay."

"Yeah?"

"Yeah."

The bell rang, and I could hear the collective groan of kids mid-game — they'd have to wait till lunchtime to pick up where they'd left off, and there'd no doubt be shouts for do-overs and clean slates. Anna Mae and I walked quietly together to the nearest school doors, side-stepping a tennis ball rolling its way down to the fences, completely abandoned by the boys who'd been playing Red Ass ten minutes earlier.

THE ASSOCIATION

Elise Levine

Where are you? Martin's mother says when he calls. She sounds groggy, not her usual self.

Martin is in Virginia Beach with his dad. Or not quite with his dad, who is here to check out—Martin's dad's words—a certain bass player at one of the bars near the boardwalk, while Martin keeps his own counsel in the motel room. *His own counsel* is a new phrase of Martin's, gleaned from one of his TV shows. Martin is eleven. His dad is in a band. After a thirteen-hour drive, he and his dad arrived straight from Chicago around dinner time and now it is well past. Martin is supposed to be in Rehoboth with his dad. His dad is supposed to take him for crab cakes and fries and hot pie with caramel sauce. He is supposed to buy Martin a boogie board, though it's June and the water will be cold. In the morning his dad is supposed to take him the short drive from Rehoboth to Gran's in Perth Amboy.

In the weeks before his dad picked him up at five a.m. this morning, Martin and his mother agreed he would only call in case of emergency. He peers at the low-stuccoed ceiling of the motel room and swipes the sweaty hair from his eyes. He crinkles the plastic bag lying next to him on the mattress cover. The labouring air conditioner barely flutters the closed curtain. The window looks out, Martin knows, onto the parking lot. The motel is near the highway and not within walking distance of the beach. None of this, Martin knows, is an emergency.

Put your father on, Martin's mother says when he doesn't respond. She sounds more alert now.

Martin pops a hard candy in his mouth. Sour cherry. He clicks his teeth against it. Next he will try the banana taffy his dad bought at the last service plaza at which they stopped.

Where is your father? Martin's mother says. Martin?

I have to go the bathroom, he tells her.

Don't hang up, she says, enunciating with the cool precision she might use with one of her patients. Put your phone down on the desk, she says. I'll be waiting for you.

There's no desk, Martin says.

All right, she says evenly. On the nightstand. Is there a nightstand?

Martin, she says in her clear, unflappable voice when he returns and picks up again.

Yo, he grunts.

I'm here, she says after a few seconds.

Here, he thinks, and pictures the old apartment before remembering they've moved. He brings the taffy close to his phone, scrunching it between his ear and shoulder, and unwraps the candy so she can hear him do it. He chews loudly.

Why don't you describe the room for me, Martin? she says cheerily.

Not much to describe, he thinks. But he will leave it to her to decide what is important and what is not. There's two beds, he mumbles.

Good, she says. Thank you. Any sounds?

Martin pulls his ear away from the phone. The mini fridge buzzes. A few sad clanks for attention from the AC unit. Surf, he tells his mother, struggling to get his tongue around the sugary plug in his mouth. Big-ass waves, he lies.

Martin, his mother says, then coughs to cover her stern-
ness at his language. See? she says, in reset mode. Pretty neat,
huh? Tell me, what colour are the walls?

He has no idea—the walls are walls. He wrinkles his nose
and swallows. The room smells bad, flobby, a made-up word
he'll tell her if she asks. He fixes on an unevenly painted square
above the TV, which is not working. There are uneven squares
everywhere, he realizes, spying another above the closet, others in spots near the ceiling. Drab, he thinks, the walls are drab,
though he knows that is not a colour.

He considers that yellow might please her. He recalls the
Post-its tabbed on the door frames and banisters of the new
townhouse he and his mother relocated to on the South Side
this past winter, the neighbourhood occasioning sneers from
his aunt and uncle—his mother's older sister and younger
brother, North Siders. His mother's flags bear hand-written
instructions—NO NOT HERE! and FIX THIS CROOKED!—
for the workmen who still arrive every week to finish what
the builder should have completed before Martin and his
mother took possession, as his mother refers to it. Martin
thinks the townhouse will never be fixed. He mostly ignores
his mother's written directives, which are not addressed to
him and which, in his view, serve as poor replacements for the
framed prints and family photographs that once hung in the
sprawling, floor-crooked Rogers Park one-bedroom he and
his mother shared with Martin's dad—mementos now stored
in the townhouse garage. As such, Martin thinks—liking the
sound of the phrase, sometimes used by an evil lawyer type on
Martin's favourite rerun series—as such the notes are also like
the mutterings of the adult world, like the continuing arguments between his divorced parents that do not concern Martin. Over his head, out of sight. Nothing he can or needs to
do about them. His mother will deal. As such, the notes make
him feel safe.

Martin?

He picks a jawbreaker from the bag and contemplates it. Yellow, he tells her.

She gasps happily. Yellow, she says. That's exactly what I was thinking.

He wakes cold out of the covers. There is a kerfuffle—his mother's word, he realizes despite his haziness—outside the motel-room door. He hears a woman's voice. A man's. Martin's dad, Martin realizes after a moment. The woman squeaks a few words Martin can't make out. Bullshit, his dad says, laughing. Martin drags his heavy legs under the covers and snuggles down. Bullshit. As such, the rest is blank.

Martin is the boy who eats all the candy and he knows it. He is a Lab Rat. This means he is smart, very. He can do what he wants, to a degree. On this July evening three weeks after the botched beach trip with his dad, Martin grabs a fistful of Gummi bears from the fancy bowl on the granite counter in the neighbouring unit, everyone cooing at the kitchen upgrades although they're here to attend a townhouse association meeting. Martin's bravado—another newly acquired word—causes the rest of the neighbours to glance meaningfully at each other and shake their heads. Martin's mother gives him The Look, reserved for moments like these when they are around other people, and which he disregards.

Moments later he hulks on the end seat of the white sectional in front of the French doors leading to the Juliet balcony—terms bandied by the milling adults—and ignores the bullshit. For example, the bullshit that is his mother's hopes that the neighbours whose unit this is will take a shine to Martin. They are a childless couple who both wear chunky sandals and stiff cargo shorts and pink short-sleeved shirts and hold doctorates in neurobiology. Jewish too—like Martin's mother's side, she has lately become fond of pointing out. She smiles like she has a secret each time the couple acknowledge Martin's existence, like right now, the man stumping toward Martin offering a glass of bullshit tap water and a napkin to wipe his sticky mouth, pointing to it with the napkin and making a wiping motion. As if Martin doesn't know his mouth is sticky.

Martin stares straight through the neighbour. The man looks confused. Frowning, he places the tumbler on the coffee table, on top of the napkin on top of a coaster, and retreats to a seat in a folding chair by the glass doors.

Martin knows a lot. Like all the solutions to the big-snore math problems at the Lab School—the school the reason why he and his mother live here, so she won't have to keep driving him every morning from the North Side where they used to live and she still works, and reverse drive in the late afternoon. Martin also tears through the outcomes to the biology and chemistry experiments, way faster than most of the kids whose parents are faculty at the university to which the Lab School is attached. Parents who, according to Martin's mother—who is not faculty at the university—receive a hefty discount on their children's education, unlike his mother. Parents who might win Nobels one day, according to their kids. According to Martin's mother too, who plumps with pride when Martin returns home from after-school science enrichment and tells her the scuttlebutt, as she calls the kids' brags. Just home from work, she adjusts the collar on her blouse and straightens from her usual exhausted hunch on the display-model couch she boasts she smartly bought for a song—a real couch, not like the futon-frame job they had in the apartment in which Martin had until now grown up. She tilts her chin and smiles her knowing smile and draws back her shoulders, displaying the remnants of the powerful upper torso of a former college two-hundred-yard freestyler champ.

Swimming was how she met Martin's dad. Martin knows the story, which his mother was once fond of relating. She'd finished her laps in the pool at Columbia U and, upon levering out of the water, a tall young man strutting the deck caught her eye. Failing to catch his, she re-entered the water and lapped him several times, hoping and failing again to impress as he crookedly backstroked and unashamedly treaded water. This went on for months, the same time once a week, but never on the same day of the six she trained. In exasperation one afternoon she full-on went for it—maneuvered herself from her fast lane into his slow, passed and then waited for him at the deep-end turn, jammed her leg into his creaky pivot and met his glare with a compliment on his stroke. They married a year later. Another year and they had Martin.

Martin knows the rest of the story too, what his mother does not relate. His parents divorced after ten years, and here Martin is now, with his mother in the neighbour's townhouse. Bullshit-bored.

More people assemble in the living room and Martin ignores them too. He concentrates on his modest earache, a recurrence of his childhood infections. He wonders if he can claim the clicking pressure in his head as a reason for returning to his and his mother's own unit. But she takes a seat in the large easy chair opposite him, her soft stomach mounding on her lap, her chin up. She's wearing her superior smile.

Martin nudges a dish of cashews on the coffee table toward himself while his mother clears her throat and leans forward. Her wire-rimmed glasses are smudged. Visible below her baggy white shorts, her legs crack with purple veins. Her frazzled, grey-streaked mane frays around the shoulders of her oversized T-shirt. She clears her throat again and everyone continues to ignore her.

I believe we have a problem on our hands, she says into the swirling chat. The problem is the easement. We're leaving ourselves wide open.

Martin scores a haul of nuts and sits back. Might as well, he thinks.

The easement? the woman neurobiologist says sharply, interrupting the various conversations, and her husband snorts into his hand, then gazes at his woolly toes.

Martin's mother squints craftily. I propose, she says, that each unit chip in, so we can hire one smart cookie of a lawyer. And see about jointly buying out the easement rights.

A few outright chortles from those assembled. Martin grinds a paste between his molars. Since his parents' separation, his mother has become an expert in lawyers. She frequently speaks of suing people—for example, the townhouse builder—and obtaining multiple legal opinions on subjects ranging from her contract at work, which leaves her underpaid and unhappy, to her living will, which she wants to redo for the third time since she and Martin's father split. Martin thinks if his mother could sue his father over Martin's latest earache she would, if only she could prove the infection was caused by his father's negligence. Had he or had he not insisted on making Martin shower immediately following his sole and unwilling dunk in the ocean? He had not. But Martin has decided on a personal policy of shrugging away any of his mother's lines of questioning concerning his dad. Things seem simpler that way.

Please, another neighbour groans. A lawyer?

I know one or two, Martin's mother says, face lit. But we should interview five or six, and make each sign a confidentiality agreement. You never know.

The neighbours seem to avoid each other's eyes, unsure of where to direct their attention. Helpfully, Martin lets his lower jaw drop open and his coated tongue protrude. He ignores the startled expressions.

His mother is looking at him but not with The Look. This is one he's never before seen. He ignores it too.

Hours after the townhouse meeting, by the gleam of his computer screen, Martin dislodges cracker crumbs from his keyboard. He tugs at the scratchy bandages his mother has wrapped over his ears and wriggles his pointer finger beneath them to poke the wadded cotton balls. He runs another algorithm then closes some of his programs for the night and turns off his screen. He stands and for a disorienting second the still-unfamiliar carpeting swells and falls. Dizzy, he considers calling for his mother, until his eyesight adjusts and he makes out the reassuring hallway light at the bottom of his bedroom door. His mother's clear voice suddenly carries from her bedroom. To whom am I speaking? On her phone again. The floor settles beneath Martin's feet and he mounts his bed, still a novelty to him. In the apartment he'd slept stretched and dreamless on a mattress on the floor of his room while his parents crashed together on the futon sofa in the living room—life when Martin's dad was still around, in those years when Martin's mother was finishing med school and then hardly sleeping at all through her internships.

Like the parents of his classmates, Martin's mother does important work too. At the VA on the North Side she is a psychiatrist who medicates criminals, as she refers to her patients. She mostly knows them by their social security numbers, not their names. Some of these people, she confides to Martin, are more criminal than others. Some of her work is Top Secret, for the government, and some of her work means the late-night phone conversations. Does Martin understand? she sometimes asks. What Martin understands—aside from Homeland Security maybe and maybe global peace—but neglects to let on is that she will never win a Nobel, like some of his classmates' parents, as the award would require everyone to know what his mother does. As such, Martin can't brag about her Top Secretness. He can only keep it secret too, storing it in his chest where he thinks of it swelling his soft stomach and floating his man-boy tits, inner keeps where he hides other secrets too, other tales he refuses to tattle, no matter the temptation. Like the one about the boogie board his dad promised and then neglected to buy Martin to make up for his missed dinner a few weeks back. Or the mere single day at Gran's—because his dad just had to book, as he called it—instead of the three Martin was supposed to have. And she was upset and had words—Gran's word—with her son—Martin's dad—and as such forgot to make the Oreo cheesecake Martin likes so much. And the trip back to Chicago taking three long days, Martin's dad stopping at crappy towns to hear bands and leaving Martin alone in the dinky motel rooms. At least he'd finally kept himself from calling his mother, watching, instead, a lot of bullshit TV.

His dad. What a fuck. For fuck's sake.

Martin arches his eyebrows and makes a mock O with his lips. He clamps his hand over them. Language, he thinks in the voice of his mother.

Martin is also not supposed to yank off the bandage itching his right ear. He wads the material under his pillow anyway and by the dim light inspects the outlines of posters on his walls. Electro, Gakutensoku—the pictures of vintage robots are among the only decorations from the old apartment his mother has allowed in the new place. Their outdated programming and vaguely human likenesses fascinate Martin. They're the past imagining the future. The future's past.

Sometimes Martin's mother tells him he's not doing his best to cope with their current situation—their referring to Martin and his mother and not his father anymore. His father, Martin understands, is now fully in the past, the future's past. But his dad is a far less good deal than the robots.

Martin's ears hiss and sputter. The sounds remind him of the surf on the late afternoon his dad finally shook off his hangover and shuttled Martin to the beach. While Martin's dad strolled the boardwalk, Martin kicked at sand flies for twenty-six minutes, according to his phone, before his dad showed up coffee in hand and ordered Martin—minus the boogie board he'd been holding out for—into the water. For fuck's sake, Martin's dad grouched, a quick dunk won't kill you. Neither will taking two minutes to get out of that big head of yours.

Later, while his dad chatted up some girls not much older than Martin, he shivered on the boardwalk, damp towel around his shoulders like a bedraggled cape, shaggy hair uncombed and filthy, he was sure, with microscopic bacteria. When the girls left, his dad insisted on buying Martin a fortune printed on a small yellow ticket stub from a mechanical fortune teller embarrassingly named Zoltar, a crap automata wearing a turban and silk vest—Martin's school pals Shehan and Jyoti would have flamed it with sarcasm, not to mention the fortune itself. You will love wisely or not at all. Lucky numbers 17, 201, 6. What bullshit, Martin's dad said, laughing.

Martin had refused to even begin rearranging his face into a bullshit cute-kid grin. For fuck's sake, he thought, splashing the words around in his big head while his dad bought him a dripping soft serve and hustled Martin into the car, no shower or change of clothes, or late real breakfast or real lunch. His dad then crawled them through rush-hour Virginia, DC, Maryland, and sped like a fiend through Delaware, cursing the tolls since he had no transponder, and on into New Jersey, stopping three times the whole trip to hit the can—as his dad, somehow looking at once sunburned-pink and puke-pale—referred to it. The can. Martin referred to nothing until two in the morning when Gran tripped down her driveway lit by her buggy landscape lights and nearly crushed him in her arms as if he were still a bullshit kid. For fuck's sake, he told her, and the shocked look on her face struck through his chest the same way it felt the day his mother announced she and Martin's dad were splitting.

But no, Martin will never divulge to his mother the extent of his father's lapses. Aside from complicating Martin's day-to-day with his mom, at some point the deadbeat bullshit might prove useful in ways Martin hasn't yet entertained. As such, he is storing the idiocies like important data, something some superbad AI might one day unleash. As such, Martin believes in keeping a lid on tight, as his mother sometimes complains of him when he refuses to answer the questions she asks. Are you happy? Can you tell me how you're feeling? Describe the room? For fuck's sake.

Martin lifts his big head—the one his dad thinks he should get out of, the one with the lid on tight—and punches his pillow into shape. He will go to MIT when he's older, where he will construct bots who wreak fuckery. He knows from information his mother has scrounged that it's in the bag—the Lab Rats have a high rate of acceptance at MIT, at anywhere they want to go.

Martin locks his hands behind his neck and sighs at the ceiling, with its poster of Michael Phelps before he got busted and entered rehab and staged a comeback. The poster is an oldie but goodie, as Martin's mother says of it, the swimmer's nearly inhuman wingspan spread wide over blue water.

Martin blows a wish-kiss Michael Phelps's superbad-angel way, even though it isn't necessary. As much as he knows anything, Martin knows his future.

Unless the cancer gets him.

Because she is smart too, his mother figured out he harbours the cancer gene. She likes to tell the story of how, when he was a baby, she had him tested not once, not twice, but five times. She was that sure. And sure enough, the last test revealed his pre-diagnosis. This is why she microwaves organic pot stickers for his dinner and serves him organic apple juice. After dinner she microwaves organic popcorn and lets him fill up while he watches his shows about evil turds and smart-girl secret agents perfect as the AI Martin himself might create some day. He bets those bots won't dream at night either.

Sometimes Martin's mother will say, Anything interesting happen last night? She's concerned he never remembers his dreams—never has, as far as he knows.

Two nights, Martin hears his mother say now from her bedroom. As if he can't hear. Ten mil Zyprexa. Restraints.

Martin adjusts his bedcovers. Now his ears squeak and rustle and he feels a phantom motion, the in-and-out tugging of waves—nausea from the antibiotics his mother has him on. He considers phoning her to say, I'm here, even though she is just down the hall. He imagines her questions, so he gives up on the idea of calling. He tries to remember his old room but his mind thickens. He removes the bandage from his other ear and presses the fabric to his nose. The wad smells metallic, comforting. He hears his mother open her bedroom door and the hallway light switches off and then she closes her door again.

His thoughts lift when he thinks of tomorrow. He will run the simultaneous localization and mapping robotic programs he downloaded tonight—SLAM, data in, reaction out. Such programs can create maps using scanning lasers and then, interfacing with a bot, use the maps to navigate in real time with other path-planning and obstacle-avoidance algorithms. It's the stuff of driverless cars, robot vacuum cleaners, maybe excellent biological adventures in the future, like nanobots in the bloodstream. Like the miniaturized submarine and crew from the golden-oldie *Fantastic Voyage* Martin and his mother streamed ages ago one Friday night in the old apartment while they waited for his dad to come home from a show at a bar and he never did. Probably such programs have military applications too. Like bomb defusers and who knows. SLAM, problem solved.

Now Martin imagines his mother in bed, falling asleep with her smudged glasses on. He tucks his head under the covers. Describe the room, he orders himself in a corny robot voice. Martin recalls his posters in immaculate detail. Problem solved, he reports. Then he laughs inside so his mother can't hear the mock-fiendish crescendo that echoes in imagined 3D over stormy seas and interplanetary space travel stations. Like something in a movie he might watch if he could convince his mother to take him to see it. He can almost get a load of the poster for it as he drifts toward sleep.

Shit, he thinks. He shakes himself alert enough to reach into his nightstand desk drawer. He tapes new bandages over his ears so his mother won't be upset when she checks on him in the morning before she leaves for work, when he is still asleep and dreamless as machines.

Martin's ears feel better in the morning but his head hurts. He's hot but the AC is turned low to save money. He tipsies down the stairs to the second floor before the workmen arrive. They never speak to him, barely nod his direction. This suits Martin fine. He drinks a glass of organic chocolate milk standing over the sink. His mother has already left.

Martin has his own work to do. He wobbles past his mother's latest Post-its to the first floor and cracks open the first-floor bathroom door. Dank air drifts out and the two cats leap from the tub to greet him. They are large, beautiful, golden with black spots. Bengals. A birthday present just before summer break from Martin's mother, with the understanding, as she referred to it, that they stay in the bathroom and Martin tend to them. This past winter, right before Martin and his mother moved, he'd seen an article on the breed in a magazine while waiting to see the dentist. The creatures made him think of Cheetah the military bot. Martin campaigned hard and accepted his mother's terms. As such, he now fulfills his part of the bargain every day, nudging the vanity under the sink open and scooping cat food while the animals purr and rub against his bare legs. He refills their water dish and replaces it in the tub. With a plastic shovel he digs through the litter in a plastic box on the floor next to the toilet and bags the waste for the trash. From a hook on the back of the door he takes the toy, a long stick with a feathered mass on one end, and dangles it while the cats jump and pounce.

August arrives. Martin's ear infection clears and his mother drives him each morning to science camp in Evanston where he applies his mad skills. Evenings, he quality times it with his shows and sometimes fails to get out of accompanying his mother to more association meetings. At least the adult talk eddies undemandingly around him while he basks in the potent AC and perfects his scowl between mouthfuls of snack foods. He is here, he understands, to keep his mother company among the hitched. As if he and his mother also form a couple, a childless one like the Jewish neurobiologists, to somewhat balance out the two South Korean pathogen-research couples who each have a daughter much younger than Martin and both of whom are also Lab Rats. There is also a white not-Jewish couple, internists both, with a large doughy baby.

Martin does find himself warming to the idea of the Jewish couple. Oddballs, his mother has recently taken to calling them, to account for their increasing stand-offishness. But of interest to Martin is the large, loud black dog they have recently acquired, an excitable pedigreed beast—a near-child only better, by Martin's count—that the man and woman parade to the nearby park. Martin would love to play fetch with the animal. By his count his own pets don't rate as full playmates or as kids, since by his mother's decree the animals exist only in the first-floor bathroom. But the couple haven't offered and Martin's mother can't get behind the idea, as she puts it. Too unpleasant that a child should need to beg, she says. I'm not begging, Martin keeps insisting to her steely smile. And I'm not a child.

There is another member of the townhouse group, who Martin sometimes forgets about. The man never attends the meetings and has refused to join the association, period, so Martin's mother dislikes him. He's a divorced financial guy, middle-aged like Martin's mother and also white. His young, pretty Japanese ex and their daughter sometimes live with him in his lot-and-a-half western end unit. So he counts as half of a couple with half a kid.

Martin's mother also dislikes the man for the money he has spent hiring an interior designer for his unit. She dislikes him for the expensive—and she means ex-pen-sive—landscaping featuring costly mature trees and heirloom perennials he has put in his yard. The man is likely on the spectrum, Martin's mother declares at the association meetings. You bet he's all about fee simple, Martin's mother likes to say in her precise, clipped voice to the other townhouse owners.

The man's teenage daughter, pretty and older than Martin—Mallory or Ashley or Allie—does not attend the Lab School. Pretty and too dumb, Martin decides, when she and her glossy friends ignore him one sweltering evening as he strolls past her dad's shady trees and shrubs, attracted by the girls' silvery laughter, their smiles flashing like minnows through the twilit-green leaves.

Martin's dad calls one night in the middle of August. They haven't spoken since the beach trip, the longest they've gone without contact. Martin is online and too busy to answer. His dad leaves a message—Hiya kiddo!—sounding drunk and also, for once, like he's trying too hard. Kiddo yourself, you fuck! Martin mouths when he finishes listening. He laughs his villainous laugh. He determines he is too busy to ever return his father's call.

Another night, after organic pot stickers and carrot sticks with honey mustard dip on the TV-dinner tray tables in front of the couch, his mother folds her arms over her chest and asks if Martin would like a dog. Summer shadows wash outside the open French doors. Soon it will be dark and Martin's mother will close the doors and shut the curtains. The room will shrink. Martin, his mother says again, eyes narrowed behind her glasses. I asked you a question.

Martin thinks. Zipping around the park with his own dog barking and nipping at his heels—until the obedience training, which Martin is sure his mom would insist on. Running into the neighbours at the park with their dog and chatting about doggie daycare, which Martin's mother would likely be into big as well. Chatting about prey drive, about the opioid-fueled significance of human-canine eye contact—which Martin has just learned about in school—and the best organic dog treats, as people settle in for the association meetings. Martin thinks hard. He thinks a dog would make he and his mother into even more of a couple.

The thought makes him feel as if his thumbs are enormous and his toes miniscule, his big head too huge for him to heft to the very park where he'd need to walk the dog. To beyond the park and far, far away.

Martin? his mother prompts.

Suck that, he says, staring at his show, though a sidelong glance tells him his mother is smiling now—as if he has cleverly provided the correct answer, the one she has in her endless wisdom known all along.

She gets up and returns with large helpings of Caribbean coconut gelato. He places his bowl on his thighs and his skin shrivels.

Martin, she says, and pops her spoon in her mouth—and spends a long time getting that ice cream down. I'm glad you're happy, Martin, she says when she is done. Her eyes behind her glasses are fog and steel. Her smile says she knows, she knows, has always known.

Knows what? A jagged impatience rips Martin's chest. His hands seem like a monsters' cupping the sides of his bowl. He thinks that tomorrow morning, when he stands next to the height measurement taped beside his bedroom door, he will discover he has cleared five-ten, a spurt of twelve inches, at least. Could be—when she's not hunched over like she's bearing the weight of the world, his mother is tall and broad shouldered and his dad is too. Once upon a time Martin's parents could have passed for twins, Martin is sure, when his mother was more lean from not working so hard and being unable to work out. A time when his mother and dumb father saw eye to eye, sort of, when his mother would shut her books and rub Martin's dad's shoulders, sore from playing a gig half the night long while she studied, and she'd cook him pancakes and feed Martin some too. A time which Martin only dimly remembers.

Martin's mother is now frowning at him.

Martin thinks harder than he ever has as he continues to stare at his mother's soft, shapeless face. If she thinks she knows he is happy, then what has she ever really known?

Martin, she says. Why are you looking at me like that?

Science camp ends. School will start soon and Martin cannot fucking wait, sorry-not-sorry. He runs algorithms, watches his shows, visits his cats. Despite his mother's mushrooming Post-its—NO! INCORRECT! HERE CROOKED FIX!—fewer workmen arrive each day and some days no one shows. Martin evilly considers writing his own notes and sticking them everywhere, a single repeating phrase he imagines used by people working black rotary phones in vintage movies. TO WHOM DO YOU WISH TO SPEAK? It's similar to what his mother says on her phone at night in her bedroom, in secret still keeping the world safe. Or so she claims, it occurs to Martin. TO WHOM AM I SPEAKING? He decides against it. These days his mother is crabby with him for not emptying the dishwasher or picking up his used towels. She makes him microwave his own food. She microwaves her own and takes it upstairs and shuts her door behind her.

School begins at last and Martin feels killer happy. Until one night during the third week of September his mother mutes the TV in the middle of Martin's show. She would like to take him for a ten-day excursion to the Bahamas, over Thanksgiving. He'll need to miss some classes.

Martin's favourite criminal jumps up and down and appears to spout zingers that come-up everyone, and which Martin is now missing. He stares and stares at the screen. What's his pal saying?

Martin, his mother says. I am speaking to you. Please respond.

Searching for correct response. Unable to locate correct response. Okay, Martin says. Ha ha.

It's when I can get time off, Martin, his mother says in that crisp, keeping-it-together voice of hers, the one she used to unleash on the dad-o. And better believe that right now I can get one smart package deal, she continues. Doesn't that sound like a good idea? Like a whole lot of fun? Martin?

Sounds fucking bat-shit, Martin says calmly, gaze still averted.

She presses unmute on the remote and they watch the rest of the show in silence. The show ends and Martin scratches his knee and his mother clicks off the TV and sits tight as Martin's lid, the one he keeps tight on his big fucking head. And then somehow the remote is in his hand, his giant hand. As if it's no longer attached to his still-puny kid's arm, his hand jerks and the remote crashes into his TV tray. Batteries explode out, bouncing and rolling. His glass of lemonade tips over.

Martin's mother flinches, her smile soured. I'm worried about you, Martin, she says quietly.

Martin feels his face flush. He is fucking eleven. What does she want from him? Yeah, he says uncertainly, voice cracking. Well, I'm worried about you.

Her face convulses. Yeah? she says, twisting the word to an ugly sneer. You mean yes? she says. As in, yes you know I'm worried? And why would you worry about me? You think you know a lot, don't you?

The living room seems vast, bottomless. Martin's feet seem

to swim and swell before his eyes. He has the odd, panicked thought he should try to catch them before they get away. Yeah, he says again, louder this time. And you don't? Think you know everything?

She stops speaking to him for a few days and then it is mostly business as usual. How was school? Will that be Wasabi Warrior or Sweet Ginger Soy? She preps his pot stickers and they eat by the TV again. By late October she complains to Martin that the financial dude neighbour has turned the other townhouse owners against her. They barely say hello. They've stopped responding to her calls for association meetings. They excluded her—and Martin too, if he can believe that, imagine doing that to a kid, she says, shaking her head—from their First Festive Fall Potluck. There goes her plan to have everyone chip in and jointly buy the easement rights to the shared guest parking lot at the end of their townhouse row—the lot adjacent Martin's and his mother's eastern end-of-group, and the rights to which are held by the offices for a childhood disability services organization that sit behind the townhouses. Martin's mother has taken to grooming through the lot after she gets home from work and before dinner for stray pieces of trash left, she claims, by the employees, garbage she captures in large freezer bags and labels by date as evidence. In case, she says.

Mid-November she pressures Martin to make his bed in the mornings. One morning, she threatens to withhold his allowance for the rest of the month when he hits his head on his bed frame and swears. Which, he protests, would not have happened had she not forced him to make his stupid—her word—bed. I'm sorry my bed is so stupid, he finishes the argument by yelling lamely, and swats a stray tear from his cheek. A tear for which he swears to loathe her forever and a day.

For Thanksgiving, instead of a Bahamian cruise Martin and his mother join her North Sider sister and brother and their families at the brother's Irving Park house, as they have for the past few years. Martin sits crammed in at a far end of the table from his mother and picks at his turkey. His cousins, seated next to Martin, are too young for anything but terrible fart jokes. His mother, at the opposite end of the table, listens expressionlessly while her brother, who is an architect, ridicules the layout of Martin and his mother's townhouse, criticizes the construction materials and finishings he saw on his only visit, hating to make the trip to the South Side. Martin's aunts and other uncle attend to their innocent, stupid brats and it occurs to Martin that once again he and his mother are a childless couple set apart from the crowd.

When dessert finally comes, Martin devours several slices of the pumpkin and apple pies his mother bought at the organic supermarket. His blood uncle cracks a few unkind jokes in Martin's direction about growing men, at which his mother chins up and stares above her brother's head. She looks like she has smelled a terrible fart, not just heard some bad jokes about them, and is taking the high road, as she often counsels Martin to do.

For the first time, Martin feels badly for her. Despite the grudges he holds over her recent general moodiness toward him, he suddenly longs to throw his arms around her as he used to when he was much smaller, when she was studying through dinner, through weekends, through his dad's frequent absences, and she'd momentarily close her books and laptop and offer her bracing smile.

Martin pushes his empty plate away and knocks back his glass of milk. He calls out the length of the table, past the unkind adults and dopey kids, to his mother. Mom, he says. Mom?

She pushes her own plate away, leaving her pie half-eaten. She coughs loudly and raps the table with her knuckles. The aunts and uncles and cousins go quiet. Martin quickly feels ashamed of having felt badly on her behalf, as if this might weaken her.

Martin? she says. I believe Martin would like to say something.

The aunts and uncles and cousins all turn to look at Martin. He clutches his stomach with both arms and rocks forward. Mom, he groans, facing into the white tablecloth. Mom, I have a stomach ache.

His blood uncle grunts and shakes his fat head. The aunts try to hide their smiles. Martin's cousins gum their pie innocently in his direction, whipped cream streaking their noses.

Martin's mother dabs her mouth with her napkin and drapes it on the table. She regards everyone solemnly, as if making a crucial determination. Then her gaze falls on Martin and she smiles as if she has found the very thing that will set everything straight. Let's get you home, she says, eyebrows arched knowingly as she over-carefully articulates each word.

Martin's mother drives slowly through his uncle's nearly traffic-less neighbourhood. She misses all the lights. It's snowing and Martin has his window buzzed down a few inches. Frigid air and the occasional flake wash in. Eventually, the impressive buildings of Lakeshore Drive swim coolly, serenely into view. Some of the high-rise apartments are lit like aquariums and Martin thinks of the people in those rooms, paddling around in lives they maybe can't leave. Some units are dark as if the people in them have drowned or not yet paddled forth from their mother's insides.

Martin? his mother says after several minutes of cruising among the few vehicles out at this time. I asked you to do something. The window, please. Up.

He ignores her. He can barely remember the old apartment in which he was a baby and then a little kid and then an older one. The chipped-enamel stove, stained bathroom sink, the sound of his dad's razor tapping against the porcelain when he rinsed it of stubble—these memories and more ripple and evaporate. Martin thinks his way toward the townhouse, mapped with his mother's Post-its toward some future perfection only she can see. He can only see parts of his own future, like shooting as tall as his parents. Like leaving the townhouse, the city, off to college.

Then what.

Martin, his mother says. Do as I tell you.

Or what. He slumps further in the passenger seat. The future, he thinks glumly, is as far away as the past.

And then it is not—Martin's mother lifts her hands from the wheel and jerks her head toward him. Listen to me, she snaps, and the car strays into the left lane.

Mom, he cries.

She rights the car and stares straight ahead. What's going on? she asks after a moment, voice again practiced and smooth.

Something thin and sharp rises within him. Buzz it up yourself, he tells her, voice as calm and precise as hers. You have the controls on your side, he tells her.

That's not the point, Martin, she says after another pause. Work with me on this.

Sorry-not-sorry, he says in his new voice. You can do and say whatever you want. Just leave me out of it.

At home Martin continues to feed the cats. He cleans their litter. He plays with them in the first-floor bathroom after school and on weekends. Hello kitties, he says. He tells them his best fart jokes. Each time he leaves, he closes the door carefully so the cats won't escape. Bye for now, kiddos, he says.

ALICE & CHARLES

Camilla Grudova

I liked to go walking at night, and so did Alice. My roommates, Edith and Elizabeth, thought I was a fool, but I always went prepared. I wore an old striped one-piece swimsuit overtop my underthings, a baggy Irish fisherman's jumper, a woollen plaid skirt, and two pairs of thick stockings. The long laces of my bovver boots were tied around my ankles like ballerina ribbons, a green beret hiding my hair. And, of course, I had Alice, whose white body glowed like the body of a cartoon ghost. She was a bull terrier, stocky, with a head worthy of a Roman emperor. At night, there were fewer women and dogs out and about, so Alice was less distracted, but it was [also?] harder to see the dog filth that was everywhere, and when I went back home, I always had to scrape some off the bottom of my boots.

Edith, Elizabeth, and I, along with our dogs, lived in a basement apartment. Inside, it was painted all white with decorative trimmings, though it had terribly low ceilings, as if our apartment were a cake in a box being squashed. The ceiling lights were round and breast-like with copper tips and trimming, as if gigantic naked women lived above us and stuck their large breasts through holes in the floor, laughing at our misfortune for living in a basement. The white radiators gave off a weak heat, and the plaster mouldings were like bits of a starved girl's skeleton. When we first moved in, we discovered an old image of a naked woman taped in one of the closets. She had no dog. It was a very old photo. Boys must have once lived in the same apartment. The thought frightened us, and we cleaned as best we could, using bleach and baking soda. Edi burned the photograph of the naked woman over the stove, the woman lingering like a grey ghost made out of smoke, much larger than when she was flat and contained in a square.

Our apartment was the bottom of a five-storey house, very thin, and made of dark red brick. The top floor had a tower covered in green shingles, it looked like a dragon's neck, and was the bedroom of a girl named Lou-Ann who slept in an armchair because the tower was too small and round to fit a bed. Lou-Ann owned a black poodle named Edgar, who was known for being clever, and together they worked in the back room of a post office, sorting envelopes and sniffing them for wicked things. Lou-Ann told us they once discovered a package full of men's hairs, addressed to a woman, and another time a drawing of a shirtless man on a horse surrounded by hearts. Lou-Ann shared the top floor with four other girls. All the apartments were crammed, with the exception of the third floor, a large three-bedroom where only two girls lived. They owned bulldogs and hardly went outside.

Our basement was a two-bedroom. Elizabeth slept on a fainting chair in the living room. Her job was picking up rubbish off the street, so she couldn't afford to rent a bedroom of her own, but neither could Edi and I afford the apartment without her. I told Edi we should just let Elizabeth have the living room as a bedroom, but Edi said that because the kitchen was so small she needed another room to sit in.

Edi didn't work. I don't think she wanted to. She received money and parcels from her father, who sent them under the name Miss Djuna-Rose. Lou-Ann made Edi nervous. It was a disgusting thing to be in contact with one's father all the time. Edi was the only girl I knew who was. She was afraid Lou-Ann would figure it out.

Like me and Elizabeth, Edi applied for a job by post after leaving school. She received a position as a file clerk. It was a good position, but she was fired after her first day because Benjamin, her dog, made a mess on a bunch of papers and bit another girl's dog.

Benjamin was a Rottweiler, and she had never trained him properly, even though it was the most important thing a girl was supposed to do. He was constantly restless, because Edi rarely went outside.

Edi was a redhead. Her hair was very long and thick and dry, her skin very freckly. The bones of her wrists, ankles, and nose were all prominent and her eyes very narrow. Her eyebrows were very light, almost blonde. She didn't trim them. From certain angles you could see tiny golden hairs down on her eyelids, high on her forehead, and also on her chin and above her thin lips. She didn't have bangs, her forehead stuck out. If she grew old, her forehead would become more and more prominent, I thought.

She kept her orange hair up with an ugly lacquered black-and-gold clip or tied it in a braid using a rubber band, the kind our dogs ate if we left them lying around. After, we'd have to feed them bicarbonate of soda to vomit them up.

Everything she wore was covered in stains because she never used protection when she had her period. Sanitary napkins were expensive: we kept them for going out, so Elizabeth and I stuffed our underwear with toilet paper or old rags from around the apartment. Benjamin often managed to get into the garbage bin and chew them up, leaving flakes of bloodied, slobbery paper and cloth around like the feathers of a butchered chicken.

Edi always came to my door and stared at me as I prepared to go outside. I knew she'd go through my things while I was gone. She borrowed my clothes and returned them dirty, dark brown bloodstains on my grey wool stockings, tea stains on my cardigans.

The air was cold, so the smell of dog filth was not so strong, though I could hear dogs barking everywhere, see them pawing at lit, uncurtained windows, wanting to go outdoors too. Alice pulled me onto a quiet, darker street and went to the bathroom on the wild lawn of a house with no lights before we continued on.

Walking towards us, on the sidewalk, was a clown.

Alice and he were the brightest things on the street. He wore a blue wig, a yellow-and-red suit with large buttons, and exaggerated saddle shoes. Alice stopped and growled, waiting for him to pass.

The clown got down on his knees and held his palms open for her to sniff, which, to my surprise, she did. His hands were shaking. He told me his name was Charles and would I like to come over to his house for a cup of coffee.

I was frightened, but Alice was no longer growling, she even wagged her tail a bit, so I said yes. I had only had coffee once before in my life, in a tearoom with Elizabeth and Edi. We each had a cup and shared a pastry that looked like a small purple hat. Our dogs whined underneath the table and we felt horribly guilty. It was a place where girls went. It served coffee, tea, and desserts.

The pastries looked stale and were all bright, fake colours. The smell of dog was everywhere—we were used to it, but some dogs were worse than others. There were many girls who didn't take care of their dogs and let them go to the bath-room wherever without cleaning it up: their fur was matted, their ears smelt like dirty socks, their nails were unclipped, their beards yellowed, their anuses unwashed. It was unpleas-ant to go somewhere like a dog-friendly tearoom We never went again. I didn't want to be around so many girls with filthy dogs.

Charles the clown was short. His wig and the heels of his clown shoes added some height, but Alice could reach his throat in a moment, if need be.

He took me to a large salmon-coloured brick house with green trim and a bunch of bicycles parked on the lawn. Men often used bicycles or the trams to get around rather than walking because there was less chance of being bitten by a dog. Dogs weren't allowed on trams or trains, and it was impossible to use a bicycle with a dog. This meant men who walked were either seen as suspicious, or as actively seeking a girl. Charles told me he walked home from work because other men made fun of his work clothes on public transport, and the clown wig flew off when he cycled.

When off work, I like to cycle, he said. He pointed to a black bicycle with a light on the front and a basket on the rear, and said that one is mine.

I knew he was telling me this so I wouldn't think him a creep who spent all his time strolling around.

We entered a green-and-yellow tiled foyer filled with men's brogues and cigarette butts. There were three fancy umbrella stands. I didn't understand why men needed walking sticks or umbrellas, since they never walked anywhere. Charles noticed me gawking and said men used them decoratively, but also used them to hit each other on the tram and in pubs. Two of the stands were painted gold, and the third was covered in some sort of oily fur. I heard birds chirping, and also music, a cheery trumpet melody drifting from upstairs. I suppose most men could afford record players and radios, and liked to keep birds as pets because of the nice sounds they made.

The halls of the house smelled like polish and sweat. There were framed photographs on the walls, of men playing lacrosse or rowing in boats. Charles held one of my hands while my other held tightly onto Alice's leash as she sniffed and growled curiously.

We went upstairs and passed through a kitchen, which was abundant with food, and filthy. Wine and beer bottles, open tins of sweet corn and beans, bags of sliced bread, a half-eaten roast chicken, crates of apples, boxes of tea and metal canisters of coffee, a large dish of butter with the cover off, potato peels, a crate full of green cabbages. On top of the refrigerator was a cake with green icing, covered with a fancy looking glass lid.

I didn't mind the mess: I supposed if Edi, Elizabeth, and I had as much food as they did, our kitchen would be messy too.

His bedroom was a sunroom, a covered balcony on the fourth floor, right off the kitchen he shared with several other men. He shut his door and opened one of the windows as the rotten apple-and-meat smell from the kitchen was also in his room.

The top of his windows had stained glass depicting pheasants and herons. The light that filtered through them was brown, green, blue. Masculine colours, I thought. Despite the smell that wafted in from the kitchen, his room was very clean and austere. The furniture was all dark green and metal. There was a wool blanket on the bed and no pillow. A shelf of paperback books with orange and white spines, a brown rug.

He owned a grey electric radiator, a metal fan, and a record player.

"Excuse me one moment," Charles said. He took a canvas knapsack that lay on his bed and left, locking the door behind him, which relieved Alice and me—the house was full of other men, after all. I sat down on the bed. It was as hard as a bench. It was only then I noticed a white plastic cage with a real mouse inside, crawling around amidst old bits of cloth and loo roll. Beside the cage was a package of fancy cream crackers.

The only thing in the room that gave hint of his profession was a black and white postcard on his nightstand, of a French clown, sitting on a half moon.

He returned, a plain, blond man with a crew cut wearing grey trousers and a blue jumper and holding two cups of coffee. He handed me one, saying careful it's hot, and put his down on his nightstand while he unlocked a metal chest and put the knapsack, now much fuller as it contained his clown costume, inside and locked it.

He gave me some cream crackers to have with my coffee, and some to Alice, too. He saw me out after I promised to come by again.

When I got home, Edi was wearing a green cardigan of mine over her nightie and sitting on Elizabeth's fainting couch with Benjamin. The living-room carpet was gone and Edi told me Tobias was really sick again. Elizabeth was washing the carpet in the bathroom. I went to help her, as Edi wouldn't.

Tobias was whining on the bathroom floor, and Elizabeth was hosing down the carpet. It wasn't the first time Tobias had made a mess.

Elizabeth had short black hair, she cut it short so filth from Tobias wouldn't get in it. We were all only nineteen, but she already had some white hairs. We tried pouring tea on her head to dye them, but when she sweated while working, her ears and neck turned reddish brown. Edi muttered to me that it was a waste of tea, and no man would get close enough to Elizabeth to see her white hairs anyway. She always wore jean overalls with a jumper over top, and smelled clean, of yellow soap, despite being in such close proximity to Tobias all the time. Elizabeth did her best with Tobias. She brushed him everyday, keeping the hair in a plastic bag before throwing it out; gave him baths, swabbed his ears, brushed his teeth, and cleaned his privates after he went to the bathroom—she carried a rag and a small glass bottle of water for this. It was like patching up a leaky old boat: he wheezed, vomited, farted, had diarrhoea, got sores on his knees, back, and behind his ears.

The free government dog food didn't sit well with him, and neither did the meat Elizabeth found, or bought when she had the money. He was so cute and goofy as a puppy, she sometimes said sadly.

When I first got Alice, she was so small she resembled a white rat and would sleep underneath my jumper, against my stomach. We were given advice on which type of dog to choose, but many girls ignored it and went for the cutest, fluffiest ones.

I didn't understand why they gave us too many options: if they only provided vicious dog breeds, fewer girls would be hurt or disappear. But the state believed in giving girls the freedom to choose what type of fate they wanted, whether a miniature poodle or a great Dane.

They brought them in boxfuls to schools, a surplus for us to choose from, yelping and pissing, the girls squealing, and some crying, realizing they were afraid of real dogs, even puppies.

Let's just throw the carpet out, I told Elizabeth, I can get another one from work, there are plenty rolled up there.

I worked at a second-hand store. We sold women's clothes, stained teapots, dolls, pots and pans, records, tapes, blankets, porcelain figurines, lamps, and what not. Mostly we sold women's bovver boots, with beige and red laces. Some were almost brand new, some had holes in the bottom and smelt bad.

We had a small selection of other women's shoes, fancy ones that some girls wore around their apartments, which wasn't very wise: if there was a break in, they couldn't run away.

I was always excited when Sophia and Violet merchandise turned up in the shop. Sophia and Violet was a book for girls that had been written when we were little, and was so popular that for a time there was Sophia and Violet everything, from Band aids to toothbrushes. At school, whenever someone won a prize, it was always a Sophia and Violet book or poster or set of stickers. I had a poster of Sophia sitting on a giant toadstool, her beautiful dog Violet below, with a butterfly on her nose. No one knew what breed of dog Violet was, she had white fur, purple eyes, long eyelashes, and a long nose like a borzoi or a collie. I was proud that Alice had a distinguished nose similar to Violet's.

In the shop window was a sign indicating we were dog-friendly, which meant men often didn't shop at our store. My co-worker Louisa said she once had a man come in and try to buy an old frilled dress, but her dog Henry growled so viciously the man left, leaving the dress, and his money, on the counter. Louisa said she used the money to buy her and Henry four cream buns with candied cherries, their favourite.

She told the story often, and each time she described the dress differently. Sometimes it was polka-dotted, other times striped. I wasn't sure if the story was true, or just an excuse to describe cream buns, which she loved, but could rarely afford.

Henry was an Old English sheepdog, whose white and grey hairs stuck to everything in the shop, especially the sombre black clothes and blankets. I particularly noticed them because I was the owner of a short-haired dog, but most girls didn't care or notice. Dog hairs and dog smells clung to everything female, more so to Elizabeth than anyone else I knew, despite her efforts to repel them, which is probably why rubbish-picking was the only job she could find.

When we came back inside from taking the carpet out, Edi was turning over the teabags she'd left to dry on one of the radiators. They looked like tiny dirty nappies, but we couldn't afford to waste anything.

Though her father sent her enough for rent and presents, Edi barely had any money for food. She was too frightened to sell her father's gifts, which included an elaborate box of make-up with a mirror on the inside of the lid and a tiny blue ballerina that, when the box was opened, twirled in front of it accompanied by a mechanical-music-box version of *A Spoonful of Sugar* from *Mary Poppins*, which we thought must be some sort of factory mistake: it ought to have played something from *Swan Lake* or another ballet.

The make-up colours were horrid: dark green, blue, black, grey, rust red, with lipsticks in fake enamel containers.

Edi never used it. The box was covered in red velvet with a cream trim, which I suppose to Benjamin made it look like raw meat. He chewed and ate the whole thing: there were coloured powders all over his fur, and bits of lipstick and mirror all over the floors. He vomited a lot, but the ballerina was never found.

The state gave us free kibble and biscuits for the dogs. Often, we ate a porridge made out of smashed dog biscuits and milk and sugar or margarine spread on the dog biscuits to have with our tea. The biscuits were alright. The kibble made us smell bad if we ate it as it was full of nasty meat. Some girls soaked it then mixed it with mayonnaise for sandwiches, you could always smell which girls ate kibble. I didn't tell Edi or Elizabeth about Charles, or about the coffee and crackers he fed me.

A few times a month a young man came by for Edi. He first visited when we had been living in the apartment for a year.

We didn't know how she met him, as she hardly went outside. Whenever he came over, Elizabeth and I hid in my room, with the door locked, our dogs by our feet.

Even though it would be three dogs against one man, we were still scared. Edi was kind enough to lend us her tape player so we didn't have to hear them in Edi's bedroom. It was a very small, old silver tape player; another present from her father.

When a tape finished, we could hear them, Edi and the man, but couldn't picture what they were doing. We had seen dogs mount each other of course, but didn't know if people were supposed to do it the same way. One of us would quickly add another tape. Efficient and mechanical in our movements, we avoided looking at each other.

I had a collection of tapes I brought home from work, soundtracks to films we had never seen: *Mary Poppins, The Sound of Music, Chitty Chitty Bang Bang, Annie, The King and I, Oliver!* The small, colourful tape cases almost looked like boxes of candy.

Neither of us liked Edi's tapes—choral, organ and banjo music—which she constantly played without regard for us or anyone else in the building.

Of course, nothing could drown out Benjamin's barking.

Edi didn't lock Benjamin in the bathroom, she didn't want him to be too far, just in case. The door to Edith's bedroom was covered in bites, dents, paw marks, and dog spittle. He had made a few large holes that Edi covered in paper. Edi locked Benjamin out, and he battled with the door, trying to get in. The man came and left through Edi's bedroom window, we could see his legs walking past my own window, there was a lot of barking from the other apartments as all the dogs could smell him. I once slipped out of my window with Alice and followed him at a distance. He walked hurriedly to a tram stop, and kept turning his head in all directions. He had a wide mouth and a scar on one cheek, a row of pink indents, the ghost mouth of a dog.

Edi would go into the bathroom and moan after he left. I think he caused her a mysterious pain she wouldn't tell us about, she'd come out walking stiffly and awkwardly. She had to bathe right away so Benjamin wouldn't hurt her because of the man's smell.

The man always left a loaf of grey-looking bread for Edi, and occasionally some jam or cheese. She acted like she didn't care about it until he left, when she grabbed the food and sometimes ate it in one sitting, Benjamin pawing at her dress and whining because he wanted some too.

Once he left her five dollars instead of food, and it lay on her windowsill for weeks. I was worried Benjamin would chew it up until, when I was going to the grocery store, Edi quietly asked if I could pick her up some digestive biscuits, eggs, and Bovril. She didn't offer me any when I came back, taking the bag into her room. I never saw her cook the eggs. I didn't like to imagine her eating them raw, sitting in bed, which she probably did.

I had read one of her father's letters before. I had found it half-submerged in the toilet.

I could only make out a few sentences, as the ink had run.

I wish I were your dog.

I imagine you have nice pink ears.

I want to take your dog away . . .

I dried it on the radiator in my room, folded it up, and put it in a jar of dog vitamins, where I knew Edi wouldn't look. Now and then I unfolded it and read it in bed; it made me feel dark and strange. My father only sent me postcards that said, "I hope you and Alice are Well. Love Dad and Mom," always in his handwriting.

I went over to Charles's house three or four times a week. Alice and I felt less afraid each time. He always gave me something to eat: pineapple rings on toast, boiled eggs, cinnamon doughnuts, slices of cake or pie, tomato soup, baked potatoes with butter, bowls of jello, preserved cherries. He did events at birthday parties and boys' schools, and sometimes had old cake, tiny sandwiches, and all sorts of candies left over from them.

I had never eaten so well. He fed Alice too. He bought special food for her from a butcher's: sausages, lamb livers, tripe, and marrowbones. I had to be extra careful to keep her beautiful white chin clean, it was always getting wet with blood.

Soon, she let him pet her, and she even licked his hands. He had never touched a live animal before, not even his mouse, which he said seemed too delicate. He had bought it in a cage and had never taken it out.

I felt jealous of the mouse, though he told me he didn't have a huge attachment to it, it didn't mean anything really, he just liked to look at it, it didn't have a name. We could get rid of it if I liked. He hadn't directly asked me to move in with him, but took it for granted, from my second visit to his house, that I would.

He kept in contact with an old room-mate of his who now lived in a couples building, there was a free one-bedroom that had its own bathroom and skylights.

He bought things in anticipation.

A percolator, which was for making coffee, he explained; a box of sanitary napkins; a strange pair of silver tongs whose ends looked like a bird's beak; bed sheets; a small rubber ball with a plastic tube sticking out of it, which he squeezed, demonstrating something unknown to me; a cookbook, with a large piece of meat covered in cherries and orange slices on the cover, whose recipes he said he was excited to try; a box of spoons and forks, laid out on red velvet like jewels; and a few nice outfits for me, including a green dress, a navy-blue pea coat, a chequered scarf, a bunch of black and beige nylons in square packages, black shoes with a thick, embossed strap, pearl buttons, and thick heels, and a pair of blue slippers with embroidered flowers on the toe. I couldn't imagine what it would feel like to wear them, the top of one's foot so exposed. Charles was used to wearing various types of shoes.

I'll buy you underthings too, of course, he said before putting everything away, neatly refolding the clothes. He kept it all under lock and key in his chest.

He bought me several boxes of sanitary napkins, an expensive brand I had never used before. I was surprised, and ashamed that he knew what sanitary napkins were, I assumed it would be something I would hide from him, but I was also relieved he had bought so many, and even a belt to hold them in place, as I would no longer have to use twists of toilet paper. Also, shampoo, which I had never used before, lipsticks, and paint for cheeks, a bar of soap wrapped in purple paper that had the words SOFT SKIN printed on it, and a tin of cotton sticks with an illustration of an ear on the lid.

I had never cleaned my ears before. I did Alice's with a wet rag so they wouldn't smell.

At home, we just had baking soda for hair and teeth, and washed our bodies with thick bars of pale yellow soap that was sold as useable for both ladies and dogs, and also laundry and floors.

Every time I went over he had more things. Metal tins filled with fancy nut biscuits, liquorice, and other treats, an iron, a bottle of feminine perfume he didn't open to let me smell. I didn't know what I would smell like as a woman who lived with a man, but the bottle had a rose on it. We spent all of our time drinking coffee, eating, and looking at everything in an orderly fashion before he put it all away again and it was time for me to go home. Mostly he saw me out, but one evening he didn't and a man in the hall downstairs opened his door to look at me. His hair was greased back. He wore make-up, so that his face looked like a young woman's, the skin of his neck tan compared to his pale, false face. He was naked. I had never seen a naked man before: I hadn't even seen Charles naked. I had only seen dog's penises. I was shocked to see men had pubic hair. The man looked like some gross amalgamation of a naked woman and a male dog, and his penis moved as he looked at me.

Alice snarled and barked. The man quickly shut the door.

I didn't tell Charles what I had seen, but Alice was agitated, no matter how many bones and wedges of cheese we fed her in the days that followed.

In Charles's backyard, there was a crab-apple tree surrounded by fallen brown crab apples no one there wanted to eat. A waste, I knew Elizabeth and Edi would eat them, regardless of the taste. Getting enough vitamin C was a worry for them. Charles gave me glasses of juice and tins of fruit salad.

I wasn't allowed in the yard. They were afraid of Alice, he said of his roommates, and didn't want her smell or her hairs around the building, which offended me because Alice was very short-haired and didn't smell at all. I made an effort to keep her clean.

I was too afraid, even with Alice, to use their bathroom, and so my visits were always regulated by how long I could go without relieving myself.

Sometimes, walking home, seeing Alice pee was unbearable, so I pulled down my stockings and squatted too, which was foolish and dangerous, and I got piss all over my bovver boots, and my underwear had marks in them from not using toilet paper. Usually I wore them three or four times to save soap, but I was worried that Charles could smell them, even under my stockings.

Charles and everything in his room was very clean, except for the mouse cage, which gave off an odour. I was glad he'd never see my apartment, the blankets covered in stains and chewed on by Alice, and Edi and Benjamin's behaviour, poor fat Elizabeth and Tobias, the bags of dog food, the cheap teabags.

After the night we met, Charles never let me see him in his work outfit, a fact I knew would change if we ever lived together. I was embarrassed by the idea of watching him get ready for work, his nice dull face hidden under cheerful make-up. I wished that Charles had such a lovely, simple outfit as the clown in the postcard on his nightstand, instead of the bright yellow and red satin and the hideous wig he had to wear, and which I knew shamed him terribly.

Charles told me he put cream on his face every night because the clown make-up wasn't very good for his skin, and he suggested I ought to do the same.

He gave me a red tin full to take home. I didn't want Edi or Elizabeth to see it, so I hid it in my drawer of jumpers wrapped up in an orange cardigan that was too ugly and moth-eaten for Edi to borrow.

Charles's hair was receding slightly at the temples, I wondered if it was because of the wig he had to wear for work. He didn't tell me if he had any special lotion for that.

Charles often kissed me, without touching any other part of my body, while we sat facing each other on his bed, his hands either sitting in his lap or fist-shaped and kneading the mattress between us. He always made sure Alice had something in her mouth beforehand.

I was home the night Elizabeth didn't come home from work.

Edi and I walked around our neighbourhood, calling, 'Elizabeth, Elizabeth' and 'Tobias, Tobias' but lost our enthusiasm after a few hours because we had half-expected it to happen; Tobias was almost worse than having no dog at all.

I was too sad, listening to all my tapes without Elizabeth, so I brought them to Charles' house. Perhaps there would be a time, when I lived with him, when I could listen to them again. I also thought if he listened to them he would understand more about me. He only listened to instrumental music, *Percy Faith Orchestra, Continental Music, Santo & Johnny, Sleep Walk, Important Symphonies of Europe, Best of Bach.*

When Edi's man came over, I lay in bed with Alice and covered my head with a pillow, thinking about Charles and nice food to eat.

I put up 'Room Mate Wanted' signs in the second-hand shop, we had a few weeks before the end of the month, and no one to cover Elizabeth's half of the rent. I didn't know when Charles planned for us to move, but I couldn't leave Edi on her own.

I noticed that all the stains on her clothes and our furniture were now familiar, there weren't any new ones, no fresh drips of blood on the toilet seat and floors.

Edi had cried for days after Benjamin was fixed; it was illegal not to. You couldn't have girls going around breeding puppies—a woman was only given one dog in her life. It was less noticeable when Alice was fixed so it was easier, she didn't look different, but I had never thought of myself, or Edi, as needing to be fixed too. Charles hadn't bought any baby things, just stuff for two grown-ups. I hadn't seen him naked yet. I didn't know what his plans were, besides for us to live together and eat liquorice. I asked Charles when we would move in together and he said, whenever you are ready, everything is prepared.

Edi was suspicious because Alice and I had both gained weight even though I didn't snack on dog biscuits anymore. She'd pull at my hips or poke me in the back but never asked outright if I was seeing a man. She wasn't secretive about her own predicament.

I'll feed it to Benjamin, a dog needs fresh meat, why not my meat, it's the only meat I can afford, she said over and over.

Not long after we moved in together, Edi and I saw a woman with a small greyhound. It barely reached her knee, and its tail was tucked between its legs. It looked frail as a bird. The woman wore heels, sheer stockings instead of wool ones, and a green dress with blue flowers on it. She was the same age as us, but taller, and prettier. What her dog, and her outfit, were meant to convey was simple:

I don't need to rely on precautions or follow conventions because I am so beautiful I'll find a nice man before it matters.

Edi kicked Benjamin and let go of his leash. He chased after them. The greyhound bolted. The woman, trying to hold onto it, fell down, was dragged, and let go of the leash. She screamed as her dog disappeared.

We quickly walked away before we saw what happened to her. Eventually, Benjamin caught up with us, wagging his tail and barking. He wasn't trained but he was still loyal. I would never have taken the risk of letting Alice off her leash outdoors.

I still hadn't found a new roommate for us when I discovered Edi lying on our living-room floor. The bottom of her nightie was all red, she had bunched it between her legs. Benjamin whined excitedly in circles around her.

It's early, it will be much smaller than expected, she said. Her tape player was on, Mary Poppins was singing, and I wanted to leave before it finished. I went into my room and began to pack before remembering all the things Charles bought. I didn't need to bring anything besides myself and Alice. Everything we owned was rubbish anyway. As I left, Benjamin was licking Edi between the legs. She had her hands on his head, and was scratching his ears and moaning.

I put Alice on her leash. As soon as we were outside she began to behave strangely and I had to pull her away from the house. She kept trying to sit down, refusing to budge. She had diarrhoea on the street. It was a vivid ochre colour, I didn't know what she had eaten to make it that shade. I didn't have time to stop and clean it up, I was starving and I wanted to see Charles. A smear of diarrhoea followed us as I dragged Alice along. She was whining, and refused to get up on all fours, no matter how many times I kicked her. It took much longer than usual to reach Charles's house because Alice was acting so difficult. When we finally arrived, I asked Charles if we could spend the night. He told me he'd have to kill Alice first, that he had bought a needle that would do it quickly; it'd be alright. He showed me the leather case that the needle was in.

It wasn't Alice who bit him, it was me. My teeth weren't used to biting, or to meat. I went for his throat, as a dog would. He made a choking sound and pushed me away, but I leaped on him and pushed him to the ground. I bit again then Alice helped me, once she saw blood, she was jolly to eat.

Soon, his face and neck were a mess. I covered him with his costume and clown wig. How to get out of the house I didn't know, and I didn't exactly want to. There was food and other comfortable things in the room, and we had nowhere else to go, but I would have to eventually because the house was full of other men, and I was just a woman with a dog. The clown costume brought attention to, didn't hide, Charles's body. Alice would have to eat the whole of Charles, every little bone so the other men would think he was just out for a long time or had moved or something. Eat, Alice, I said. Eat, Alice.

I wasn't sure if women who lived with men were allowed to leave their houses or not, and there was nobody to ask. I should have asked Charles before. I had never seen a woman wandering around the city in the company of a man, dog-less, but who knew, perhaps there was special transportation and places for couples I didn't know about but would soon discover.

WHEELERS

Alex Pugsley

My mother's maiden name is Wheeler—in her early roles she's credited as Mary-Margaret Wheeler—and the Wheeler family ethos, as my father would tell you, from time to time possessed everyone in our household. For my father and I lived in a house of girls and women. Imagine a back hall of scuffed figure skates, rubber boots, ballet slippers, mismatched high heels, a broken flip-flop. Picture a second floor where dance routines are rehearsed at all hours of the morning, doors are perversely slammed, sweaters are illicitly borrowed only to be returned "completely reeking of fucking cigarettes." My four sisters competed for clothes, friends, time in the bathroom, nights with the car. They competed to be heard. There were skirmishes, schemes, hormonal swings, unburdening emotionality. Nights could be loud. When I was young, I tried to make connections between all factions—I let them give me manicures, I let them put my hair in braids—only to later explode in survivalist anger. MY SISTERS TALKING: "Remember when you ripped off your Tarzan pajamas? What a psycho!" "Mom's right. You need therapy." "You know when you mooned me and Faith? We saw your balls and they looked shrimpy. In your *face*! And fuck off because I actually *don't* talk about other people." How to respond? The unstable spin of feminine non-logic can overwhelm a single guy and, after the age of twelve, I vowed to never again take anyone's side or get sucked into any argument. My mother presided over these histrionics from afar and seldom intervened. When indifference was futile, she could commit to the scene with the full force of her personality and in these moments the female members of my family seemed united in a singleness of lunacy. It was rampant in the house and halls and provoked in me a confusion of sympathy so absolute I had no idea where their contradictions ended and my own instabilities began. So, with such *Sturm und Tollheit* looming overhead, I can tell you most of what follows occurred some thirty years ago on a slushy late December afternoon when my mother began the proceedings sound asleep in a full bathtub in the house on Dunvegan. For the second time in an hour, Katie, my youngest sister, called to my mother that she was wanted on the telephone. But this information did not really infiltrate my mother's dreaming brain. She lay in the bathwater, her head at an awkward angle, her mouth a smidge above the water's surface. Katie, on the other side of the door, stood listening for some kind of response or movement, but, hearing none, returned to the staircase. It was only when Katie's footfalls faded from the doorway that my mother stirred, eyelashes fluttering, elbow twitching, finally awakening. "Who's there?" She pushed herself into a sitting position, a pink mesh sponge slipping from her shoulder. In another second the swirl of her dreams would dissipate and her full identity return to her, bringing with it all the concerns, perplexities, and divinations that free-float on any given day. "Ditsy?" She stood up, bathwater rinsing from her, and reached for an orange beach towel draped over a nearby radiator. She sniffed the towel, feeling where it was damp from earlier use, and quickly swabbed her shoulders, arms, legs. She called a second time and stepped out of the tub, careful to avoid the debris on the fringed bathmat at her feet, debris she seemed surprised to see. Which was: a three-pack of miniature Henkel Trocken champagne, a red Lego brick, and a water-warped paperback copy of *Anne's House of Dreams*. The first item had been liberated earlier that afternoon from a reunion luncheon for Dalhousie University's School of Nursing, Class of 1955. It was a degree my mother abandoned to go into acting but she'd been convinced to crash the reunion by two of her classmates. The Lego piece belonged to my mother's first and, at the moment, only grandson. The book had been hers since childhood. Frowning a half-moment, she picked up the Lego piece and paperback, brought them to the sink, and placed them on a built-in tiled shelf. Why this frown? The whirligig of my mother's likes and dislikes, and where it might spin on a given day, was something few could figure or predict and what was obsessing her on this winter afternoon was anyone's guess. It could be the reminder of being a grandmother at fifty, or the memory of a ringing telephone, or Neptune Theatre's current season, or some theatricals still to be played. Whichever—with sudden compulsion, as if she felt the present scene needed fresh energy—she turned away from the sink and reached into the tub to pull out its rubber plug. She took a plaid bathrobe, not her own, from a two-pronged hook on the back of the bathroom door and, threading her arms through the sleeves, walked out the door into the hallway. Fading behind her in the bathroom was a sense of fragrant vapours—the down-draining water redolent of Pear's Transparent Soap, lavender bath oil, and the everyday assorted effluence of an adult woman's metabolism. "Hello?" she said, tightening the bathrobe's belt. "Where are you? Ditsy?"

My four sisters—Carolyn, Bonnie, Faith, and Katie—went by the family nicknames of Itsy, Bitsy, Titsy, and Ditsy, although my father often changed that third appellation to Mitsy, especially in formal correspondence. My mother did not always care for formality—nor did she stand on ceremony. "Ditsy," she called down. "Who was on the phone?"

"Nan."

"She probably wants to know when she's getting picked up. Not that I haven't told her three times."

"No. She said she's not coming. And the real estate lady called for Dad."

"Not coming? She complains and complains she's not invited then when she *is* invited she's not coming?"

"She said she's sick."

"Sick?"

My maternal grandmother, Evelyn Anne Wheeler, known to us as Nan, was spending her first winter in Nova Scotia in some time. She and my grandfather, known to us as Dompa, had wintered in Sarasota but with my grandfather dying of congestive heart failure three years before, and my grandmother suffering a small cerebral hemorrhage at the Trimingham's perfume counter in Bermuda—after which she'd been on a more or less constant stroke watch—my mother decided it best to move her back to Halifax and into Saint Vincent's Guest House.

"With Nan," said my mother. "It's always a little more complicated. She likes to play head games, you know. And she likes to be in control."

"She was using her Big Whisper Voice."

"And after getting me to give up my hair appointment for her?" My mother came down the stairs, her hand sliding along the bannister. Framed on the walls around her were posters for productions of *Deathtrap*, *Chapter Two*, and other plays she'd acted in. "Imagine," she said. "Thinking you can get a hair appointment the week before Christmas. But you know Nan. It's all about her hair. She's on the phone, it's about her hair. She's opening a bottle of wine, it's about her hair. She's down at Emergency, it's about her hair." At the front door, my mother stooped to gather the day's mail. "Maybe it's better she's not coming. I mean Nan's a wonderful woman. No, she is. Until that third drink. Third drink and she's peeing on the floor."

Standing up, my mother stared through a glass panel in the front door and considered the house-under-construction across the street. It was vertically composed, made with red cedar and solar panels, and very unfinished. Not only was it out of style with the street's other houses, but its incompleteness—the lot disordered with backhoe tracks, cinderblocks, and two-by-fours—gave the place a raw, defective quality. "That mess of a house," said my mother, with fresh awareness of nuisance. "It just looks like shit. Bringing property values down, my God."

There was, I should say, a For Sale sign on our house. For four years there'd been a For Sale sign on our house. Some eons earlier, my parents had divorced, only to reunify. But complications—familial and financial—persisted. The material takeaways were an enormous short-term debt and my mother's wish to move to a smaller, cheaper house. But, to avoid further tribulation, she wasn't going to buy until she sold. "I wake up in the middle of the night," she said, sorting through the mail. "And I have visions of that For Sale sign blowing in the wind for the next twenty years. By then the roof's fallen in, the windows broken. No one's buying houses right now. No one." Turning from the front door, she said, "Did Carolyn show up with the salmon? Ditsy, where are you?"

My sister Katie lay watching television in the living room, her head somewhat acutely propped up by a baseboard, her feet in striped toe socks. Katie was fourteen, but a very young fourteen, and, unlike my sister Faith, who at fifteen was drinking and dating her way through multiple social circles, Katie dwelled in a protracted teenybopperdom. She was slim, quick, "coltish," as the heroines were described in the YA books she daily demolished, and for the last months she'd been trying out a series of obsessions. Her latest fascination had begun with my mother's appearance in a revival of *The Gingerbread Lady*, continued through repeated viewings of *The Sunshine*

Boys, and recently resulted in her commitment to a dialect I'll call Generic New York Wisecrack. Which is why, when my mother took a step into the living room, Katie, without shifting her gaze from the television, simply said, "Hey, Ma. Dinner's when?"

"Guests are invited for seven. Kids can eat any time. Did Itsy bring the salmon?"

"She went to the cat clinic."

"Cat clinic?"

"Cat clinic, bird clinic. Who am I—Marcus Welby?"

"Ditsy? Enough." My mother crossed to the television and was about to switch it off when she recognized someone onscreen. "Is that Walter Matthau? Christ, he's looking old. Katherine McKee—" My mother faced Katie. "Look at me. Where'd she put it? The kitchen or the basement fridge?"

"I'm fourteen years old! I should know where the fish is?"

"The salmon, Ditsy."

"Fish, salmon. You're going to nitpick?" Katie rolled on to her stomach. "Adults get salmon. Kids get what?"

"Shepherd's Pie."

Katie nodded, judicious. "Is the shepherd fresh?"

"Ditsy—" My mother shook her head. "I forbid you to watch any more Neil Simon. You're cut off. Did she drop it off or not?"

"*Yes.* Kitchen fridge."

My mother flipped the mail on a hall radiator and returned to the stairs. "I'm going to get dressed. If Nan calls again, Ditsy, let me know."

Getting up to press rewind, Katie shrugged. "The thing about salmon," she said to herself. "It's not funny. Pickerel? Pickerel is funny. Kippers is funny. But salmon?"

Not four seconds later, the front door swung open and my father entered the house carrying a box of Perrier. Plastic bags containing bottles of wine were hanging from his wrists and a red Twizzler licorice dangled from his mouth. Without taking off his shoes, he carried his purchases to the kitchen and eased them onto the kitchen table. "Bitsy, Ditsy?" he said. "Which one are you? Could one of you crap-artist kids help with the groceries?"

Katie came to the doorsill and looked in. "Out of left field he comes running with the craziest questions."

"Christ," said my father, tripping over an empty milk carton. "Could we have one day in this kitchen when there *isn't* an open garbage bag on the floor?" He glanced at Katie. "Peanut? Go find your mother. She's got a dozen people coming over for dinner."

"Find her yourself. She's upstairs."

My mother, now wearing a full slip over tea-stained sweatpants, appeared at the stair-top and gazed down at my father with—what would be called in the stage directions—an amused air of distant suspicion.

"There she is," said my father, beaming. "Look at you, twisting your hair, you get more and more beautiful every day. How about some kisses?"

"Did you remember the Campari?"

"Campari? Who drinks Campari?"

"*I* don't drink it, genius. But your esteemed colleague, Roz Weinfeld, newly appointed to the bench, drinks it and she's the reason we're having this dinner. Remember? It was the one thing I asked you to get."

My father considered this with narrowing eyes, the Twizzler dangling from his lips. "All right, Little Miss Mums." He shifted the licorice to the other side of his mouth, like a backroom bookie rearranging a cigar. "Make a list and we'll get Baby-boy to get it. Because, God knows, whatever Mumsy needs, Mumsy gets."

"It's whatever *Lola* wants, Lola gets."

The line in question was from the musical *Damn Yankees* and, for my parents, another installment in a never-ending game of name-that-quote. Both had strutted and fretted some time upon the stage and had within their imaginations a number of dramatic parts. So the evening might see variations on Elyot and Amanda, Nathan and Adelaide, George and Martha. My parents moved within a series of personas but to what extent they were using these personas, and to what extent the personas were using them, was not always easy to establish.

"Some days I hate that goddamn law firm," said my mother, musing. "Do you ever wonder what it's done to us?"

"As fun as that sounds, Mumsy, wondering what might've been, do you mind terribly if we stick to the here and now? You might want to get dressed."

"Oh, McKee. You've lost the plot. You've lost the plot, kid."

"Sure, sure," said my father. "You contain multitudes, Mums. Now would you mind containing dinner?" He smiled again. "And I better get some kisses around here or there's going to be real trouble."

Just then, Katie bumped open the front door and traipsed in with four bags of groceries. As she moved past my father, he snatched at her shirttail. "When I met her, Ditsy. She was nothing. She had half a degree and two dirty jokes."

"Dad! Don't stretch my shirt! And that lady called you back."

"Just a second, Peanut. I'm trying to tell you something about your horrible mother."

My mother arrived at the bottom of the stairs and, pushing shut the front door, said to him, "Quit terrorizing the children, would you, darling?" Ambling into the kitchen, she whispered over her shoulder, "And fuck the firm."

"Did you *hear* what you said?" He was staring at her as if this remark were perhaps the absolute zenith of her derangement. "You're a *terrible* person."

"Honestly, Stewart. Why do you talk? Why do you even open your mouth? Some lawyer." She opened the refrigerator and searched for the rumoured salmon. "You want to tell me where you've been the last hour? The Halifax Club?"

"For your information, I was taking discovery on a case."

"Which case?"

"Well," said my father. "I'm not at liberty to discuss it."

"Stewart—" My mother whirled around. "Tell me it's not Gregor Burr."

My father adjusted his tie. "I said I can't discuss it."

"Gregor Burr?" She sighed. "I personally can't stand him. What kind of guy who, when he's elected Member of Parliament, starts messing around with teenagers? He's a goddamn sleaze. And such a tendentious son-of-a-bitch. He could be a role model for the youth of this province and instead he's assaulting high-school girls in the stairwell of the Lord Nelson Hotel. Why can't he go to a prostitute like a normal person?"

"Do you *hear* what you're saying?"

"Don't give me that rise-above-it bullshit. Why are you always defending the bad guy?"

"That's yet to be determined, my dear."

"That's not what I heard."

"And what did you hear, Mary-Margaret Wheeler, pray tell?"

"Well, asshole, what I heard was a different story. Like the city hasn't heard a different story."

"That's enough of this talk, thank you."

"Oh, I'm not allowed to say anything?"

"No, you can say whatever you like. You can print it in the paper if you like. But if the people you describe take your remarks to be defamatory you may be forced to prove what you allege in a court of law."

My mother tilted her head, unimpressed.

"This isn't all my doing, Mums. It's just we have something here called the rule of law—"

"I'm familiar with the fucking *rule* of law, Stewart. I'm also familiar with this man's history. He stuck his tongue down Caitlyn Jessup's throat. Marge McLean, he pinned her up against a car in the Sobeys parking lot. Marge McLean! I mean how drunk do you have to *be*? And Bev Noonan, he muckled on to her at the bar convention, lifting up her dress at the coat check. And God knows how many more there are."

"Those are not the sort of stories you want to repeat."

"Why? Because they happen to be *true*? And from what I've heard about this teenager, he finally went too far. It's tantamount to raping her."

"Mackie—"

"Well, what would you call it? The teenager said penetration and the RCMP identified the semen on her skirt as his." My mother looked at my father, severe. "Did he admit it?"

"I can't repeat what's said in-camera. You know that."

"Ian Pulsifer tells Connie—"

"How would *you* know that?"

"She told me!"

"Exactly. Look, I can't discuss the facts of a case with you. Or what a client says in discovery. You know I can't. And that's final."

These arguments, sound as they may have been, did not have a wholly persuasive effect on my mother. "Listen," she said. "I applaud Tiggy for standing by him but come on, Stewart. Everybody knows what this man's like. Every single person in the Conservative Party knows what he's like and they're all letting him get away with it. That's what makes me so sick. It's like with an alcoholic. They're enablers. If someone doesn't say, 'No, this isn't right,' then who's to stop him? *He* obviously can't stop himself. But they won't say anything because everything's going so well up in Ottawa right now. Yeah, well, stick around." My mother saturated her next word with contempt. "*Men*. Puh. There ought to be a revolution."

"I feel it's underway."

My mother glanced at my father before looking up towards what, in a theatre, would be the first row of the balcony. "When the hurly-burly's done," she said. "We'll look back and wonder what we've done on this earth. And what we'll we say? That's the sixty-four thousand dollar question, Stewart. What'll we say then?"

Before my father could answer, the doorbell rang.

Dodie Rumboldt was a sweet, dithery woman who dropped by our house for the flimsiest of reasons. She worried about everything and lived in a tizzy of worsening possibilities. My mother was loyal to her because they'd grown up next door to each other in Truro. "Dodie Rumboldt has wanted to be my best friend for forty-six years," she said, on her way to the door, seeing who it was. DODIE: A SELECTED ORAL HISTORY: "She was always big, you know? I mean *big*. I never knew her when she didn't look like a tent coming toward you. And her wardrobe went purple for a while. She was one of those ladies in purple. Like you don't know how much weight she's gained because you're distracted by all the purple? Let me tell you something. You're not fooling the cheap seats. Then she got a boyfriend. Did wonders for her. She lost over a *hundred* and fifty pounds. Jogging with weights. Eating right. Looked great. But now? She's gone too far. Can't stop. Some thin. Scared skinny. She's going to give herself a nervous breakdown. Well, her mother's had terrible Alzheimer's. Her mother's in Saint Vincent's on the third floor just out of it. Not much fun having a mother whose memory's gone. But Dodie and her father have been bricks. Visiting every day. Every day one of them's gone to see her."

The doorbell rang again. Composing her face into a smile, and with a very convincing demonstration of calm, my mother opened the door.

"It's Dad," said Dodie, putting a hand to her throat. "First it was his heart. Now it's his hip. He fell doing the snow-blower. They have him at the hospital and I think they're going to keep him overnight. You just never know if this one's—"

"Oh, Dodie," said my mother. "His hip? I'm sure he'll be fine. He's had a replacement before, hasn't he?"

211

Dodie nodded. "I could just *feel* something was going to happen this month. All month I could feel it. My mind's just been *racing*. I mean I know life's what happens when you're doing something else, but this?" She pressed her lips together. "I've been down at the hospital all afternoon. I just left."

"Was he awake when you left? Were you able to talk to him?"

Dodie was nodding again when she spied Katie in the dining room. Katie had her hands full of silverware and was setting fourteen places for dinner. "Oh?" said Dodie. "Mackie, you have company coming. I should go."

"Don't be silly. Wouldn't dream of it. You stay for supper."

"But I'm not dressed for it."

"We'll find you something. You come talk to me. Ever peel a potato?"

"Well," said Dodie, with a surprised giggle, as if this might be the third funniest thing she's heard in her life. "I might've peeled one or two."

And so the evening, for some minutes, advanced without further ruckus, my youngest sister setting the table, my father shaving in the upstairs bathroom, and me rising from the basement, while my mother sat Dodie down with a glass of white wine at the kitchen table. Which is where Dodie learned of my mother's plans to poach a salmon in the dishwasher. "I have *never* heard of anything like that," said Dodie, watching my mother drizzle two large fillets with white wine, lemon juice, and butter. "In *tin* foil? On a wash cycle? Mackie, honestly, I've never." My mother, holding in buttery hands a bottle of chardonnay, was pouring herself a glass of wine when the telephone jingled. She glanced into the dining room and with a look indicated that Katie should answer it. Katie walked to the kitchen and shyly picked up the receiver. "Hello?" After a moment, she covered the mouthpiece to say, "It's the real estate lady again." She held out the receiver to my mother who was wiping her hands with a blue J Cloth. Which is when my father entered and, with a nimble two-step, filched the receiver from Katie's fingers.

"What are you doing?" My mother turned to Dodie. "What is he doing?"

"Sh, Mumsy," said my father. "Go have an olive."

"An *olive*? Give me that phone."

My father turned his back to the room, effectively blocking all access to the telephone.

Deciding on another course of action, my mother grabbed her glass of wine and was on her way to the hall extension when my father, after several curt, somewhat inaudible, but mostly professional-sounding instructions, replaced the receiver.

With glaring eyes, my mother re-appeared. "What did she say? What did you tell her?"

"There's an offer."

"The couple from Vermont?"

My father nodded.

"I knew it."

"They made an offer this morning and—"

"What is it?"

"It expires tonight at six o'clock."

My mother glanced at the clock on the stove-top. It showed two minutes to six. "How much?"

"Well, I suggested—"

"I don't care what *you* suggested! I want to know what the offer is."

"Three seventy-two."

"Take it."

"I said we'd only consider bids over three eighty."

"You did not. You did not—" She studied him. "Stewart, are you out of your mind? This house, need I remind you, has been on the market for four fucking *years*! We get one offer in four years and you think you're John Kenneth Galbraith?

Call her back this instant. No—just—*move*. I'll call her."

"You will do nothing of the sort," said my father, disconnecting the telephone.

From somewhere inside my mother burst a howl—a melismatic mixture of crying and laughter—and with a vicious spin of her wrist she flung her wineglass at the window. After it smashed against the windowsill, she stared at my father, livid. "Why would you do that without talking to me? When you know I've been out of my mind with worry. *Why* would you do that?"

"Mumsy, you're behaving badly." My father felt his neck, above his shirt collar, for shards of broken glass, then extended his hand toward Dodie, who was still sitting at the kitchen table, her eyes wide with panic. "Dodie, I'm sorry to say, your friend's gone berserk."

"Stewart," said my mother. "I have met some jackasses in my life—"

"Beautiful, you love me. You wouldn't change a thing."

"I've got news for you—" In the back hall, my mother grabbed a ski jacket and guided her feet into two rubber boots. "If I had to live my life over again, I'd do it alone."

"Performance to follow. Applause, applause. Fanfare, trumpets, exeunt omnes."

"No. Just mine." She raised her voice. "Aubrey! Get your coat—"

"Mackie?"

"Because I'm leaving. I've had it. I'm through. My nerves can't take it."

"Sure, sure, Mums."

"Stewart—" My mother's voice weakened with a note of frailty. "Why would you *do* that? Without talking to me? Why?"

My father reached for her hand. But she shuddered away from him, fiercely blinking her eyes, and marched into the hallway. "Don't *touch* me!"

Silent on the stairs, Katie and I watched our mother zip up the ski jacket, yank open the front door, and charge outside into the sleet and snow.

To me she was incomprehensible—a possible narcissist, a perpetual actress, a charmer, a drinker, a Fury. "Your mother's larger than life, kid," my father would say. "She's something else, a singular sensation, and one of the great unsolved mysteries of maritime history." My mother was twenty when she quit nursing and went into the theatre and, very arguably, her life from that point became one long unfinished performance. She started as an ingénue of shaky self-esteem. Feelings of nervousness and shy defiance were useful for some roles—Miss Julie, Juliet, Ophelia—but further vitalities were needed. A FEW DIGRESSIONS: my mother holds the record for most appearances in productions at Neptune Theatre and ringing the walls of the administrative office on the second floor is a succession of her head shots. Not only do these form a year-by-year photographic biography of my mother but they also showcase a sort of folk history of commercial photography and period hair styles. Around the time of her Medium Wavy Shag, she and my father divorced. During the years of their estrangement, many were the conversations among my sisters regarding how my parents' nights were spent—wondering who got together with whom and for how long. "*All* Dad's friends have crushes on Mom, you dink. Don't you want to know who she was with?" I knew my mother cultivated friendships with Art College types, sculptors in cable-knit sweaters, potters with kerchiefs and mandolins, and dwelled for a time in a Volkswagen van with a man named Elkin Duckworth. This was a New Brunswick actor, effeminately gay, the lead in a celebrated local production of *Godspell*, and afterward known to us as Jesus of Moncton. Their relationship, my mother maintained, was a love affair in all ways but sexual. She and Elkin took a cabaret to BAM, Strasberg on Fifteenth Street, and acid on

Halloween, before he transmigrated to Laurel Canyon and she returned to take custody of my two younger sisters. From America, she arrived supercharged. She'd been radicalized. My mother lived less than three months in New York but, for the rest of her life, auditioning for roles in Halifax's two-and-a-half professional stages, she rather carried herself as if she were only three steps away from walking onstage at the Lyceum Theatre in midtown Manhattan. The expectations of the Halifax audience were irrelevant now. In her time away, she'd gained access to a more primordial emotional life. She'd learned to "go there," to trade and traffic in her emotions, emotions all the more potent if she actually believed in them. And believe in them she did. There was conflict in her acting now, vulnerability alternating with impatient superiority, and the friction between the two sparked true *frisson*. She was celebrated. She was profiled. She acquired groupies. There was a dental hygienist—known to us as Stalker Don Walker—who did not miss an opening night in twenty-three years. (During my teeth cleanings, he had the somewhat exasperating habit of asking about my mother's shows when his soap-scented fingers were far inside my mouth.) Donald's companion was the Dartmouth actor Brandon Merrihew, known as Uncle Brandy. Onstage he was Jimmy to my mother's Evy, Sir Toby to her Maria, and offstage he was her pal and drinksy confidante. Brandy was enamored of, borderline obsessed with, my mother, and his holiday compliments were so effusive as to veer into a dementia of over-flattery. His remarks after my mother's turn in *Streetcar*: "There she is! Nothing really astounds me but you, Mary-Margaret, *you* astound me. You confound me. You wear the crown for me. When I saw you on stage, I said to Donald, 'There *is* magic in the world. That Mackie McKee has done it again.' No one can touch you, can they? Not then. Not now. Not ever. Really, Mackie. Hail to thee, blithe spirit." Emotive disturbance and evidentiary emotionality—these were her new vitalities but such Method did not belong to my father's process. Societal and practical exigencies played their parts in my father's flight from playhouse to courtroom but he contained multitudes all his own. And he would learn it was not really in his professional interests to be emotionally open or emotionally uncontained. The practice of law, which was to be his calling and prevailing vocation, demanded he think first, strategize second, emote never. It actually took me *years* to figure out I was raised within these two mighty monarchies and, digressions done, now might be the time to check in with the subject that was me.

There in the moving car, beside my mother, very much in the passenger seat, sits the lurking figure that is Me at Nineteen. This Aubrey McKee seems a faraway incarnation, a gorky kid beset with contradiction and compulsion and greatly incomplete. A growth spurt has sent me over six feet but left me awkward, pimply—I am known to my sisters as Treetop and Pizza Face—and my signature has not stabilized in years, the capital K of my surname lurching wildly ahead of the final two letters. As earlier explained, it is my tactic, in these *Walpurgisnächten*, to keep calm and follow the example of my oldest sister. For Carolyn is the sane sibling in a crisis, supremely self-controlled, and largely aloof from family politics. So, as my mother fulminates, I suppress All Feeling and mutely stare at a softcover actor's copy of *Hedda Gabler*, published by Dramatists Play Services, which has been left in the slush of the plastic floor liner.

"Why is he doing this?" My mother punches at the steering wheel. "A month ago he was willing to drop the price to three fifty but *now* he wants to play tough guy? I would've offered three seventy-nine to let them know we're willing to budge. No one knows. No one knows what I have to put up with. Do up your seatbelt, please." She checks the rearview mirror and swings up Jubilee Road. "Your father acts like everything's fine. This unfounded optimism he has, thinking everything's going to work out. Well, unless you take steps to make *sure* things work out, I want to tell you, they don't. Do up your seatbelt, Aubrey."

I grab carelessly at the seatbelt but the retractor pulls it from my fingers, the metal latch smacking against the window. My mother does not appear to notice and seems disposed only to stare out the windshield. The evening, I feel, has become for her a primal assertion of self and despite her questions I do not think there is a part for me in her one-person show. I do up the seatbelt and peer out the window. Fog is everywhere in the city, the falling snow has changed to wetting sleet, and my window reflection is smeared with moisture.

"We owe three hundred thousand dollars! I was always taught to live within your means. Your father spends it as soon as he gets it." Speeding into the intersection with Oxford Street, she turns sharply left, our tires slipping sideways on the paint of the wet crosswalk. "I'm fifty years old. I'm too old to be in debt. I say drop the price and rent a place. I don't care where we live. But your father wants the right address. Maybe he needs it to have the confidence to win cases but—Jesus— who's this asshole?" My mother squints into the rear-view mirror where the reflection of high beams from an upcoming vehicle has begun to blind her. "For the love of Pete." She pulls over to allow this vehicle, an ambulance, to pass. After it has gone by, its rotating light flashing on my mother's cheek, she checks over her shoulder and swerves back into the laneway.

I am still studying my reflection in the rainy window, the Christmas lights of St. Thomas Aquinas shimmering outside, when somewhere in my memory shimmers a scene from four years before, when my family is split and I am wandering smashed on Kempt Road and I see my father inside a brightly-lit Harvey's restaurant. He is alone at a booth, his table covered with case briefs, legal pads, an orange cheeseburger wrapper. As I teeter outside, a stranger exits the front doors and with this airstream the wrapper breezes off the table but my father does not notice, so absorbed is he in his preparations. He has this day ninety-two files in various stages of discovery, development, and trial, and he seems so solitary, eating by himself at ten o'clock on a Friday night, when once we'd eaten together as a family, and I consider the ideals he once pursued—a life where his wife wasn't running off, where his family life was secure, where he could manage everything through diligence and force of will—and I think to wave hello to him, impulsively, absurdly excessively, in a way we sometimes had, but as the doors reclose and within their glass my scruffy reflection appears, I am too ashamed to say hello and have him see me fall-down-drunk—and all of this is getting close to the crux of my feelings of what-the-fuck powerlessness regarding my father and mother and sisters and me and so, returning to the scene-in-progress, and sidebarring for a moment my instinct to punch a fist through the windshield, I twist in the car to ask where, exactly, we are going.

My mother sighs, sensing a change in my manner, and asks, "Do you have the list your father gave you?"

I say I left it at the house.

"Well—" She rubs the bridge of her nose. "Can you remember what's on it? The Campari, Gouda, the what-was-it?" She glances at me, irritated. "I don't have time for one of your moods, Aubrey. If you're going to be like this, I can stop the car and you can get out. In fact, here, I'll do it myself." She spins the steering wheel, beginning a very unstable U-turn—which sends me into the armrest of the door—the car coming to a skidding stop on the other side of the street. She gets out, steps over a rain-melting snowbank, and slides toward a payphone beside the Oxford Theatre. As she inserts a quarter and dials, I become aware that her get-up—ski jacket, full slip, sweatpants, rubber boots—is not quite suitable for public walkabout. I am thinking again of Evy from *The Ginger-bread Lady* and her last-chance struggle with, what she calls, this "human being business," when my mother hangs up the phone, her face grim with new information. "It's Nan." She stands very still, the falling sleet fluorescent in the lights of the theatre marquee. "Saint Vincent's called to ask if we picked her up." She makes a fluttery sigh. "No one knows where she is."

My mother lived the first years of her life in an orphanage. My grandmother had become pregnant before she and my grand-father were married and the stigma of being an unwed mother, in those days, was such that she chose to give her first-born away. "It's not as if she was a pregnant teenager," my mother recalled later. "She was twenty-*four*, for Christ's sake. But Nan grew up in the Depression. In that era, respectability was the most important thing. Respectability, security, appearances." After my grandmother's figure recovered, after she'd entered properly into wedlock, and after she'd given birth to a legiti-mate daughter, my grandfather prevailed upon her to repos-sess the first and so my mother, at thirty-one months, rotated back into the Wheeler ménage. "Dompa loved Nan. But so did everybody else. So did half the city. And in those days, you didn't get divorced. What you did was argue. And drink. Their marriage was like a lot from those years, I guess. And during the war, that was a party every night. Up at the Officer's Club." My grandmother drank. Liquor was a magic fundamental to her spirits. Dipsomania was everywhere in the years of my childhood, in all waters, someone or another was always sloshing towards the end of the line, and you learned from an early age not to take it personally. At family dinners, you'd see her sneak away from the table, totter into a hallway, only to later rejoin the room, talkative, flirtsome, hilarious. She was then at ease with herself and her various energies expressed themselves in sweetness and light and contagious unpredict-ability. She let you operate the electronic ice-crusher for her Crème de Menthes. She sent you a cheque on Labour Day. She grabbed your hand and sang high harmony on "Happy Birthday." But over the years there was a gradual running down and aspects of her behaviour—the monomania, the suggestion of paranoid self-involvement, a drift toward delusion—seemed to darken every scene and family occasion. My father, whose preference was to speak well of everyone, conceded his mother-in-law had become "a bit of a loose puck."

"After Dompa died," my mother explained. "Things took a turn." My grandmother became quite close with a widower in Tampa but, when he couldn't commit, she focused her attentions—briefly—on a tennis instructor, after which she made a move to Bermuda. "You should've seen her in Bermuda! Now Nan's a good-looking woman—big bosom, long legs—but there are age-appropriate clothes, you know? Your father and I arrive in Bermuda and here's Nan tricked out like a Vegas showgirl. Seventy-three years old in hot pants and a lace-up tube top with matching headband?" My grandmother's bachelorette adventures resulted in some confusion and real infirmity so she'd been relocated, not without protest, to Halifax. "Here's the thing with Nan. All she wants is a man. She doesn't care what kind. She just wants someone to make her feel special. Well, her parents spoiled her. Her husband spoiled her. Her boyfriends spoiled her. But when there's no one left to spoil her, what's she going to do then?"

When we arrived at Saint Vincent's, the ambulance that had passed us was flashing in the parking lot, a paramedic loading through its back doors someone strapped to a wheeling stretcher. "Good God," said my mother, as the ambulance rolled on to Windsor Street, its siren sounding. "Who do you suppose it is?" My mother walked across the yellow-painted lines of the parking lot, her face set in a pensive frown, as if there were two or three plot twists still to be endured. Inside, we moved into the hallway past the reception desk, and there, at the end of the hall, as if only a few beats behind cue, my grandmother appeared, frail and quivery and checking behind her, as though persecution might arise from some new quarter. Summoning her strength, she began to walk very evenly, with chin held high and a frozen smile—the expression of a visiting head-of-state—and she stared at a point in the hallway ahead of a heavyset elderly woman in a Lindsay tartan dress. Though I vaguely recalled this second resident as a family acquaintance, I saw that, for the moment, my grandmother was choosing not to favour her with recognition.

My mother, sensing something very unfinished about this interaction, but reassured to see my grandmother among the quick, was about to greet both women when my grandmother—spotting my mother—stumbled for her and grabbed her hand, as if on the verge of complete collapse.

"Oh Mackie," she said, her voice shaking. "There's been the most horrible accident." She took a stagey sort of breath. "It's Dolly Hollibone. We were coming out of the service and this little boy came roaring around the corner—some people here don't care *who* their children knock into—well this boy banged right into Dolly and her glasses went flying and she fell and—*crack*—she's broken her wrist. The ambulance just came and took her away."

My mother, while listening closely, was also noting my grandmother's slightly overdone appearance. Her bouffant curls and blonde highlights had been newly maintained and she was wearing hoop earrings, burgundy lipstick, a low-cut burgundy dress, and matching slingback high heels. "You look awfully nice, Mum. What service was it? I see you got your hair done."

"This? Same thing I always do." My grandmother sniffed. "It just breaks your heart. Here she was, all set to go to her granddaughter's concert, and Dolly ends up being taken to the hospital!"

My mother nodded and asked, "Was that Elsy Horne in the tartan dress?"

"Life's full of surprises, I suppose," said my grandmother, her face twitching with worry. "But my God, that could have happened to *anybody*."

As my grandmother talked, we'd travelled—without particularly deciding to—down the hall toward the elevators. Stepping into the nearest car, my grandmother resumed her earlier, imperial manner, and I saw she was performing in her imagination an entirely different drama from many of Saint Vincent's other residents, one of whom, in an inside-out turtleneck sweater, shuffled towards us looking fully bewildered.

"He lives in the Twilight Zone, that one." My grandmother pushed at the close-door button. "Sometimes you can get a straight answer out of him. Other times? Jabberwock." She shook off a shiver. "And homely? Imagine having to kiss that every night."

Taped inside the elevator was a variety of colour photocopies. These announced Jazzercise sessions, Christmas carolling, prayer groups. I was reading a bulletin about a memorial service when my grandmother said, "That's what Dolly dragged me to this afternoon. I didn't mind going to funerals when they only happened once in a while. But this place?" She made a pained smile, as if there were further details to be divulged. "And do you know what hymn they chose? Mackie, you won't believe what hymn they chose. 'They whipped and they stripped and they hung me high and they left me there on a cross to die.'" She smirked at us, as if her own dismay had just been wonderfully validated. "I mean it's the tackiest, most Godawful hymn you can imagine. For a *funeral*?"

My grandmother sat at her dressing table re-applying her mascara, the table surface busy with poinsettias, an eyelash curler, a slim rouge brush, a silver hand-mirror, a square-bottomed decanter of bourbon, two cut-glass tumblers, an unopened box of Thank You notes, and, in a pine frame, a photograph of my grandfather, the print so dislodged most of the image was lost within its matting. A smell of floral perfume pervaded the environment, seeming drenched into everything from the padded coat hangers in the closet to the embroidered linen doilies on the dressing table to the white lace collar of my grandmother's burgundy dress. A television, in another resident's room, was loudly tuned at the moment to a Christmas special where a tenor was quavering through "O Holy Night."

"I used to know the name of that song," said my grandmother. "Is that Andy Williams?"

My mother, after a brief frown—for my grandmother's failure to remember a favourite Christmas carol was another of the day's mysteries—sat on the bed and, following a moment of private deliberation, gaily leaned into the room. "So, my dear, how are things in Glocca Morra?"

"Well," said my grandmother. "Seventy-four isn't sixty-four, I want to tell you. I've got three more years and then my looks are really going to go." She reached for the decanter of bourbon and, with a slight palsy in her right hand, poured herself a drink. "Now normally I wouldn't take a drop of hard liquor—"

"No," said my mother. "Just a forty-ouncer."

"But my nerves today are shot. Put everyone in such a state, what happened to Dolly." She raised the glass, a bit erratically, spilling a dewdrop on her wrist. "Cheers, my dears."

For the last few minutes my grandmother had affected a mood of playful detachment but, as she smiled and over-sniffed some moisture in a clogged nostril, the rest of the room began to sense the mood's essential falsity. My mother was about to say something, probably to inquire after Saint Vincent's reasons for thinking my grandmother missing, when footsteps approached in the hallway.

My grandmother turned and directed a radiant smile toward the doorway. When this visitor, an elderly lady in bifocals, hobbled past, it was clear this was not whom my grandmother was expecting and she reacted with a series of micro-expressions—a spasm of annoyance, a flinch of pain, and finally a slow-building pout, as if she were concerned a conspiracy was being somewhere set up against her.

"Who's that?" asked my mother.

"Joyce," my grandmother replied, firmly, clutching her glass of bourbon. "Her daughter, Mary-Lou, she sings with St. Martin's-in-the-Fields. She won a Bafty— She won a Bafter— She won an award. Her mother's a Morrow. Well—" My grandmother inclined her head. "Was. All the old families are gone. The Mairs, the Morrows. They hardly exist anymore. Oh, people used to care about each other. But it's all segmented now."

"Who are you kidding? You never cared about anybody. You couldn't wait to get away."

"Well," said my grandmother, bitter. "I still can't." She stared at her jeweled wristwatch as if she feared it might be broken. "I've got to get out of this place. I've *got* to."

"And go where? Back to Florida?"

"How am I going to do that? I have no money."

"What about Dompa's pension?"

"Ha! I drank that away."

"Well," said my mother, reaching for something on the floor. "As long as it didn't go to waste." She picked up a fold of toilet paper. It was vivid with a smear of lipstick where someone had blotted their lips. "You're looking pretty good, Mum, for someone who's supposed to be sick—"

"I called to say I wasn't coming."

"So why get your hair done?"

"For the—the service."

"Mmm-hmm. This is the real world. The one I have to live in. Hoop earrings and high heels? For a funeral? Something's going on."

Nan's attention was drawn again to the doorway where a looming shadow preceded the appearance of the woman in the Lindsay tartan dress. For some minutes, this woman had been lurking like Hamlet's ghost—a rather portly, slow-moving

Hamlet's ghost—and she now looked in and fixed my grandmother with a distasteful, vindictive stare.

"She's always got something up her skirt, that one," whispered my grandmother, going to the door. "Making a big to-do. I'd just as soon trip her."

A few murmurs passed between the two women before my grandmother carelessly swung the door shut.

"That *was* Elsy Horne," said my mother. "Dodie's godmother. What'd she want?"

"I have no idea." My grandmother flipped her hair. "The Catholics, they're always ganging up on people. Thinking their way is the best because it's the oldest. Well, let me tell you, I was in Rome once and I'm so glad I'm *not* Catholic. All that blood."

"What'd you say to her? Because you said something."

"I don't know," said my grandmother, reaching for the decanter of bourbon. "Go screw yourself and your dispensation from the Pope." She refilled her glass. "Oh, she gives me the pip, that Elsy Horne."

My mother was frowning. It was the day's starkest frown, a sort of intricacy of thoughtfulness, but in another moment all frowns would vanish as the pieces of the play for her came together. "Oh, Mum." She stared at my grandmother with real helplessness. "You did not. Tell me you didn't. Tell me you're not carrying on with Dodie's *father*."

Moisture came unbidden to my grandmother's eyelids. Another commotion of expressions began to form in her face but none really seemed to take. It was all somehow terrible to see.

"*That's* who you were expecting? But he didn't come today, did he?" My mother rose off the bed. "Mother. Look at me. His wife's *upstairs*. She's right upstairs. What in the name of God were you thinking?"

My grandmother was staring at us, but staring without any recognition. Attempting to speak, her mouth began to form words but no sounds were coming out and instead she made a simpering, crooked smile. Pushing on the dressing table, she suddenly started out of her chair, went over on a high heel, and toppled to the floor. She lay where she'd fallen, shivering.

My mother knelt beside her and felt for a pulse. At this touch, my grandmother screamed, as if she'd been stabbed with a letteropener, and clutched at the foot of the dressing table. There was real madness in her eyes, a sort of feral cunning that showed no idea but resistance.

"Aubrey—" My mother stood up. "I'm going to tell the duty-nurse to call a doctor. Stay with Nan. And—" She looked at my grandmother's wristwatch. "It's six-forty. Remember that time." She opened the door and fled in rubber boots down the hall.

My grandmother's face was pale beneath smears of rouge, her eyes gleaming with tears, her lower lip dribbling a gossamer line of phlegm. I was aware of a smell of raw urine— there was a dampening in her burgundy dress—and when I got down beside her she made me understand she wished to be taken to the bathroom. We rose to a hunchbacked, standing position and I guided her to the bathroom, her hand feebly shooting for and grabbing the diagonal safety bar on the wall beside the toilet. After a few side-to-side leveraging movements, I was able to remove from the crumples of her dress and pantyhose her incontinence pad, the absorbent lining for which was thoroughly soaked through. She pulled up her dress, established herself on the toilet, and waved me out of the room. I closed the bathroom door and went to the hallway, wiping my hands on my jeans. I scanned the hall. Seeing no one, and mindful of my mother's direction to stay put, I went back and opened the bathroom door, startled to see my grandmother sitting naked on the floor beside the toilet, a moist bit of feces mysteriously balanced in the groove of her collar bone. The burgundy dress, pantyhose, foam-cupped brassiere, and high heels were discarded on the floor-tile. She

sat stricken with fright, vulnerability, and—what was worse—
an absolute confusion as to where she was and what was happening. Which was when my mother returned. Flicking the
dirt from my grandmother's shoulder, she said, "Let's get you
to the bed, Mum." I helped heave my grandmother off the
floor. A flush of sweat had risen all over her, making her skin
slippery, and I dug my fingers tightly into the wattles of her
underarm to make sure she didn't slide away from us. We stag-
gered across the room and bumpily lowered her to the bed.

Scarcely conscious, making no effort to conceal her nakedness, my grandmother sprawled on the bedspread, a hoop ear-
ring bending under her cheek.

"Aubrey," said my mother, watching her. "Go see what's
taking so long."

My sprinting steps in the hall overlapped with a second
shriek from my grandmother and, swiveling around, I saw,
framed in the proscenium of the doorway, both women lying
on the bed, my mother looking alertly into my grandmother's
eyes. "You be strong, Mum. Doctor's coming any minute. You
squeeze my hand. Just like that. That's it. You hold on now. I'm
right here."

CONTRIBUTORS'
BIOGRAPHIES

Caroline Adderson is the author of four novels (*A History of Forgetting, Sitting Practice, The Sky Is Falling, Ellen in Pieces*), two collections of short stories (*Bad Imaginings, Pleased To Meet You*) as well as books for young readers. Her work has received numerous prize nominations including the Sunday Times EFG Private Bank Short Story Award, International IMPAC Dublin Literary Award, two Commonwealth Writers' Prizes, the Scotiabank Giller Prize longlist, the Governor General's Literary Award and the Rogers' Trust Fiction Prize. Winner of two Ethel Wilson Fiction Prizes and three CBC Literary Awards, Caroline was also the recipient of the 2006 Marian Engel Award for mid-career achievement.

Frankie Barnet is the author of *An Indoor Kind of Girl*. Her short stories have been published in places such as *PRISM International, EVENT Magazine, Washington Square Review*, and *With/Out Pretend*. She is a graduate of Syracuse University's MFA program.

Shashi Bhat's fiction has appeared in *The Malahat Review, The New Quarterly, The Dalhousie Review, Best Canadian Stories 2018, Journey Prize Stories 24 & 30*, and other publications.

She was the winner of the 2018 Journey Prize, and a 2018 National Magazine Award finalist for fiction. Her debut novel, *The Family Took Shape* (Cormorant, 2013), was a finalist for the Thomas Raddall Atlantic Fiction Award. Shashi holds an MFA in fiction from The Johns Hopkins University. She is the editor-in-chief of *EVENT* Magazine and teaches creative writing at Douglas College.

Christy Ann Conlin is the author of two acclaimed novels, *Heave* and *The Memento*. *Heave* was a finalist for the Amazon. ca First Novel Award, the Thomas H. Raddall Atlantic Fiction Award, and the Dartmouth Book Award. Her short stories have been published in numerous literary journals and long-listed for both the Commonwealth Short Story Prize and the American Short Fiction Prize. She lives in the Annapolis Valley in Nova Scotia.

Kai Conradi is a queer and trans poet and short-story writer from Cumberland, B.C. He is currently finishing a degree in writing at the University of Victoria. Kai's work has been published in *Poetry*, *The Malahat Review*, and *Grain*, and has been nominated for the Pushcart Prize and the National Magazine Awards. "Every True Artist" is his first published story, and also appears in the 2019 Journey Prize Anthology.

Adam Dickinson is the author of four books. His latest book, *Anatomic* (Coach House Books), involves the results of chemical and microbial testing on his body. His work has been nominated for the Governor General's Award for Poetry, the Trillium Book Award for Poetry, and the Raymond Souster Award. He was also a finalist for the CBC Poetry Prize and the K.M. Hunter Artist Award in Literature. He has been featured at festivals such as Poetry International in Rotterdam, Netherlands, and the Oslo International Poetry Festival in Norway. He teaches at Brock University in St. Catharines, Ontario, Canada.

Zsuzsi Gartner is the author of the Scotiabank Giller Prize-shortlisted *Better Living through Plastic Explosives* and the story collection *All the Anxious Girls on Earth*. Her fiction has been widely anthologized, broadcast on CBC and NPR, and won National Magazine Awards. She is the editor of the award-winning anthology *Darwin's Bastards: Astounding Tales from Tomorrow* and was the inaugural Frank O'Connor International Short Story Fellow for Cork, Ireland, in 2016. Her novel *The Beguiling* will be published by Penguin Canada in 2020. Zsuzsi lives in the Republic of East Vancouver. "The Second Coming of the Plants" was written at Banff Centre for Arts and Creativity during the Literary Arts Fables for the 21st Century residency.

Camilla Grudova lives in Edinburgh, Scotland where she works at a cinema. Her first book *The Doll's Alphabet* was published in 2017.

Elise Levine is the author of the story collection *This Wicked Tongue*, the novels *Blue Field* and *Requests and Dedications*, and the collection *Driving Men Mad*. Her work has also appeared in *Ploughshares*, *The Gettysburg Review*, *The Collagist*, *Blackbird*, *Best Canadian Stories*, and the *Journey Prize Anthology*, among other publications, and was named a finalist for *The Best Small Fictions 2018*. She has taught creative writing at Johns Hopkins University and American University, and lives in Baltimore, MD.

Lisa Moore has written three collections of short stories, *Degrees of Nakedness*, *Open*, and *Something for Everyone*, and three novels, *Alligator*, *February*, and *Caught*, as well as a stage play based on *February*. Lisa has also written a young adult novel called *Flannery*. *Something for Everyone* won the Thomas Raddall Atlantic Fiction Award and the Alistair MacLeod Prize for Short Fiction.

Alex Pugsley is a writer and filmmaker originally from Nova Scotia. His work has appeared in *The Journey Prize Anthology 24*, *Best Canadian Stories 2017*, and *Best Canadian Stories 2018*. "Wheelers" is taken from the ninth chapter of the novel, *Aubrey McKee*, forthcoming from Biblioasis.

Zalika Reid-Benta is a Toronto-based writer whose debut short story collection *Frying Plantain* has been longlisted for the 2019 Giller Prize and has been on numerous "must read" lists from *Bustle*, *Refinery29*, *Chatelaine Magazine*, *Toronto Star*, *Globe and Mail* and more. She was the June 2019 Writer in Residence for Open Book and she was listed in CBC's "6 Canadian Writers to Watch in 2019." In 2011, George Elliott Clarke recommended her as a "Writer to Watch" and her work has appeared on Town Crier, in *Apogee Journal*, *TOK* anthology and the CBC website. She received an M.F.A. in fiction from Columbia University, is an alumnus of the 2017 Banff Writing Studio and was the 2019 John Gardner Fellow in Fiction at the Bread Loaf Writers Conference. She has been the recipient of the Literary Creations Project grant by the Ontario Arts Council as well as has been awarded an Individual Writers Grant by the Toronto Arts Council. She is currently working on a young-adult fantasy novel drawing inspiration from Jamaican folklore and Akan spirituality.

Troy Sebastian | nupqu ʔak·ɫam is a Ktunaxa writer from ʔaq̓am. His writing has been published in *The Walrus*, *Ktuqc-qakyam*, *The Malahat Review*, *The New Quarterly*, *Quill and Quire* and *Prairie Fire*. Troy is a recipient of the Hnatyshyn Foundation's Reveal-Indigenous Arts Award and a graduate of the Banff Centre's Indigenous Writers program. He is a MFA student at the University of Victoria's Writing program and was longlisted for the 2019 Writers' Trust Journey Prize.

Mireille Silcoff is the author of four books of fiction and non-fiction. She won the 2015 Canadian Jewish Literary Award for her short story collection *Chez l'Arabe*, which was also shortlisted for the Danuta Gleed Literary Award, shortlisted for the Vine Award, long listed for the Frank O'Connor International Short Story Prize, and was voted Canada's favourite work of short fiction on CBC's Canada Writes. She has been a longstanding columnist with the *National Post*, a frequent contributor to the *New York Times Magazine,* and has written extensively for all kinds of publications including *the Guardian* and *Ha'aretz.* Mireille has been a senior editor at numerous Canadian publications, including the *National Post*. She is the founding editor of the literary journal *Guilt & Pleasure Quarterly*, and has organized many events designed to instigate conversations about culture. She lives in Montreal.

Cathy Stonehouse's stories have been published in a wide range of periodicals and anthologies, including *Best Canadian Stories 10.* Her first collection *Something About the Animal* came out with Biblioasis in 2011, and her first novel, *The Causes*, comes out with Pedlar Press in September 2019. She also writes poetry, creative nonfiction and literary reviews. Find her online at www.cathystonehouse.com.

ACKNOWLEDGEMENTS

"Again, The Sad Woman's Soliloquy" by Frankie Barnet first appeared in *EVENT*.

"The Most Precious Substance on Earth" by Shashi Bhat first appeared in *The New Quarterly*.

"Late and Soon" by Christy Ann Conlin appeared in *Watermark* (House of Anansi Press, 2019). Reprinted by permission of the publisher.

"Every True Artist" by Kai Conradi first appeared in *The Malahat Review*.

"Commensalism" by Adam Dickinson first appeared in *Joyland*.

"The Second Coming of the Plants" by Zsuzsi Gartner first appeared in *The Walrus*.

"Alice and Charles" by Camilla Grudova first appeared in *Canadian Notes & Queries*.

"The Association" by Elise Levine appeared in *This Wicked Tongue* (Biblioasis, 2019). Reprinted by permission of the publisher.

ACKNOWLEDGEMENTS

"The Curse" by Lisa Moore first appeared in *Eighteen Bridges*.

"Wheelers" by Alex Pugsley first appeared in *The Walrus*.

"Pig Head" by Zalika Reid-Benta appeared in *Frying Plantain* (House of Anansi Press, 2019). Reprinted by permission of the publisher.

"Tax Ni? Piǩak (A Long Time Ago)" by Troy Sebastian first appeared in *The Walrus*.

"Upholstery" by Mireille Silcoff first appeared in *The Walrus*.

"A Room at the Marlborough" by Cathy Stonehouse first appeared in *The Fiddlehead*.

"Young Warriors in Love" by Richard Van Camp first appeared in *ndncountry*, a collaboration between *Contemporary Verse 2* and *Prairie Fire*.

The following magazines were consulted: *Brick Magazine, Canadian Notes & Queries, Canthius, Cosmonauts Avenue, Dalhousie Review, Eighteen Bridges, enRoute, EVENT, The Fiddlehead, Geist, Grain Magazine, Humber Literary Review, Joyland, Lemon Hound, Maisonneuve, The Malahat Review, The Nashwaak Review, ndncountry, The New Quarterly, paperplates, Prairie Fire, PRISM, The Puritan, Room, SubTerrain, Taddle Creek, This Magazine,* and *The Walrus*.